THE
MATHEMATICS
OF TAWHID

THE MATHEMATICS OF TAWHID

Divine Solutions For Unity And Universality

A K SAYED

authorHOUSE®

AuthorHouse™
1663 Liberty Drive
Bloomington, IN 47403
www.authorhouse.com
Phone: 1-800-839-8640

Published by AuthorHouse   10/24/2012

ISBN: 978-1-4772-3960-5 (sc)
ISBN: 978-1-4772-3961-2 (hc)
ISBN: 978-1-4772-3962-9 (e)

ACKNOWLEDGEMENTS

In The Name Of God, Most Gracious, Most Merciful

How can I ever stop thanking my Allah (Arabic for The God)? He created me out of dust, gave me life, intelligence and the most perfect knowledge and guidance of Islam. Furthermore, He gave me water to drink and wash, air to breathe, and fruits, vegetables and meat to eat. In addition to this, He gave me beautiful parents, families and friends, who make me proud. My greatest bounty from Allah is my sujood (prostration and submission) to Him in my daily salaah (prayer). I thank You, Allah (SWT)!

In this world, I have not shown any respect to any person more than the Prophet, salallah alaihi wassalam (peace be upon him). He is my eternal mentor, teacher and leader. How he managed to understand and teach post modern Islam fourteen-hundred-years-ago is a miracle. If he did not succeed to become the greatest person in history, I would have failed to bring yaqin (belief and faith) on the Qur'an, today. May Allah (SWT) shower His endless blessings upon him, his families and companions and all the other Prophets of God that came before him?

In my endeavor to write this book, I have many people to thank for their marvelous support and encouragements. May Allah (SWT) reward them with an esteem place in jannatul-firdose (paradise)? Special thanks are due to Anwar Suleman, Abdool Rahim Sayed, Muhammad Sayed, Mehmood Moosa (Mems), Ismail Adam, Dawood Suleman, Dr Rasheed Shaukat, Ashraf Khan, Hussain Dildar-Mia and Khadija Sayed (my precious daughter, for assisting with the flow charts and diagrams in this book).

Salaams and Duas to all of you (Greetings and blessings)

A K SAYED.

info@tawhidiislam.co.za

SUMMARY OF WEB SITE DOCUMENT

www.tawhidiislam.co.za

WELCOME

In this book, I use the worldview teachings and practices of Tawhid (unity and universality), which are found in the Qur'an (Muslim Holy Book), to explain all true teachings and practices of Islam.

I then use these teachings and practices of the Qur'an (Word of God) as the Al-Furqaan (The Criterion), to expose all the different teachings and practices of all the present day sects, madhabs, silsilas and khanqahs that have deviated from the true teachings and practices of Islam.

The express purpose of this book is to unify the ummah (Islamic society) by establishing one true knowledge and understanding of the Qur'an and Sunnah (pure practice of Qur'an over all time and place), according to the knowledge of Tawhid, completely independent of the book of Hadith (recorded sayings and doings of the Prophet in the context of his time and place, which restricts some universal explanation of the Qur'an over all time and place) and the kitabs (religious books) of the different ulama (plural for religious scholars in this sense) and saints of all sects, madhabs, silsilas and khanqahs, or religious denominations.

WORLD-VIEW

In simple form, the worldview teachings of Tawhid include the teachings of unity: of God; in the teachings and practices of all the Books and Prophets of God; between the Word of God and the sayings and doings of the Prophets; between the Word of God and the Work of God in the signs and science of nature and in the history of religion; between the world of God and the world of Caesar, and so on.

In a more sophisticated form, it includes a very intricate balance between the seen and unseen, secular and religious, individual and community, national and international, this world and the akhirah (hereafter) and so on.

Each teaching of Tawhid demonstrates haqq (divine truth) and how the ummah has deviated from it, showing Tawhidi causes and Tawhidi solutions thereof.

QUR'AN

The most explicit purpose of the Qur'an is to explain Islam according to haqq, over all time and place.

Together, we can perform this very vital function of the Qur'an, if we all agree that ISLAM is an Arabic word meaning SUBMISSION, which is derived from the root-word S'LM, pronounced "salm" meaning PEACE.

Mathematically, this can be written down as follows:

$$ISLAM = PEACE + SUBMISSION$$

Since PEACE is he first term of the above equation, the whole issue of SUBMISSION to the Will of God in Islam depends on the understanding the Islamic perspective of PEACE, which contain the components of DIVERSITY, UNITY and JUSTICE, vital for our coexistence, not only with Muslims, but the entire creation.

The pivot or fulcrum, on which all the teachings and practices of the Qur'an exist, is religion, which is the one compartment of our life, which does not have a rational boundary. Therefore, in surah 69 verses 43 to 46 and surah 10 verse 15, Allah (SWT) gives strict instructions to the Prophet (SAW), not to say or do anything in the Islamic way of life that was not revealed to him in the Qur'an, especially in religion.

If Muslims wish to revert to the true Islam that was practised by the Prophet (SAW) and the Sahaba Ikram (companions of the Prophet), they must start by limiting every issue of religion to the exact Words of God, not Hadith or kitabs of any persons. It is the only way to establish the Tawhidi balance between the seen and unseen, secular and religious, individual and community, national and international and so on.

SUNNAH

In Islam, according to the worldview teachings and practices of Tawhid, QUR'AN, SUNNAH, SHARIAH and REALITY are one and the same thing in different forms.

For example, the injunctions of jihad, which is Qur'an, is for all time and place, but the weapons of warfare differ with time and space, because the Qur'an does not stipulate them or make it an injunction.

From this point of view, the Sunnah (exact practice of Qur'an over all time and place) of wudhu (ablution) and salaah (five daily prayer) are different, because the Qur'an does not only give us the injunctions of wudhu and salaah, but it also stipulates the procedures, which we call faraiz (compulsory acts) of wudhu and salaah, making it impossible to change with time and space.

Thus, the Sunnah is the variable term of the Shariah (Islamic law and jurisprudence), where Shariah = Qur'an in the form of the Sunnah, which varies with the diversity of our culture, custom, tradition and compartments of our lives, over all time and place, keeping up with the changes in reality as it is affected by it, at the same time observing all injunctions of the Qur'an.

EXTREMISM

To accept any teachings and practices of religion that contradicts the Qur'an tantamounts to religious extremism.

Take for example, a Muslim who believes in taqlid, aqidah, sects, madhabs, silsilas, khanqahs, and sainthood. He or she is labelled extremist because he or she believes in that part of religion that is contrary to the Qur'anic concept of ilm-ul-yaqin (certainty of knowledge by inference or reasoning), ayn-ul-yaqin (certainty of knowledge by seeing and observing) and haqq-ul-yaqin (absolute knowledge, like this is a pen, etc).

Similarly, a Muslim fundamentalist is one who fixes all the teachings and practices of Islam to the time of the Prophet (SAW) according to the 7th century Islam of the Hadith. They are the ones who insist that it is the Sunnah to keep a beard because the Prophet (SAW) kept one, and it is wrong to use the microphone in the mosque because the Prophet (SAW) did not use one in the mosque.

DILEMMA

The problem with the 7th century Islam of the Hadith is that it is extremist and fundamentalist. The problem with the rational teachings and practices of Islam according to the worldview teachings and practices of Tawhid that are found in the Qur'an is modernist and secularist. The former retards progress and development with time and space, and the latter seems like a compromise with the West and the secular.

Throughout history, the Muslims were faced with this dilemma of the Qur'an and Hadith.

Every time they found that the Hadith put them backwards, they changed according to the modernists and secularist teachings and practices of the Qur'an, to secure progress and development with time and space.

Similarly, when they found that the modernists and secularists teachings and practices of the Qur'an diluted their identity, custom, tradition, etc, of the Hadith, they reverted to the religious extremist and fundamentalist teachings and practices of the Hadith.

Unfortunately, every time they changed from one form of Islam to the other, they did not do it in a peaceful manner. They did it with a great loss of Muslim lives like the Taliban and the secularists and modernists governments of Pakistan and Afghanistan are doing at this moment.

FLOW DIAGRAM

FLOW DIAGRAM EXPLAINING THE TRUE TEACHINGS AND PRACTICES OF ISLAM

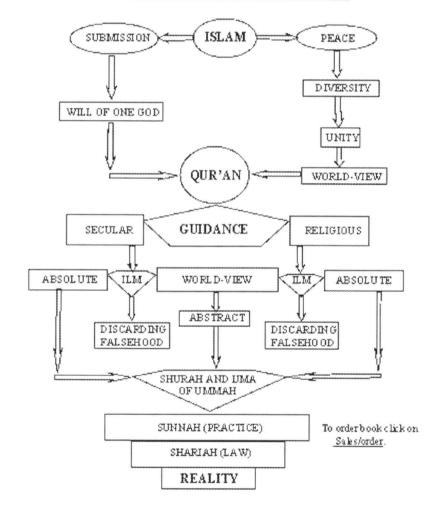

To order book click on Sales/order.

PREFACE

In this book, I am concerned with two core issues of our deen (Islamic way of life, which is as much secular as it is religious). These are as follows:

1. The global perspectives of the Qur'an (Muslim Holy Book).
2. The diversity of our creation.

To explain this, let us take, for example, the oneness of the Islamic way of life, where there is no dichotomy of the secular and religious. We have no doubt that we cannot maintain this balance and way of life, unless we educate and develop ourselves according to the divine teachings and practices of ilm-ul-yaqin (certainty of knowledge by inference or reasoning), ayn-ul-yaqin (certainty of knowledge by seeing and observing) and haqq-ul-yaqin (absolute knowledge, like this is a book, this is a pen, etc), in both the secular and religious levels of our lives.

Therefore, by inference, with reference to the above, it is wrong to educate and develop the ummah (Islamic society) according to the ultra-religious method of taqleed, aqeeda, silsila, khanqah, saints, sects and madhabs because such a teaching and practice of religion will upset the intricate balance between the secular and religious and make Islam a religion rather than a way of life. For example, an Aalim who does so will not be a scholar, but a priest. And since there is no priesthood in Islam, all his teachings and practices of Islam will be totally contrary to the Qur'an, like we will, insha-Allah, demonstrate in this book.

Similarly, in Islam, due to the oneness of the secular and religious, an imaam is not only a religious leader, but also a political leader; and the mosque is not only a place of worship but also the Assembly of the Ummah (our house of parliament) at the local community level. Likewise, it is wrong to recite the Qur'an and perform salaah for the religious purpose of sawaab (blessings) of the akhirah (hereafter) or to neglect the secular education and development of the ummah stating that it will not help in the akhirah. Unless we do not superimpose the religious on the secular according to the teachings and practices of ilm-ul-yaqin, ayn-ul-yaqin and haqq-ul-yaqin and the haqq (truth) of the Qur'an, we will not be able to distinguish the deeni perspective of Islam from the religious perspective that contradicts the haqq of the Qur'an.

According to the above injunctions of the Qur'an and relevance of these injunctions to both the secular and religious aspects of our lives, it is apparent that Islam is not a religion but a unique way of life, which accepts all secular teachings and practices of our life, which do not deny the existence of God, and rejects all religious teachings and practices of our lives, which disturb the balance between the secular and religious, which are not mentioned in the Qur'an. Therefore, in Islam, the secular and religious do not coexist by agreeing to disagree but coexist by agreeing to agree in every issue of their lives according to the injunctions of the Qur'an.

Likewise, in the Islamic way of life, the secular compartment of our life dominates the religious compartment, based on the injunctions of the Qur'an and sound reason, logic, experience, proof, history, etc. In other words, Islam is not interested in the mysticisms and myths of religion based on the ultra-religious teachings and practices of taqleed, aqeeda, sainthood, priesthood, silsilas, khanqahs, sects and madhabs. It is interested in the secular and scientific progress and development of the human life, both spiritually and materially, according to the Qur'anic injunctions of ilm-ul-yaqin, ayn-ul-yaqin and haqq-ul-yaqin.

Unfortunately, although the majority of the Muslims and their ulama (plural for Aalim) agree with me that Islam is not a religion but a way of life, and there is no priesthood in Islam, everything they say and do in the name of it is religion. They give me the impression that they really don't know what's the real difference between a religion and the Islamic way of life, where there is no dichotomy of the secular and religious. Therefore, when I state that it is un-Islamic to believe in saints, taqleed, aqeeda, silsilas, sects, madhabs, khanqahs, ulooms (religious schools), jamiats (councils of churches), etc, they think I am the one who has lost his way and is bordering on kufaar (non-beliefs), not them.

It is not very easy for me to explain the Islamic way of life in the global perspective of the Qur'an and the diversity of our creation especially after the majority of Muslims and their ulama have been indoctrinated by the teachings and practices of their sects, madhabs, silsilas and khanqahs. Therefore, I wish to appeal to all Muslims and their ulama, for the sake of truth and unity, not to support the narrow-minded teachings and practices of their sects, madhabs, silsilas and khanqahs. It will not help to conquer the post-modern era of the 25th century, let alone the hereafter.

Just quoting a few verses of the Qur'an at random, totally out of context, or in the context of your sect and madhab, does not make one an expert in religion or in Islam. One has to have an in depth knowledge of the Qur'an and Sunnah (exact practice of Qur'an) to know how Islam intersects the secular with the religious, seen with unseen, individual with community, national with international, this world with the akhirah, and so on, according to the worldview teachings and practices of Tawhid, which are found in the Qur'an, not Hadith (recorded sayings and doings of the Prophet). This does not mean that only the author of this book has the true knowledge and understanding of the Qur'an and Sunnah and that everybody else is wrong. All the author of this book is saying is that, according to the global perspective of the Qur'an and diversity of our creation and way of life, the Muslim majority and their ulama do not make sense, in almost everything they say and do in the name of Islam.

Therefore, after gaining a very comprehensive knowledge and understanding of Islam, according to the global perspective of the Qur'an in the context of the diversity of our creation and way of life, I have absolutely no place for their sectarian behavior based on the book of Hadith. I think that it is not only a complete contradiction of the Qur'an with time and space but it also teaches religious extremism and fundamentalism, which is a great threat to the true existence of Islam. For example, like the Qur'an integrates, assimilates and intersects the universal knowledge and understanding of the secular and religious, it also integrates, assimilates and intersects different cultures, customs and traditions of this world, with the Islamic way of life. Muslims who do not recognize this natural diversity of our life are a threat not only to the non-Muslims but also Muslims who differ with them.

Their sectarian behavior is in complete contradiction of the global perspective of the Qur'an and the diversity of our creation. It does not only condemn the union of the secular and religious by stating that secular education is western, worldly and Christian, and will not help in the akhirah, but it also condemns present-day inventions like the microphone, printing press, etc, making it bid'ah (innovations) because the Prophet (SAW) did not use them. Likewise, it is responsible for creating the 7th century Islam of the Hadith, which is completely against the integration, assimilation and intersection of Islam with different cultures, customs and traditions of this world with time and space. It clearly states that Muslim men, who do not keep a beard, wear the kurtha, etc, and Muslim women who do not cover their heads or faces in public, are not good Muslims.

What Muslims who follow the 7th century Islam of the Hadith do not understand is that we are not against Muslim men who keep a beard, wear kurtha or Muslim women who cover their heads and faces in public. We are against those who claim that it is Sunnah and Shariah to do so, which, according to the Qur'an, is an extremely false definition of the Sunnah and has nothing to do with the true teachings and practices of the Shariah. According to the Qur'an, the Sunnah is nothing more than the exact practice of the Qur'an in its global perspective and the Shariah is Islamic law and jurisprudence like it is explained by the Qur'an in its universal sense. Hence, without the correct teachings and practices of Qur'an and Sunnah, it is virtually impossible to accept Shariah in the post-modern era of the new millennium.

For example, if the French government stated that it was banning the burqa because it was "oppressive", the Shariah court will turn down such a request by the French government. It will argue that such a ban is invalid, even according to the secular laws of the state because the French government did not have a formal complaint from the majority of women who wear the burqa to state that it was "oppressive". Therefore, it was depriving them of their right according to the secular constitution to don the burqa. Similarly, the Shariah court will support the French government, if the French government stated that it was banning the burqa in all public buildings because of security reasons, not only because it is in the interest of the public security, but also because the burqa is not an injunction of the Qur'an, and an act of taqwa (piety), and imaan (faith).

The Shariah is a means of showing justice to the secular, cultural and religious by inspiring the exact balance between them. In the same way, if the secular government stated that we should not slaughter animals for ritual purposes like qurbani in densely populated areas like the cities for health reasons and should do so in farms, the shariah will be in favour of such a request by the secular government in the interest of proper growth and development of human life. In the 21 st century, not to allow the Muslims to create the exact balance between the secular and religious or integrate and assimilate with different cultures, customs, traditions and compartments of our lives, will lead to the demise of Islam.

Thus, according to the above, it is apparent that the SHARIAH = QUR'AN + SUNNAH and not QUR'AN + HADITH and the SUNNAH = THE PATH + THE PRACTICE of the Qur'an. If the SHARIAH was equal to QUR'AN + HADITH then according to the HADITH, we would be forced to fight our wars, which is an injunction of the Qur'an, with bows, arrows, spears, etc, because it was the way in which the Prophet (SAW) and the Sahaba Ikram (RA) fought their wars. If we did not do that then, according to the HADITH, we would be violating a very important Sunnah of the Prophet (SAW) and acting in a very un-Islamic manner. Could this be the reason why we are not winning our war with the West or is it because the ulama (religious leaders) have not understood the correct meaning of the Sunnah with the advancement of time?

According to the HADITH, is it not the case that the Prophet (SAW) did not use the car for transport therefore we should not use it and ride around on horseback or on a camel? Similarly, we should not use the microphone in the mosque, computer tills in our shops or play modern sports like tennis, soccer, cricket, etc, because the Prophet (SAW) did not do these things. This also applies to all the electrical appliances we use at home and in the office. Then, tell us, "Who exactly is following the Sunnah according to the book of HADITH, except for those that keep a beard, wear a kurtha and kneel and drink water?" Or is it the case that the Sunnah of the Prophet (SAW) is the universal teachings and practices of the Qur'an in every sphere of our life according to time and space? Or is it the case that the Qur'an and Sunnah are one and the same thing in different form, one, the Word of God and the other the practice of the Qur'an in the human form, which modernists and secularists Muslims follow in its global perspective?

Normally, when I tell the Muslim ummah that the recorded sayings and doings of the Prophet (SAW), which are found in the book of Hadith, are not the Sunnah of the Prophet (SAW), they wish to know from me then what is the Sunnah way of performing wudhu (ablution) and salaah (prayer)? In other words, they state that, since the Qur'an does not tell them how to perform wudhu and salaah, how would they know how to perform this without Hadith? Unfortunately, when I tell them that the details of wudhu and salaah that are given in the Qur'an are the details of the wudhu and salaah, they dispute this fact with me. They state that what is written in the Qur'an about wudhu and salaah are the faraiz (compulsory acts) of wudhu and salaah, which do not include the Sunnah of the Prophet (SAW).

Unfortunately the majority of the Muslims are not educated enough in both secular and religious aspects of our lives to understand the universal meaning and message of Islam in the global perspective of the Qur'an and diversity of our creation and way of life, to understand the answer to such a question on wudhu and salaah. Therefore, when I tell them that the rituals of wudhu and salaah cannot be different for the different creations in their different forms, they fail to understand the universal testimony of my declaration. For example, according to the worldview teachings and practices of Tawheed (unity and universalism), the Sunnah of the wudhu cannot be different in the ordinary form from the tayammum form (using clean sand instead of water). It has to be the same. Likewise, the salaah is no different from that of the inanimate objects that cast their shadows from dawn to dusk in prostration of their Lord.

If the wudhu is performed according to the Hadith, it would not be the same because, according to the Hadith, the Sunnah of the wudhu includes the brushing of the teeth, gargling of the mouth and blowing of the nose, which is absent in the tayammum form. Hence, if the Prophet (SAW) performed the wudhu exactly like the Qur'an told him to perform it, there would be no difference between the ordinary and tayammum forms of the wudhu.

This viewpoint that there is absolute unity between the Word of God and the Sunnah of the Prophet (SAW) cannot be doubted, even from the point of view of the Hadith because it is recorded in the Hadith that Bibi

Ayesha (RA) states that the Prophet (SAW) brushed his teeth before he made wudhu. Therefore, what is wudhu? Is it not what is written in the Qur'an and not what is written in the book of Hadith? Insha-Allah (if God willing), in the same way, we will discuss the real difference between the salaah taught by the Qur'an and the Hadith in an appropriate chapter of this book, verifying from the Qur'an, the significance of the unity between the Word of God and the sayings and doings of the Prophets.

In this book, I am not interested in the 7th century Islam of the Hadith, which states that it is the Sunnah of the Prophet (SAW) to keep a beard, wear the kurtha, kneel and drink water, etc, and to play only certain sports like swimming, horse-riding, sword-fighting, running, etc. Likewise, I am not interested in the 7th century Islam of the Hadith, which states that it is against the Sunnah of the Prophet (SAW) to use the microphone in the mosque and to do astronomical calculations to determine the birth of the moon for the day of Ramadhaan and Eid.

Similarly, in the global perspective of the Qur'an, I do not believe in an Islamic identity, sign, symbol, culture, custom, tradition, dressing, politics, medicine, science, etc, based on the teachings and practices of the Hadith because according to the divine teachings and practices of Tawhid found in the Qur'an, there is no universal sight, sound, image, custom, culture, tradition, dressing, language, politics, science, etc, in the unified field of the Islamic way of life. This means, that all true teachings and practices of Islam, or all the injunctions of the Qur'an, apply to all cultures, customs, traditions and compartments of our lives, to guide it to a meaningful way of life that will benefit and uplift humanity as a whole in the proper context of their diversities and peace.

Hence, in view of the above, I am forced to discard the book of Hadith even for wudhu and salaah, because, if Muslims persist with the book of Hadith to inform us about Islam, we will end up distorting the true teachings and practices of the Qur'an and Sunnah, dividing the ummah and our leadership, according to the selected teachings and practices of the Qur'an and Hadith, like all the different sects and madhabs are doing at this present moment. Therefore, in this book, I am looking for the universal teachings and practices of the Qur'an and Sunnah, which apply to all customs, cultures, traditions and compartments of our lives, both secular and religious, maintaining their diversity and purity according to the Qur'an. This means that I do not condemn music, singing, dancing, modern sports like soccer, tennis, cricket, etc, or secular education or secular and scientific development of the human life, which do not disturb the purity, diversity, progress and development of our life both on this plane and eternal plane. I believe that all aspects of our life contain a positive and negative part, except for those aspects of our lives that Allah (SWT) makes haraam (prohibits) in the Qur'an. Hence, Muslims are advised to enhance the positive and suppress the negative according to the Qur'an.

For me, the most intriguing aspect of the Islamic way of life is that the Qur'an and Sunnah apply equally, individually and collectively, to every culture, custom, tradition and compartment of our life. Therefore, in Islam, the cosmic truths and realities are the same for all the aspects of our lives. Logically, it should be the same, but the beauty of this sameness is that if certain teachings and practices of Islam are not clear in one compartment of our life, they can be made clear in another compartment of our life. Let's take, for example, the health or business sectors of our lives. If things are not going right, some people might advice us to recite certain verses of the Qur'an or conduct certain rituals to change our luck. But, according to the true teachings and practices of Islam, is this the right thing to do, or should we also advice the afflicted person to see a specialist for the problem in health or business?

Some people might say that, as a Muslim, it is necessary to do both. In other words, just relying on prayer or the treatment alone is not enough. But is this true according to the true teachings and practices of Islam? For example, let us take a child who has not learnt his or her work at school. Will such a child survive on prayers alone and what is the sense of saying the prayer when one has done one's work, unless, such a prayer was there to remind the child to fear God and not to cheat? Similarly, if a cricketer cannot play spin-bowling, how is he expected to score a century against world class spin bowlers on prayer alone? Therefore, in this book, I have taken many different topics from many different compartments of our lives to explain some of the injunctions of the Qur'an or teachings and practices of Islam, which are unclear in both the business and religious segments of our lives, but, are clear in sports or the science sectors of our lives.

Therefore, my main ambition in this book is to establish the same truth and reality for all compartments of our lives and cultures, customs and traditions of this world, in their most pure forms, according to the true teachings and practices of Qur'an and Sunnah. If I don't, I will end up saying and doing one thing in one compartment of our life and another thing in another compartment of life, contradicting myself, not understanding the oneness of the secular and religious in Islam. Therefore, it should not matter to Muslims, whether they are preoccupied with the secular, religious or sports compartments of their lives. They should not forget that the Qur'an is their constitution, and that according to it, Muslims will have to live a life according to the Shariah, which is the same for all the compartments of our lives, cultures, customs and traditions of this world.

For example, it should not matter to us whether a person's name is Steve or whether he is clean-shaven, wears a suit and a tie and plays music for a living. As long as such a person has declared the shahada (formal declaration of faith) and lives a life according to the universal teachings and practices of the Qur'an, we will always believe that he is a good Muslim, because according to the Qur'an, it is not a condition of Islam for him to change his name, keep a beard, wear a kurtha or to stop playing music, like Cat Stevens (Yusuf Islam) was forced to do. But it is the injunction of the Qur'an, to believe in God, not to attach partners with Him, not to commit zina (adultery, fornication), gossip, cheat, etc.

If Cat Stevens (Yusuf Islam) did not change his European culture and kept his career in music, he would have demonstrated to us how to engage in the practice of the Qur'an in the context of his European culture, custom, tradition and career. It is a pity that we have missed the opportunity to see a personality of his calibre and culture, custom and tradition operate according to Shariah, which was based on Qur'an and Sunnah, and not Qur'an and Hadith.

Therefore, the focal issue of this book is to have the correct interpretation of the Qur'an in the diversity of our creation and way of life, which was not very easy to do. About thirty years ago, when I made up my mind to write a book on the worldview teachings and practices of Tawhid (unity and universalism), I asked Ahmed Deedat, may Allah (SWT) grant him an esteemed place in jannatul firdose (paradise), ameen, for advice. Unfortunately, this happened one very busy Saturday morning at the Verulam market, which did not give me enough time to enjoy his company.

Nevertheless, in the very brief meeting with him, he said "Be careful Sayed Saab, even the devil can write a book and quote from the Qur'an." His sincerity for his deen demonstrated his humility and simplicity. From that day onwards, I developed a consciousness and strategy to control my emotions and sentiments, interact with all diversities that existed in the universe, both in Islam and outside of Islam, both in the realms of the material and religion, according to the divine teachings and practices of peace and Tawhid (unity and universalism), that are found in the Qur'an, and are the prime objectives of Islam.

Long before I spoke to Deedat, I had already concluded that the devil was my enemy, because there was nothing else the devil hated in this world more than the divine teachings and practices of peace and Tawhid, which would make all the people of this world live in peace and harmony with one another in the purity of their beliefs and diversities, where there was no place for the devil. Actually, my threat to the devil about the teachings and practices of peace and Tawhid was so great that every time I spoke to an Aalim (singular for ulama) or a mufti (highly qualified Muslim religious leader) about peace and unity of the ummah, the majority of them were uninterested, because it did not suit the devil.

They said, "Peace and Tawhid was impossible because the Prophet (SAW) had predicted that there would be 73 sects and if I tried to unite the ummah, I would be failing his prediction". What they did not understand is that the predictions of the Prophet (SAW) were not the cause of our division or even the misunderstanding of the Qur'an and Sunnah. And, that in this context, I was trying to find the causes and solutions for our division in the most neutral and universal way by exploring the worldview teachings and practices of Tawhid that were found in the Qur'an. The devil liked what he heard from the ulama, because he hated nothing more than the peace and unity of the ummah. Hence, my whole effort to write this book is to achieve that peace and unity within ourselves, our families, the nation and the international community and defeat the devil and his companions.

My task is onerous. Firstly, I have to overcome the distorted knowledge of Qur'an and Sunnah that has plagued the ummah and has been spread by the ulama and the muftis of the past and present. Secondly, I have to convince the majority of Muslims of what are the true teachings and practices of the Qur'an and Sunnah, according to the divine teachings and practices of peace and Tawhid, which are the prime objectives of Islam. Thirdly, I would like them to point out to me what is wrong with the way I reason in religion and the Islamic way of life.

I have always maintained this in my previous book, "An Islamic Revolution for Peace and Unity" and in this book that I will never claim that I am right in any teachings and practices of Islam, unless the majority of the Muslims decide according to the shurah (mutual consultation) and ijma (consensus) of the ummah (not ulama), that my knowledge of the Qur'an and Sunnah is correct, and that there is no alternative to what I have to say. It is the path, which Allah (SWT) has planned for us, to protect us from the devil.

Therefore, in the context of the diversity we experience in all the aspects of our lives in this world, both inside and outside of the ummah, none of us who represent any one of the diversities can claim that only the teachings and practices of our diversity, sect or madhab are correct, and all the others are wrong. This is the very first law of diversity in Islam, because all diversities that are the creation of the creation are imperfect. Even if they were the creation of God, the justice of God requires them to be equal, where one diversity is not greater, or better, than the other, in its pure form.

The second law of diversity states that only the true Word of God can be used to determine "the all truth" and reality of our creation, and solve all the problems of our diversity in all aspects of our lives. There is no other way to do this. Therefore, the search for the true Word of God is a very important function of Islam in determining what is true and what is false. In Islam, we are fortunate that we can claim, without any doubt, that the

Qur'an is the infallible Word of God, which we managed to keep pure since it was revealed to the Prophet (SAW).

The third law of diversity requires us to establish the true teachings and practices of the Qur'an and Sunnah by the shurah (mutual consultation) and ijma (consensus) of the majority of Muslims that represent the Islamic way of life, according to the divine teachings and practices of peace and Tawhid, which are the prime objectives of Islam. In Islam, there is no jamiat of the ulama (council of churches) of any one sect or madhab (the four schools of thought) that truly represents the diverse viewpoints of their own sects and madhabs, let alone the ummah. That's why they are divided into many different khanqahs (denominations) within their own sects and madhabs that do not agree with one another, and stay aloof from one another.

Finally, it is very important to mention once again that I am not experts in the true teachings and practices of the Qur'an and Sunnah, or in any other spheres of our life like science, politics, religion, mathematics, diversity, sports, etc. All I wish to do is to demonstrate the fact that we do not have to rely on any of the sectarian teachings and practices of any of the sects, madhab, silsila (order of saints) and khanqah and the book of Hadith to understand the Qur'an and Sunnah or Shariah. And that the only independent and universal interpretation of the Qur'an and Sunnah or Shariah can be found according to the divine teachings and practices of peace and Tawhid, which are not only found in the Qur'an, but, are also the prime objectives of Islam.

It stands to reason, because Islam is a dynamic way of life, which is revolutionary and proactive with time and space. To copy its teachings and practices from the past and make it unchangeable with time and space is completely against its nature and character. Thus, in this book, I ignore most of what was said and done in the past because the revolutionary nature and character of the Qur'an leaves me with no other choice.

CONTENTS

CHAPTER 1

Introduction

It is almost ten years since I published my first book, "An Islamic Revolution for Peace and Unity". Unfortunately, the position of the ummah (Muslim society) has not changed for the better. Some of the repercussions of the present situation are as follows:

1. The ummah is divided into many different sects, madhabs, silsilas and khanqahs, according to the knowledge of their ulama and saints. About four to five years ago, when I published my first book, "An Islamic Revolution for Peace and Unity", the division of the ummah was almost entirely religious and I did not think that it could get any worse. Only the religious institutions like the mosques, jamiats, ulooms, religious radio stations, etc, were divided into the different religious sects and madhabs. According to my knowledge and understanding of the Qur'an and Sunnah, none of these belonged to the mainstream of the ummah.

2. Today, the division of the ummah has become even worse, because religious extremists are also using western style democracy to gain political power. In Palestine, after fighting a common enemy for 60 years, Fatah and Hamas got divided, and now after killing one another for many years, they decided to unite in May 2011. In Saudi Arabia and Pakistan, after supporting the Taliban for the last 20/30 years, the Saudi and Pakistan governments are now hunting down and killing them. About two years ago, there was a massive, "No" to the Shariah law in Turkey. In addition to this, here in South Africa, the unexpected has happened. The Transvaal Wahabi Jamiatul Ulama has after nearly 50 years of undivided and solid existence, is now divided (which we did not expect). Nowadays, there are many more silsilas within each sect and madhab than ten years ago.

3. In this division of the ummah, the majority of the Muslims do not have the same knowledge and understanding of the Qur'an

and Sunnah. For example, the Bareillys do not believe in that part of the Qur'an that states that the Prophet (SAW) is an "ordinary person" (Al-Qur'an 18:110 and 7:188) and it is wrong to believe in saints and karamets (the veneration of the graves of the saints). In addition to this, they believe in urs, forty-day and one-year ceremonies for the dead, etc, which are totally contrary to the true teachings and practices of the Qur'an and Sunnah. Likewise, the Deobandis do not believe in that part of the Qur'an that does not compel their womenfolk to cover their faces in public, and their men to keep a beard, wear kurtha, kneel and drink water, etc. They also believe in saints but they do not venerate the graves of the saints. Their biggest problem is that they have become fundamentalists and extremists by giving greater preference to the Hadith than the Qur'an.

4. In this division of the ummah, there is no freedom of speech or expression. One Aalim of one sect is not allowed to lecture in the institution of another sect. Similarly, when I proclaim the pure knowledge and understanding of the Holy Qur'an and Sunnah according to the worldview teachings and practices of Tawhid, completely independent of the Hadith, I do not expect them to accept my knowledge and understanding of Islam. This is mainly due to the fact that they are totally ignorant of the pure knowledge and understanding of the Qur'an and Sunnah independent of the Hadith. Besides, it is wrong to use a lower book like the Hadith, which is written by man, to give meaning to a higher book like the Holy Qur'an, which was revealed by God.

5. The ulama (religious leaders) have lost their way, and do not know the real problems of the ummah. They refuse to be analytical, and blame everybody else except themselves for the present state of the ummah. For example, one of the first things that they claim is that the majority of the Muslims are insincere whereas the rest of the non-Muslim world is of the opinion that "Muslims are most sincere to God". Likewise, they blame it on Bush, Blair, on our western education, influence, etc, for the failure of the Muslim ummah. They go as far as possible to blame other people for the present condition of the ummah. They even use natural disasters like earthquakes, floods, tsunamis, etc, in Muslim

countries to frighten Muslims to believe in religious extremism and fundamentalism.

6. There is no doubt that they also blame God and the Prophet (SAW) for the present situation of the ummah. They state that it is a punishment from God or that He is giving us a difficult life in this world to give us a better life in the Hereafter. Likewise, they state that the Prophet (SAW) predicted that there will be 73 sects and there is nothing anybody can do about it. I have already explained this argument of theirs in the preface.

There are many different causes for the above situation of the ummah. Muslims are required to investigate these causes according to the worldview teachings and practices of Tawhid, so that they can rectify the situation and understand some of the reasons for writing or reading this book. Some of these are as follows:

1. The ulama who divide themselves into sects and madhabs consider themselves to be the real scholars of Islam (ulama-e-haqq) and true representatives of the Prophet (SAW) or waris-ul-ambiya, yet they fail to agree with one another as to what are the true teachings and practices of the Holy Qur'an and Sunnah. Take for instance Maulana Fazlul Rehmaan Ansari. He was a professor of Islamic studies at the University of Karachi, and a patron of the Muslim Youth Movement (MYM) in South Africa. He has a large following in South Africa. In his book "Islam and the Modern Minds", he states that keeping a beard, wearing a kurtha, sitting on the floor and eating, etc., has nothing to do with Islam and that these teachings and practices of religion are those of "a cult movement" within the ummah. He further states that if we do not believe in saints, we do not have imaan (faith). Unfortunately, from this point of view, he does not agree with Sheik Najaar, who was the former President of the Muslim Judicial Council (MJC) and a very highly respected religious leader of the Malay community in South Africa, which is also a very large Muslim community in South Africa.

2. In his book, "I am a Muslim", Sheik Najaar does not reprimand the men in his community for not keeping a beard, which was a very common practice among them, or the women in his community

for not covering their faces in public but he reprimands them for believing in saints and venerating the graves of the saints (which is also a very common practice among them), stating that it is totally against the true teachings and practices of the Qur'an to believe in saints and venerate their graves. Therefore, it boggles my mind, that after 1400 years of the study of the Holy Qur'an, the majority of the ulama of haqq and waris-ul-ambiya do not agree with one another as to what is written in the Qur'an and what is not, and what is Sunnah and what is not. It is the first time since I published my first book, "An Islamic Revolution for Peace and Unity", in which claims were made not to believe in saints, that I came across an Aalim in South Africa, who agreed that it is wrong for Muslims to believe in saints, and make it a condition of their faith to do so.

3. In this division of the ulama, the Deobandi and Wahabi ulama have no regard for "scholars" like Sheik Najaar and Professor Ansari, who do not belong to their sects. They state that I should just follow the teachings and practices of their ulama and saints, who follow Hadith. For example, if the Hadith tells us to keep a beard, wear the kurtha, etc., then we should just do that and not question it. Hence, they do not worry about the universal teachings and practices of the Holy Qur'an and Sunnah, with time and space and the diversity of our creation. Sometimes one wonders if they and their institutions are not working for the CIA, when they state that I am a munafik (hypocrite) when trying to correct them. Hence, I do not think that these differences in the knowledge and understanding of the Holy Qur'an and Sunnah by different ulama of the different sects and madhabs are co-incidental and trivial. Some of these are deliberate and others are due to ignorance. No matter how trivial, they destroy the true knowledge and understanding of the Qur'an and Sunnah, divide us and destroy our leadership. Our enemies know that. Therefore, they have a large hand in sowing seeds of our divisions.

4. The majority of the Muslims and their ulama do not understand why Islam is not a religion, but a life guide and a way of life. For example, they do not understand that, if they believe in a life guide and a way of life that is based on sound reason and logic, then it is wrong for them to believe in saints and taqleed

(the blind following of religion), and to divide the ummah according to the different religious sects and madhabs like they do. Therefore, in view of this, they have to understand that if Islam is not a religion, then they must not say and do anything in religion that contradicts the Qur'an. For example, let us take the mimbar in the musjid (mosque). In our ordinary way of life, it is just a political platform in the assembly of the ummah, from which the speaker delivers his speech so that he may be seen and heard by the people in the back row of the assembly. Now if we gave the same mimbar a religious connotation, which is contrary to the Islamic way of life, then we will have to be very careful how we climb the mimbar with the right foot and what we recite when we climb the mimbar, and so on and so forth.

5. Recently, one naath reciter refused to sit on the third step of the mimbar like the previous reciter had done because, according to him, it was not permissible for any Muslim to sit on the third step of the mimbar because the Prophet (SAW) occupied that position of the mimbar. Hence, when we attach a religious connotation to any one aspect of our life like salaah, mimbar, asaa, musjid, nikaah, talaaq, zakaat, hajj, nikaab, beard, etc., which is contrary to the Islamic way of life, then it becomes very difficult to explain any of these things according to science, logic, reason, politics, diversity, or in any other rational or intellectual manner. For example, how can we explain to the Aalim who recited the naath that it was alright for him to sit on the third step of the mimbar because, in the Islamic way of life, the mimbar was a political platform and not a religious platform, because, Islam was not a religion but a way of life, which had very little to do with religious beliefs and practices that were contrary to the balance between the secular and religious. As a religious extremist and fundamentalist, he was not any better than a Christian who believed that Jesus is God and the Son. No amount of reason could have persuaded him to believe otherwise.

6. The majority of the Muslims are like that. For example, the owner of a very large bookshop here in South Africa refused to buy or sell my previous book entitled "An Islamic Revolution for Peace and Unity" because I did not believe in saints, silsilas and khanqas. He said he was not prepared to listen to any reasons on

the matter because it was the cornerstone of his belief system to believe in saints, silsilas and khanqahs. Therefore, out of respect for my age he was prepared to offer me a cup of tea but was not prepared to do business with me. It is a shame, that after 1400 years, the majority of the Muslims who are selling Islamic books, and who call themselves scholars are unable to distinguish the fact why Islam is not a religion but a way of life. There is only one conclusion to this: they give preference to the Hadith, and not the Qur'an to support their views on Islam.

7. Therefore, the other big problem in the Muslim ummah is that we have two religious books, namely, the Qur'an and the Hadith, which contradict one another, like it was mentioned in my website and preface. According to the divine teachings and practices of Tawhid, we are supposed to have only one religious Book, and one (and only one) true knowledge and understanding of the Holy Qur'an and Sunnah by shura and ijma of the ummah. By attaching a book like the Hadith, which did not collaborate with the true teachings and practices of the Qur'an with time and space, it's like attaching partners to God. And it was because of this mistake Muslims have now not only distorted the whole teachings and practices of the Holy Qur'an and Sunnah with time and space, but have also divided the ummah into the many madhabs, sects, silsilas and khanqahs, and cannot find a true leader to represent the ummah. If we did not have a book like the Hadith, we would not have got involved with Islamic religious fundamentalism and extremism, and would not have religious schools such as the ulooms and religious institutions like the jamiats, which are no better than the Council of Churches in Christianity. We would have had only one assembly of the ummah, with a unified and universal knowledge and understanding of the Qur'an and Sunnah.

8. Not long ago, before the last general election in Turkey, the majority of the Turks rejected the shariah law in Turkey not because they rejected the Qur'an, but because they rejected the fundamentalist and religious extremist teachings and practices of the Hadith. Since, then they have embarked on a procedure to rewrite the Hadith to reinstate the shariah so that it can be collaborated with the true teachings and practices of the Holy Qur'an. I think that

this is virtually impossible to do because the worldview teachings and practices of the Holy Qur'an are so complete and perfect, and so revolutionary with time and place, that any amount of rewriting the Hadith will not complete, and perfect, it. What is the point in making the teachings and practices of the Hadith to collaborate with the Qur'an when we have the Qur'an in the most complete and perfect form, which the Hadith will never be able to replace? Thus, I think, that the only way to make the meaning and message of the Holy Qur'an complete, and perfect over all time and place, is to make constant shurah and ijma of the Holy Qur'an like the Prophet (SAW) and the Sahaba Ikram (RA) did in the assembly of the ummah, in the context of our culture, custom and tradition of our time and place. Hence, it's my contention in this book that Muslims should completely disregard the Hadith and focus completely on the Qur'an like it was stated, and explained, in my website and preface of this book, and many other chapters.

Therefore, following the ulama and choosing your sects, madhabs, silsilas and khanqahs, according to their knowledge and understanding of Islam, which contradicts the true teachings and practices of the Qur'an and Sunnah, is like taking other gods other than Allah (SWT) to conduct our affairs in this world. The following verses of the Qur'an will convey this Message to you:

> "Turn back in repentance to Him, and fear Him; establish regular prayer, and be not among those who join gods with God.
>
> Those who split their religion (deen), and become (mere) sects, each party rejoicing in that which is with itself".

> (Al-Qur'an 30: 31-32)

The only "straighwt way" of choosing the true teachings and practices of Islam, is by studying the Qur'an, (without the influence of the Hadith and their sectarian teachings), according to the worldview teachings and practices of Tawhid (unity and universality), which are found in the

Qur'an. These teachings and practices of Islam, which I have explained in great detail in this book, will not only assist us in getting rid of all the sects, madhabs, silsilas and khanqahs, but will also assist us to unite the ummah, according to one true knowledge and understanding of the Qur'an and Sunnah.

The division of the ummah is not nice for us. The primary issue with it is that it makes us hate one another for what we teach, practice and believe. For example, a few decades ago, one so-called "Sunni" brother was killed in a clash with the so-called "Tabligh Jamaat" in Azaadvile (Johanessburg). This kind of thing can happen again and again, within and between sects, with time and space. For example, now that the Wahabi Jamiat of Ulama is divided, some of its former supporters, who have divided, hate them, by calling their jamiat a "no name brand jamiat", their leader "Reverend Bham" and their radio station "Radio Shaitaan". No doubt, if we were living in Muslim countries Iraq, Syria, Afghanistan, Pakistan, etc, we would be killing one another as mercilessly as they are doing at this moment in our history. This is a curse from Allah (SWT) on us for dividing, and not practicing the true teachings of Allah (SWT) on unity, but following the sectarian teachings of the ulama.

Another very important issue of our division is that it does not provide us with true leadership and direction according to one true knowledge and understanding of the Qur'an and Sunnah, either at the local, national or international level. Hence, we are functioning in a much unorganized manner at all levels in our lives. Although, the majority of the Muslim might not feel the pain of their division at the local level, it does have national and international repercussions. For example, we are unable to give our government an answer to the Muslim Marriage Bill for more than a decade because we are divided on the true knowledge of the Qur'an and Sunnah. Likewise, on the international level, we are badly marginalized politically, socially, militarily and otherwise. How our women and children are suffering throughout the world because of the unintelligent way in which we are conducting ourselves is a disgrace.

There is not a single Muslim in South Africa, who does not desire the unity of the ummah. In the last thirty-to-forty years, the majority of them have tried everything like forming the Islamic Council of South

Africa (ICSA), the Unity Council and the United Ulama Council, but unfortunately none of these have succeeded. One of the reasons why they have not succeeded is because they wish for unity without giving up the teachings and practices of their sects and madhabs and tribal affiliations. In other words, they wish to come to the unity convention only to agree to disagree and not to agree to agree, even if truth stands out clear from error. In addition to this, they do not provide shurah and ijma of the ordinary Muslim at the grassroots level, where people like me, who do not subscribe to their organization, have a voice.

According to the above situation of the ummah, it is apparent that there are two major problems with the Muslim ummah. One is the difference in their knowledge and understanding of the Holy Qur'an and Sunnah and the other is their religious division into the different sects, madhabs, silsilas and khanqahs. Obviously, these two problems are related. Mathematically, they can be written down as follows:

Differences in the knowledge and understanding of the Qur'an and Sunnah
= The division of the ummah.

Conversely or alternatively, this can be also written down as follows:

Unified knowledge and understanding of the Qur'an and Sunnah
= The unity of the ummah.

Fortunately, in the true teachings and practices of the Islamic way of life, we do not have to wait for the Madhi or Jesus (PBUH) to come to unite us and tell us what are the true teachings and practices of Islam. Likewise, we don't have to form any organizations like ICSA, the United Ulama Council, etc. All we have to do in order to unite the ummah and establish one true knowledge and understanding of Islam at the grassroots level, is to find out what are the divine teachings and practices of Tawhid that are found in the Holy Qur'an, and in some of the Sunnah of the Prophet (SAW) that collaborate with the Qur'an. Some of these teachings and practices of Tawhid are as follows:

1. **Unity of God:** All Muslims know what are the true teachings and practices of the unity of God. What they do not understand is that it is a great offense in Islam to follow the teachings and practices of any one Aalim or saint who contradict the Holy Qur'an and Sunnah. It is like attaching partners to God. Therefore, if Muslims wish to attain salvation in the akhirah, they must make sure that all the teachings and practices of their ulama and saints are according to the Qur'an and Sunnah, which does not conflict with the Qur'an. If not, they will pay a very heavy penalty in the akhirah. Hence, it is the duty of every Muslim to find out for themselves, what are the true teachings and practices of the Holy Qur'an and Sunnah and not to rely on what the ulama are saying and doing. One way of doing this at an individual level is by taking the English or Urdu translation of the Qur'an or any translation of the Qur'an and to jot down all the ayahs of the Qur'an that deal with a specific subject like salaah, zakaat, the Prophet Muhammad (SAW), women, sects, believers, non-believers, munafiks, science, politics, business, etc. Hence, knowing what is written in the Qur'an and what is not, in any aspect of our lives, is a very important priority of our life. In other words, if we do not have a very exhaustive knowledge of the Qur'an, we should refrain from teaching Islam and religion or defining the Sunnah.

2. **Unity between the word of God and the sayings and doings of the Prophets:** All Prophets were given strict instructions not to say and do anything in the Islamic way of life that was not revealed to them. Hence, the Sunnah of the Prophet (SAW) is limited to the absolute knowledge and understanding of the Qur'an. Therefore, the keeping of the beard, wearing of the kurtha, etc, which was the Arab culture and custom of the time of the Prophet (SAW), is not his Sunnah because it was not revealed to him that he should do or not do these things. Thus, those who seek the unity, progress and development of the ummah with time and space, must recognize the true definition of Sunnah and bid'ah. Otherwise they will make Sunnah and bid'ah what is not Sunnah and bid'ah and vice versa, and divide the ummah. If all the people of all religions taught the true Word of God, which was given to their Prophets, it would be easy to conclude that not only their religion was one, but their God was also one.

3. **Unity between the individual and the community:** The individual and community are supposed to have the same knowledge and understanding of the Qur'an and Sunnah so that they may understand one another on every issue of their lives and support one another in every matter of their lives. The best way to achieve this is by participating in the shurah and ijma of the ummah in the assembly of the ummah in your local masjid. Hence, those who commit themselves to the shurah and ijma of the ummah commit themselves to the Shariah, otherwise they betray the trust of the ummah. The converse of this teaching and practice of Tawheed is also true. For example, the knowledge and understanding of Islam by the individual is determined by the progress and development of the community or the nation. If the community is backwards in all the compartments of their lives, means that the individual has not done enough to understand the Qur'an and Sunnah, and develop the community accordingly.

4. **Unity between the world of God and the world of Caesar:** In this teaching and practice of Tawhid, like in all its teachings and practices, there are many other teachings and practices of unity, which overlaps this teaching of unity. One of these is the unity between seen and unseen, which states that as the seen part of the creation, we should see the unseen according to the knowledge and understanding of the seen. For example, we know that God exists because we can recognize His existence through His creation but we cannot see His shape and form and His partners through His creations. Therefore, we are not permitted to state that He created us in His image or He has partners, etc., unless the Qur'an told us so, because we cannot prove these things through the seen. Likewise, another important teaching of Tawhid in this category is the unity between the secular and religious. In this unity between the secular and religious we are requested to believe in only those teachings and practices of God, His Revealed knowledge and His Prophets according to haqq, which is based on science, reason, history, experience, etc, according to the criteria and guidelines of the Qur'an. In other words, we are supposed to believe in all the teachings and practices of the secular that do not deny the existence of God, and reject all teachings and practices of

religion that disturb the balance between the secular and religious, according to the injunctions of the Qur'an.

5. **The unity between the national and international:** The Islamic way of life was designed to achieve world peace. It teaches peace within the individual, his family, community, nation and international community. All these teachings of Tawhid apply to all the cultures, customs, traditions and compartments of our lives, preserving the purity of their diversities according to the injunctions of the Qur'an. This means that Islam is tolerant to all the people of all the cultures, customs, traditions and compartments of lives and values multilateralism in all the affairs of the international community. Therefore, to limit Islamic identity, culture, custom and tradition to only the Arab culture, custom and tradition of the time of the Prophet (SAW) and the compartment of religion is totally contrary to the true teachings and practices of the Holy Qur'an and Sunnah of the Prophet (SAW).

6. **Unity between this world and the akhirah:** According to this teachings and practices of Tawhid, we are not supposed to just read the Qur'an, perform salaah, give zakaat, etc., just for the sawaab of the akhirah. But to use these institutions to build our nation in a very dynamic manner like our Prophet (SAW) did. For more information on this subject refer to the chapter entitled, "The Difficulties of Finding the Straight Way".

7. **The unity between the teachings of all the Books and Prophets of God:** For further information on this very important teachings of Tawhid refer to the chapter entitled, "The Vision and Mission of Prophet Abraham (PBUH)".

Thus, according to the divine teachings and practices of Tawhid, it is apparent that if we desire the unity of the ummah then we will have to by-pass the book of Hadith, the ulama of different sects and madhabs that contradict the Qur'an and Sunnah, and establish the Shariah according to the shurah and ijma of the ummah like it was done by the Prophet (SAW) and Sahaba Ikram (RA). In a diagrammatic form this can be represented as follows:

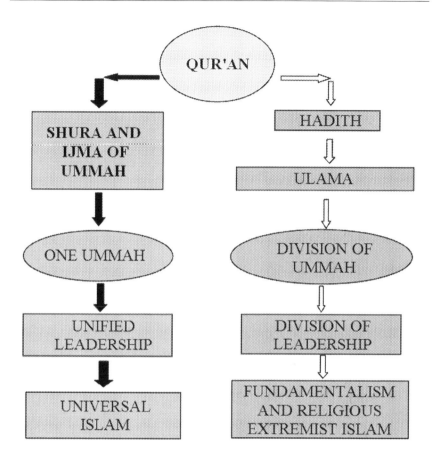

PATHS THAT UNITE AND DISUNITE THE UMMAH

Our fathers and grandfathers who came from India a little more than a century ago followed a very similar type of Islam that I advocate in this chapter and this book. Some of the things they said and acted upon are as follows:

1. They did not separate the boundaries of science, politics and religion in their lives, making them separate and exclusive. They gave the same priority to building a hospital, a school, a university, etc., like they gave to building a mosque and a madressah, which they called a vernacular school, (never a madressah). Similarly, they made tremendous progress in politics and business. Some of their landmarks still stand, for example, the ML Sultan Technikon,

the RK Khan Hospital, the Grey Street Mosque, etc. If we are enjoying many kinds of benefits, (social, political, economical or educational), it is mainly due to their efforts, which they achieved in a very short period of time, about fifty-to-sixty years after coming to this country.

2. They hardly quoted the Hadith and rarely lived a life according to the teachings and practices of the Hadith. For them Islam did not appear to be a religion and the Sunnah of the Prophet (SAW) was not the practice of Hadith. But it was the practice of the pure teachings of the Holy Qur'an. Therefore, we hardly found them keeping a beard, wearing a kurtha, sitting down on the floor and eating or telling their womenfolk to wear the veil or the niqab. Like they interacted, interrelated and intertwined with the politics and the business of their time according to the injunctions of the Holy Qur'an, they interacted, interrelated and intertwined with the customs and culture of their time. Hence, they were mostly clean-shaven, wore suit and tie, sat on chairs and table and ate their food (sometimes with forks and knives), and even played music, went to the cinema, played sports and did gardening. And, knew exactly what was haalal and haraam in every compartment and level of their lives.

3. They planned and developed their lives according to the shurah and ijma of the ummah. Besides having three to four general meetings in a year regarding the affairs of the mosque and madressah, they made constant shurah and ijma with our mothers and grandmothers at a wedding or funeral house after the event. They usually sat in a circle with the men occupying one half of the circle and the women occupying the other half of the circle and discussed everything about their lives from politics to the education of their children. They did not let the ulama dictate the shariah to them according to the shurah and ijma of the ulama. In those days the molvies were also different. They hardly quoted the Hadith from the mimbar probably under the instructions of our forefathers who employed them. Hence, from the mimbar they read from the Holy Qur'an, gave tarjuma (translation) and related the application of those verses to the affairs and current affairs of the day.

4. They sent both their boys and girls to schools and universities to get educated and pursue a career. Hence, their children did not let them down. They studied very hard and became lawyers, doctors, pharmacists, engineers, scientists, educators, politicians, businessmen and women, etc. They excelled in every compartment of their lives. Thus, their children were well educated in the secular way of life and never lost the slightest touch with their imaan (faith). Therefore, besides organizing debates on Islam at primary, secondary and adult levels and attending the lectures by Ahmed Deedat in the city hall, they formed the MYM, MSA, ICSA, SANSAF, IPCI and many other organizations in Islamic trade and industry, Islamic banking, etc. Hence, they were as much religious as they were secular.

5. During their time they were very well respected by all the non-Muslims of this country for their efforts in all the compartments of their lives. For example, in the previous year (2008), Pat Poovalingum, a well known Durban attorney wrote in "The Leader", a weekly newspaper, that the Tamil and Hindu community is very grateful to the Muslim community for building schools and universities, where many of them were educated, because in those days they had very little funding from the apartheid government to fund their education and health services. Largely, the Muslim community dug into their pocket to make such facilities a reality. Furthermore, I do not believe that our forefathers did not have true knowledge and understanding of the Holy Qur'an and Sunnah. And that whatever they did in this country was natural and that anybody would have done what they did. To the contrary, I think that they had a very in-depth knowledge and understanding of the Holy Qur'an and Sunnah because they did not only come from the ancient civilization of India, but they were also greatly influenced by the Moguls, the Ottoman Empire and the British Raj, and any interested Muslim with such experience and influence would have a very extraordinary knowledge and understanding of the Holy Qur'an and Sunnah.

There was only one weakness with our forefathers. They did not have a well-organized assembly of the ummah. Hence, they did not have a well-organized and highly qualified executive or leadership that could give them expert advice on any serious decision that they had to take in their lives. They were mostly business people. Their shurahs and ijmas were informal, without proper documentations and leadership at the regional or national level. Hence, one day they had to make a very vital mistake, and pay a very heavy price for this weakness. For example, in the nineteen sixties they had to make a very important decision that affected all the Muslims in South Africa. They wanted to know what to do with their boys who were not doing well in school. Somebody suggested that they should send them to India to become hufaaz and ulama. This was their big mistake because in Islam religion is taboo and when one takes a religious decision one has to be very careful. Religion is like a tsunami, and if you are not careful it will take you away without any mercy. Therefore, restricting all knowledge of religion to that of the Qur'an is a very important function of Tawhid.

Our forefathers learned the hard way and left many lesson in this regard for us because when the ulooms in India heard that the South African students were coming in their numbers to their institutions they got very interested. The main reason was that the South African students were big business at that time not only because we paid well but also because our Rand was stronger than the dollar in the Rand/Dollar exchange rate. Hence, the Indians came down in their numbers to canvass for our business. The Bareilly's offered melaad, the forty days ceremony for the dead, urs, etc., and the Deobandi's offered the fundamentalist Islam according to the Hadith. The majority of the Urdu speaking Muslims and the Memons joined the Bareillys and the majority of the Gujrati speaking Muslims joined the Deobandis. Ever since then our communities are divided according to their languages, tribal, social and religious affiliations.

Unfortunately, the majority of the Muslims and the ulama do not approve of the type of Islam I advocate and the type of Islam our forefathers followed in this country more than fifty years ago. They say that it is un-Islamic and not religious enough. They state that Muslims, who do not keep beard, wear kurtha, etc., and go to the cinema, play music, etc., are not good Muslims. Sometimes, I also feel the same way but I am always assured that I am not wrong because most of Islam of the Qur'an is a compromise between all the people of the different customs, cultures, traditions and compartments of our lives, with time and space and that I am indoctrinated to believe it is wrong to live with such a rational and intellectual teachings and practices of the Qur'an and Sunnah, according to Tawhid (the divine teachings and practices of unity and universalism).

Thus, so far, according to all the things that I have mentioned in this book, our task is to do the following:

1. Not to believe in religious leaders like the ulama and muftis and not to rely on the knowledge of religious institutions like the jamiats and ulooms, mainly because Islam is not a religion but a way of life.

2. To believe that Islam is a way of life that intersects the knowledge of the seen with unseen, secular with religious, and accept only that part of the knowledge of the unseen and religious that is completely compatible with science, reason, history and human experience, according to the injunctions of the Qur'an.

3. To establish the assembly of the ummah in all local masajid and give power to the majority of the people to establish Shariah according to the shurah and ijma of the ummah. And not according to the shurah and ijma of the ulama who are divided into sects and madhabs.

4. To understand that the worldview teachings and the practice of the Holy Qur'an are Sunnah, and not the fundamentalists and extremists teachings and practice of the Hadith or the kitabs of their ulama and saints.

5. To believe that God's guidance was sent to preserve the diversity of all the cultures, customs, traditions and compartments of their lives in their pure form, and not only that of religion and the Arabs of the time of the Prophet (SAW).

6. That men and women have equal rights and its wrong not to allow a woman to drive a car, go to school, work with men, perform salah with the congregation in the masjid, etc., or compel her to cover her face in public like in Saudi Arabia and Afghanistan under the Taliban. According to the Qur'an, the only restrictions on her in public are that she cannot assume the leadership of the ummah in the form of a caliph and has to cover her jayb (chest) when in public, otherwise, she can own a property, do business, etc.

CHAPTER 2

Miracles Of The Holy Qur'an

Before, the Qur'an was revealed to the Prophet (SAW), the pagan Arabs were totally ignorant and most backwards people in the world. Similarly, the Prophet (SAW) was unknown. Besides being "a village boy" and "ummi" (unlettered), he ran a business for Bibi Khadija (RA), whom he married later. He had no position in the community, like the leader of his tribe, mayor of his town, etc. Yet after the Qur'an was revealed to him, he became the greatest person in history, and the Arabs ruled the world for 800 years, making great contribution to science, history, education, mathematics, etc.

The question now arises, "Why does the Qur'an not have the same kind of impact on us like it had on the Prophet (SAW) and the Arabs of his time?"

According to the worldview teachings and practices of Tawhid, there are several reasons for this. Some of these are as follows:

1. We don't focus all our attention on the knowledge of the Qur'an. We focus a lot of our attention and energy on other books like the Hadith, etc. We are unable to grasp the fact that the Qur'an is "the mother of all books" and no other person or book can explain the Qur'an better than the Qur'an.
2. We refuse to rely on the most diverse and challenging viewpoints of the ummah in interpreting the Qur'an and Sunnah. We are afraid of their universality. We prefer to rely entirely on the sectarian viewpoints of the different ulama of the different sects, madhabs, silsilas and khanqahs.
3. We are reluctant to be adventurous (dynamic and revolutionary) in the interpretation and understanding of the Qur'an and Sunnah. We like to copy the past and be content with it. We think only the

teachings and practices of the Hadith of the 7th century Islam is the pure teachings and practices of Islam over all time and place.

4. Like the "secularist" and "modernists" Muslim, we do not wish to establish Shariah by the shurah (mutual consultation) and ijma (consensus) of the majority of the Muslims who live in the vicinity of our local masjid. We wish to do so by forming elitists' movements like the jamiats, khanqahs, Vision 20/20 or like-minded Muslims around the Internet, etc.

Therefore, according to the above, it is a very important requirement of Tawhid to make the mosque the nucleus of our development, because, when we go to the mosque for the five daily salaah, we go there to fulfill two very important functions, or to be more precise, two very important relationships of Tawhid, which are as follows:

1. **The unity between the individual and his or her Creator:** This usually happens during the salaah, when the individual recites the Qur'an (the infallible word of God) and prostrates to God in complete submission to Him, which is his or her submission to His word, found in the recitation of the Holy Qur'an. Therefore, if there is any teaching and practice of our life that does not collaborate with the true teachings and practices of the Holy Qur'an, then we cannot state that we are in complete submission to God. If we do, then we will be guilty of associating partners with Him. For example, according to the Qur'an we are not compelled to keep a beard, wear the kurtha, etc. If we insist that it is the Sunnah of the Prophet (SAW) then we associate partners with God by listening to those people, who insist it is Sunnah, because the Prophet (SAW) was given strict instruction by God not to say and do anything in religion that was not revealed to him. Besides, when we contradict the true teachings and practices of the Holy Qur'an and Sunnah in this way, we destroy the universal knowledge and understanding of Islam making Sunnah and bidat what is not Sunnah and bidat and vice versa. Basically, we are expected to exhaust the knowledge of the Qur'an first before deciding what Sunnah is because the Sunnah of the Prophet (SAW) was established only after the Qur'an was revealed to him.

2. **Unity between the individual and the community or the nation:**
   This teaching and practice of Tawhid has been already explained in the previous chapter and preface. What we have to stress in this chapter, is that the Qur'an also plays a very instrumental role in acquiring this relationship between the individual and the community. For example, in order to secure the unified knowledge of the Qur'an and Sunnah, the community is dependent on all individuals in the community for their input and consensus in all the aspects of their lives. In addition to this, another important teaching and practice of Tawhid that takes place in the mosque or the Assembly of the Ummah is the application of the Qur'an and Sunnah in the natural growth and development of the ummah in all the compartments of our lives, according to the diversity of their natural experience, not only in religion. Unfortunately, such a unity between the individual and the community does not exist in our masajid anymore because the shurah and ijma and the Assembly of the Ummah does not exist in our masajid anymore.

In a diagrammatic form, all the above teachings and practices of Tawhid can be represented as follows:

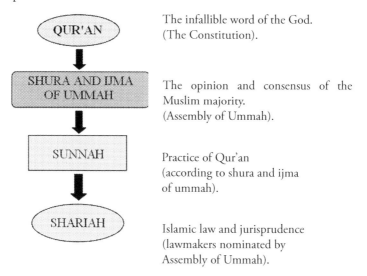

QUR'AN — The infallible word of the God. (The Constitution).

SHURA AND IJMA OF UMMAH — The opinion and consensus of the Muslim majority. (Assembly of Ummah).

SUNNAH — Practice of Qur'an (according to shura and ijma of ummah).

SHARIAH — Islamic law and jurisprudence (lawmakers nominated by Assembly of Ummah).

MUSLIM ASSEMBLY ESTABLISHING GOD'S RELATIONSHIP WITH THE INDIVIDUAL AND COMMUNITY

In the above relationship between God, the individual and the community, it is important to explain why its improper to use a lower book like the Hadith, which is written by man, to interpret the true teachings and practices of a higher Book like the Holy Qur'an, why the Hadith is not Sunnah, why the shurah and ijma of the ummah is more important than the shurah and ijma of the ulama of the different sects and madhabs, and why its wrong to believe in saints and spiritual mentors according to the true teachings of the Holy Qur'an. All of this cannot be done in just one chapter of this bsook, because the ulama and the muftis of our time have corrupted the above path to the Islamic way of life to such an extent, that it will take several chapters of this book to sort out the mess, especially because the majority of the Muslims have more faith in the ulama and muftis of the present day than us.

Therefore, the most important feature of the Assembly of the Ummah is that it promotes a very intricate and intimate relationship between the Holy Qur'an and the ordinary Muslim with God and the community according to the shurah and ijma of the ummah. The reason why this intimate relationship between the Word of God, (Qur'an and Sunnah), the ordinary Muslim and the community has not materialized in the last 500 years is because the ulama have told us a lot of lies about the Qur'an and the ability of the ordinary Muslims to read and understand the Holy Qur'an according to the shurah and ijma of the ummah, like they have done with many other important teachings and practices of Islam. For example, they state that only the ulama, not the ummah, is qualified to read and understand the Holy Qur'an and therefore, it is not proper to establish shurah and ijma of the ummah to establish Sunnah and Shariah.

Furthermore, when some of us tell them that its the instruction of the Holy Qur'an and the Sunnah of the Prophet (SAW) and the Sahaba Ikram (RA) to apply the shurah and ijma of the ummah to establish the true teachings and practices of the Holy Qur'an and Sunnah, they say we cannot compare ourselves with the Prophet (SAW) and the Sahaba Ikram (RA) and the instructions of the Holy Qur'an that were given to them because they were not ordinary people like us.

According to the divine teachings and practices of TawhId, this statement is totally untrue, firstly because they undermine the injunctions of the Holy Qur'an that compel us to promote the shurah and ijma of the ummah, a very important Sunnah of the Prophet (SAW) and the Sahaba Ikram (RA). And, secondly, in the way in which, they destroy the whole democratic process of the assembly of the ummah. If the Prophet (SAW) and the Sahaba Ikram (RA) were not ordinary people like us then how would we relate to them and how could they become a perfect example for us?

The Holy Qur'an is explicit that the Prophet (SAW) was "an ordinary person like us who had no knowledge of the unseen". This fact is confirmed by the following verses of the Holy Qur'an:

> Say: "I am but a man
> Like yourselves, (but)
> The inspiration has come
> To me, that your God is
> One God: whosoever expects
> To meet his Lord, let him
> Work righteousness, and
> In the worship of his Lord,
> Admit no one as partner."

(Surah 18: 110).

> Say: "I have no power
> Over any good or harm
> To myself except as God
> Willeth. If I had knowledge
> Of the unseen, I should have
> Multiplied all good, and no evil
> Should have touched me:
> I am but a Warner,
> And bringer of glad tidings
> To those who have faith."

(Surah 7: 188).

Similarly, there are many teachings and practices of Islam where the Deobandis and Bareillys do not agree with one another. But what I do not understand about the Wahabi ulama is why do they tell us that the Prophet (SAW) and the Sahaba Ikram (RA) are not ordinary people like us, while they tell the Bareillys that "The Prophet (SAW) and Sahaba Ikram (RA) are ordinary people like us"?

Some Christians also have a very similar problem with the majority of the Christians who believe Jesus is God and Son of God. For example, some Anglican church-leaders have questioned "The Myth of God Incarnate". They wish to know how can Jesus be an example for them when Jesus is God and Son of God or how can they relate to the true teachings and practices of the Holy Bible when they are ordinary people and not the incarnate of God and Sons of God like Jesus (PBUH)? They say that they have to be God and Son of God to relate to the true teachings and practices of the Holy Bible or alternatively Jesus has to be a figure like Gandhi or Mao Tse Tong for them to relate to the true teachings and practices of the Holy Bible.

Amazingly, unlike the ulama of our jamiats, their church leaders admit that there is something wrong with their belief in the myth of God incarnate. But they say that there is nothing that they can do about it because all the dogmas and doctrines of the Church are so closely interrelated and intertwined that if they admit that Jesus is not God and Son of God then all the dogmas and doctrine of the Christian Church will collapse. Hence, the Christian Church is in a dilemma. They have to live with their lies, and it is for this reason that many Christians have lost interest in their religion.

But, do we have to live with the lies that the ulama and saints of the different sects have created for us about the Holy Qur'an and the Prophet (SAW)? Can we not comprehend in the above formula of the Assembly of the Ummah that the ulama have nothing to do with the shariah making process of Islam except as ordinary members? In other words, they can be totally left out of the equation except as ordinary members of the ummah in the Assembly of the Ummah and it will not make an iota of difference to the true teachings and practices of the Holy Qur'an and Sunnah. Try it. In fact, it will improve our situation.

Unfortunately, the Muslims are doing the same thing that Christians have done to their way of life. Like Prophet Muhammad (SAW), Jesus (PBUH) never preached religion. He always propagated a rational way of life, which was clearly distinguishable from a religion that was based on blind faith, which was the modus operandi of all the Prophets of God. They always taught a way of life that was rational, intellectual, practical and comprehensible. The Prophet Muhammad (SAW) was given the task to "complete and perfect" all the teachings and practices of Islam, which was in essence the religion and way of life of all Prophets that descended from Prophet Abraham (PBUH).

Therefore, it is very important for Muslims to distinguish the difference between a religion and a way of life. For example, it is religion to state that the Prophet (SAW) is a cosmic human being who did not have a shadow and performed many miracles like splitting the moon, giving life to the dead, etc. Such kinds of religious statements about the Prophet (SAW) do not conform to the Islamic way of life because we cannot prove such facts about the Prophet (SAW), according to the Qur'anic teachings and practices of ilm-ul-yaqin, ayn-ul-yaqin and haqq-ul-yaqin. We can only do so if we believe in the religious teachings and practices of taqleed, aqeeda, etc, which conforms to blind faith. It is just like the Christian belief that Jesus (PBUH) "is God and Son of God", which is based on blind faith, and which if we do not believe, the Christians will tell us, we have no faith.

This is typical religion and contrary to the true teachings and practices of the Qur'an. For example, in the Islamic way of life, if we wish to speak about the greatness of the Prophet (SAW), both in the Islamic world and the non-Muslim world, then it is important that we demonstrate his greatness in world history like La Martine, Boswell Smith, Michael H Hart, etc, have done, and not according to the religious teachings and practices of taqleed, aqeeda, silsila, khanqah, etc, like he split the moon, did not have a shadow, etc. In addition to this, it is important to explain all the teachings and practices of Tawhid in all the aspects of our lives to demonstrate how Islam embraces all the natural diversities of this world in their pure forms, never discriminating or dividing, but always caring, loving and being inclusive. In other words, it would appeal to humanity if we make the Prophet (SAW) relevant to the realities of our lives, not myths.

Similarly, another relationship or condition that exists between the Qur'an and the Prophet (SAW) is that he was not allowed to say or do anything that was not revealed to him. These injunctions also apply to us. Hence, some verses of the Holy Qur'an that support our rationale are as follows:

Say: ".... I follow
Naught but what is revealed
Unto me: if I were
To disobey my Lord,
I should myself fear the Penalty
Of a Great Day (to come)".

(Surah 10: 15).

"(This is) a Message
Sent down from the Lord
Of the Worlds.

And if the apostle
Were to invent
Any sayings in Our name,

We should certainly seize him
By his right hand,

And we should certainly
Then cut off the artery
Of his heart".

(Surah 69: 43-46).

In Islam, the prime issue in the worship of God includes our observance and practice of the exact Word of God that is found in the Qur'an, and not in the words of the ulama and saints who are sectarian. For example, the perfect salaah is one where we function according to the exact words of the Qur'an that we recite in the salaah. If we don't then such a salaah is meaningless. This means that when we deviate from the Word of God, distort it or even show ignorance to it, our claim that we worship our Lord is false, even if we perform the five daily salaah. The following verse of the

Qur'an explains why the worship of God is so strongly associated with the Word of God:

> "Do you not see that to Allah bow down in worship all things
> that are in the heavens and on Earth, the sun, the moon, the
> stars, the hills, the trees, the animals, and a great number among
> mankind? but a great number are (also) such as are fit for
> Punishment: and such as Allah shall disgrace, none can raise to
> honour, for Allah carries out all that
> He wills".
>
> (Surah 22: 18).

Thus, in the context of the above and the divine teachings and practices of Tawhid that are found in the Holy Qur'an, the most important miracle of the Holy Qur'an is that it can be understood in any language. I, as the authors of this book, hardly know a word of Arabic, let alone Qureshi Arabic in which the Holy Qur'an is written, yet I am able to tell more about what is written in the Holy Qur'an, like I have done in this book, than people who know Arabic. For example, I did not have to know Arabic to know that the Qur'an teaches unity in all the compartments and levels of our lives and that these teachings and practices of unity are the same for all people, Muslims and non-Muslims, over all time and place.

Likewise, I did not have to know Arabic to know that when I apply all the simple injunctions of the Qur'an in my life that I will develop a very intricate balance between the seen and unseen, secular and religious, individual and community, national and international, this world and the akhirah and so on. And that, all these teachings and practices of my life, apply to all the people of all cultures, traditions, customs and compartments of my life. Similarly, I did not have to know Arabic to understand that the jamaat salah was a prelude to the assembly of the ummah, that Islam was not a religion, that there was no priesthood in Islam and that the Sunnah of the Prophet (SAW) was the absolute knowledge and understanding of the Qur'an and had nothing to do with the Arab culture and custom of the time of the Prophet (SAW).

How some people, both modernists and religious extremists have come to the conclusion that one has to have a sound knowledge of the Arabic language to understand the Qur'an is difficult to fathom? Look at verse 4 of surah Ibrahim. It clearly states:

"We sent not an Apostle except (to teach) in the language of his (own) people, inorder to make (things) clear to them".

Likewise, Allah (SWT) reminds the Prophet (SAW) that He sent the Qur'an in the Arabic language to him and his people, so that they should not claim that they did not understand it. Besides, if the same Muslims claim that all Prophets brought the same Message, then what difference did their language make to the Message? Truth does not change with time and space or the language we speak. It remains the same. For more information on this subject refer to notes 3228 and 3229 in Yusuf Ali's translation of the Qur'an.

According to Qur'an, it is not a condition of shurah and ijma of ummah to know the Arabic language. But, it is a condition of the shurah and ijma of ummah that those that make shurah and ijma should know what is written in the Qur'an in the language they speak and should be regular for salaah. This is because the salaah establishes the submission of God through the recitation of the Qur'an in the salaah and both the individual and the community who are present in the assembly accept this fact. Thus, there is no indication in the Holy Qur'an that we have to have a sound knowledge of Arabic to have a good knowledge and understanding of it.

But, there are many verses that indicate that we should have a good education and we should be men and women of understanding to read and understand the Qur'an in the diversity of our creation and way of life. Therefore, when the ulama state that we are unqualified to read and understand the Qur'an, they are lying, mainly because they do not have the true knowledge and understanding of the Qur'an. Secondly, because they do not like to lose the power and position they occupy in their communities. And thirdly, because they do not wish to be exposed to the fact, that they do not have the true knowledge and understanding of the Holy Qur'an and Sunnah.

Likewise, another very important miracle of the Holy Qur'an is that it is not only a Book of religion but it is also a very comprehensive political document and a scientific journal. For example, in the Assembly of Ummah, if we fulfill all the political, social, economical and scientific obligations of our lives according to the Holy Qur'an, then automatically we are considered to have fulfilled all the religious obligations of the Holy Qur'an. This is because the Qur'an is a life guide which acknowledges only that part of religion that is compatible with science, reason, history, experience, etc., and is the will of God.

In the previous chapter I have explained how the Qur'an handles all the teachings and practices of all the compartments of our lives in the context of the diversity I experience according to the Qur'anic teachings of Tawhid. In this chapter, I explain some of the nation building programs of the Holy Qur'an, which superimpose the political and scientific aspects of our lives with our religion. These are as follows:

1. Our nation cannot be built on sentiments, emotions, myths and mysticisms of religion. Therefore, in view of this fact, the Holy Qur'an wants us to do away with religion as far as possible and take the secular path of logic to develop our lives according to the guidance of the Holy Qur'an. In other words, the Holy Qur'an does not want us to be part of any stupid childish superstitious beliefs and practices of religion that will be detrimental to the progress and development of the human life. This means that we are permitted to embrace only that part of religion that is compatible with the true teachings and practices of the Holy Qur'an or with our human reason, logic, science, history, experience, etc, according to the true teachings and practices of the Holy Qur'an and not according to the fundamentalist and religious dogmas and doctrines of the Hadith, which are based on emotions and sentiments, let alone myths and mysticisms.

2. In addition to this, its important to be aware of the fact that according to our history and experience, religion is a dangerous ideology and a major cause of our division and war. And that in many countries of this world, including many Muslim countries, our secular governments are spending a major part of their resources and energy fighting religious fundamentalism and extremism instead of using the energy and the resources to develop the ummah. Of course, jihad is permissible but not without

knowing what is right and what is wrong and what are the true teachings and practices of the Qur'an and Sunnah. In other words, how can we proclaim jihad on our secular governments when we are wrong or if we do not know what are the true teachings and practices of the Qur'an? For example, the Taliban have declared jihad to establish fundamentalism and religious extremism, not Islam. According to the Qur'an, is it right to do so? If they have declared jihad on foreign troops only for the occupation of their land then that is another matter, but to govern it according to the Hadith and the dogmatic teachings and practices of religion is totally un-Islamic.

3. The Holy Qur'an is very aware of the fact that it is virtually impossible for us to build a nation without a very comprehensive knowledge and understanding of science and maths. For example, Allah (SWT) created this entire creation using the laws of physics and mathematics. He wants us to do the same in every aspect and dimension of our life. Refer to the chapter on "Qur'an and Science" for more information on this subject. Recently, some experts in our nation-building program here in South Africa stated that our nation-building program was so sophisticated nowadays that it was not sufficient to have only a bachelor's or master's degree. They stated that we required people with a PhD in every field and compartment of our life. For example, in science, business, politics, agriculture, education, communications, building, mining, health-care, arts and culture, tourism, mining, accounting, law, sports, entertainment, etc. Muslims who limit their tertiary knowledge to medicine, accounting, etc, which they believe do not conflict with Islam are foolish.

4. One of the most important features of the Holy Qur'an and the Sunnah of the Prophet (SAW) is to promote democracy from the grassroots level of our society. For example, although the Prophet (SAW) was the greatest Prophet of God, he was humble enough to establish the Shariah by the shurah (mutual consultation) and ijma (consensus) of the majority of the Muslims of his time. Unfortunately, many Muslims do not see the shurah and ijma of the ummah as a democratic process. They think that it is the antithesis of democracy, which gives us the right to alter the injunctions of the Qur'an. Unfortunately, they misunderstand the

concept of the shurah and ijma of the ummah. They are unaware of the fact that it also provides us with the opportunity to accept all the injunctions of the Qur'an and its interpretation, in our present day life, according to the shurah (mutual consultation) and ijhma (consensus) of the majority of the Muslims. Furthermore, the western world is now in search of a democratic government or authority which begins from the grassroots level and not from the party politics level of the present system. Refer to the chapter on the "Assembly of the Ummah" for more information on this subject. What a pity that we Muslims have the ideal structures for such an authority and government but fail to implement it.

5. According to the true teachings and practices of the Holy Qur'an, our accountability and morality is not only subject to the fact that we submit to the will of God according to our recitation of the Holy Qur'an in our salaah but, it is also subjected to the fact that we are committed to our consensus in the Assembly of the Ummah. Hence, unlike in the non-Muslim world, where they render unto God what is God's and unto Caesar what is Caesar's, we are accountable to both God and man in a very spiritual and rational manner for everything we say and do in every aspect of our material life. At the present moment in our history, we have also lost our sense of morality and accountability in almost every issue of our lives because we have separated the secular from the religious, which is totally contrary to the true teachings and practices of the Holy Qur'an and Sunnah.

6. Likewise, we have discarded our commitment to our community by discarding the shurah and ijma of the ummah. Thus, betraying the trust of our brotherhood, which we are supposed to secure in the Assembly of the Ummah, if it existed, would be like betraying the amanah (trust) of God, His word, and there is great punishment for it both in this world and in the akhirah. Therefore, in order to improve our morality and accountability, Muslims should consider the idea of reinstating the Assembly of the Ummah, because today, if there is a major problem in any nation-building program, it is our morality and accountability, and by reinstating the Assembly of the Ummah would not only enhance our commitment to God but it will also establish our commitment to our community in a partnership with God.

7. One of the most important items on our nation-building program should be to secure a very strong military power so that we can defend any aggression on our nation and the amanah entrusted to us by our God. The Holy Qur'an is very serious and open about it. Hence, jihad is a very important topic of discussion on the Muslim agenda. It is not only directed towards striving for taqwa (purity) but it is also highly recommended to defend the truth, property, lives and the sovereignty of the Muslim ummah. Fourteen hundred years ago, Allah (SWT) told us in the Holy Qur'an to read, write and educate ourselves. Likewise, He told us that He put iron in the ground and that there were many uses for it. Hence, with jihad He prescribed technology. He did not expect us to fight our wars during the modern era with bows and arrows. But unfortunately, the fundamentalist ulama failed to heed this very important message of the Holy Qur'an by telling us that secular education was western, worldly and Christian and will not help us in the akhirah. Hence, we failed to extract any benefit from the iron that Allah (SWT) gave us.

8. Our loss was the gain of the western world, which paid attention to secular education and used the iron not only to benefit mankind in many different ways but also to build sophisticated weapons and military equipments to defeat us. It now seems that Allah Paak is punishing us for listening to ulama and not listening to Him. In this world we have to have a very sophisticated army and defense system because we cannot trust the so-called "civilized" nations of the Western world to defend us or solve any problems of international proportions by the consensus of the majority. Look how they have destroyed the credibility of the League of Nations and the UNO. Muslims would be mad to trust them anymore. We have no alternative but to build a powerful defense system and join the non-aligned nations of the world, not the UNO, which is made up of rouge nations of the West.

What the Muslims do not understand is that we are capable of building the most modern and sophisticated society in the world because we have the best constitution in the world in the form of the Qur'an, and structures of parish level democracy, which does not exist in the non-Muslim world. I am not saying this because I am Muslim and it is natural for me to say so. I am saying this because I have contested this issue in the mass media with the non-Muslim world. For example, in South Africa, one self-proclaimed atheist stated that the constitution of the new South Africa was the best in the world and that Muslims should change their Scriptures accordingly. I did not agree with him. My reply to him was published in The Star newspaper of Johannesburg, entitled, "Islam less flawed than the constitution". It reads as follows:

MF Mahamed is arrogant. He thinks he knows more than God.

As a self-proclaimed atheist I expect him to think so but, as a philosopher and reformer, I think he should be more tolerant (Criticising religion within my rights", The Star, April 29).

His statement that we should change our scriptures according to the constitution is wrong.

For his information, the constitution is not the ultimate document of this universe.

My experience with the constitution is as follows:

- It is new. It has still to be tested.
- It is extremely secular. It has still to combine all the true teachings of all levels of our lives.
- It makes the individual more important than the nation.
- It was built on the guilt and grudge of apartheid.

The Holy Qur'an and Sunnah are much more tolerant. These two books of God gave great glory to the pagan Arabs who were insignificant in world history.

For 800 years after the coming of the Prophet Muhammad (PBUH), they ruled the world and made great contribution to science, maths, geography, history, philosophy, medicine, etc.

Hence, according to Michael H Hart, in his book The 100 most influential people in history, Prophet Muhammad (PBUH) was the greatest because he was the only person in history who was "most extremely successful in both the secular and religious levels".

Muhammad (PBUH) also combined all the true teachings and practices of all the books and prophets of God.

Therefore, in the death penalty debate, it was not unnatural to state that in Saudi Arabia the state conducted the murder trial and the victim's family was given the choice to take a life for a life, according to the Old Testament, or forgive, according to the New Testament, or take blood money.

Likewise, it was not unnatural in the evolution debate for a Muslim to state, "Godless science is an impaired vision." Thus, the Islamic system is flexible.

Furthermore, in a true Islamic system there is no place for either religious or secular extremism.

Therefore not only atheism is prohibited but also priesthood and sainthood. In the last three centuries, Muslims allowed priesthood and sainthood to take charge. They became extremists.

I hope my book, An Islamic Revolution for Peace and Unity, will correct the situation. Likewise, in our country, if we allow people like MF Mahamed to control the constitution, we are expected to see the decline of religion and tradition with great repercussions in the long term.

In the above letter I stated that the Qur'an and Sunnah were "two great books of God" which "gave great glory to the pagan Arabs". Some knowledgeable Muslims rightly wanted to know, "What two great books of God?" They were under the impression that I thought that the Hadith was a book of God. In my reply to them in The Star newspaper which was entitled, "Islamic law falters from skewed views", I explained that Sunnah was not Hadith but it was an indirect revelation to the Prophet (SAW), which the majority of the Muslims mistook for the Hadith, and it was due to this misunderstanding of the Sunnah and Hadith that the purity of the Shariah was suffering today.

In view of the above, there are many miracles of the Holy Qur'an. For example, it is the only Book of God that can do the following:

1. Decide what haqq (eternal truth) is in all cultures, customs, traditions and compartments of our lives. For example, if we did not have the Qur'an, how would we know that we are permitted to slaughter certain animals for food or marry more than one woman (up to four) at any one given time? Likewise, if we did not have the Qur'an, how would we know that we must not believe in

saints, taqleed, priesthood, etc, and not to make them the partners of Allah (SWT) by listening to them and believe only in what is written in the Holy Qur'an?

2. Establish the balance between the seen and unseen, secular and religious, individual and community, this world and the akhirah and so on, by establishing haqq. Hence, it is the only book in the world that does not separate the boundaries of science, politics, business and religion and allows all the compartments of our lives to develop with great harmony with one another in a very constructive and pure manner.

3. Wipe out religious extremism and fundamentalism from the surface of this earth and unite all the people of this world (both Muslims and non-Muslims) who are against religious extremism and fundamentalism in their lives.

4. Establish the sovereignty of God on this earth because it is the only Book of God that can provide suitable solutions and guidance to all the affairs of our lives. Furthermore, it has a very comprehensive plan to build a nation by total submission to the will of One God.

5. Uplift the worst nation on earth and make it the best nation of the world. For example, before the Holy Qur'an was revealed to the Prophet (SAW), the Arabs were the most insignificant nation in world history but after the coming of the Prophet (SAW) they ruled the world for 800 years and made great contribution in science, maths, geography, history, philosophy, medicine, etc. Even today, the Holy Qur'an has the ability to make us the foremost nation in the world if we are prepared to listen and pay heed to its message and content.

In conclusion, I wish to state that the Holy Qur'an is the most powerful document in the world. It has the power and potential to make us the foremost nation in the world once again. We have to know how to use it. If we are going to use it to make taweez for shifa and protection or recite it for the sawaab of the akhirah and many other religious purposes for which it was not sent for then according to the worldview teachings and practices of Tawhid (unity and universalism) we will derive absolutely no benefit from it.

If we wish to derive maximum benefit from it, and change our condition overnight then we will have to discard all false uses of the Qur'an, and give all our attention to learning it and applying it with all the energy and resources at our disposal. This can be done by discarding the study of the Hadith, the recitation of the Qur'an for the sawaab of the akhirah, making taweez, closing down the ulooms and the jamiats which spread religious extremism and fundamentalism and so on and by giving all our time, energy and resources to the study and application of the Qur'an in all aspects of our lives according to shurah and ijma of ummah, in the Assembly of the Ummah.

CHAPTER 3

⬩•⬥•⬩

The Union Of The Secular And Religious.

All teachings of Tawhid (unity and universalism) have to perform many different functions of Tawhid. Some of these are meant to establish the following:

1. Which of the diversities of this world are the dominant power and forces of our lives in any one relationship of Tawhid. For example, in the relationship between the seen and unseen, the Holy Qur'an establishes the seen part of our creation as the dominant power and force of our life because we belong to the seen part of our creation and we can only see and understand that part of the unseen that is compatible or relative to the seen. Let's take for example the Quranic concept of God. We can only see that part of God and His attributes that we see in His creations. No more no less, because we cannot see His shape and form nor His partners, sons and/or daughters. Thus, when we take this dispute to the Qur'an, it confirms that He has no shape nor form nor any partners, sons and/or daughters. Likewise, in Islam, in the relationship between the secular and religious, the Qur'an confirms that the secular is the dominant power and force of our life because the Qur'an commands us to accept only that part of religion that is compatible with science, reason, history, our experience, etc, according to the teachings and practices of ilm-ul-yaqin, ayn-ul-yaqin and haqq-ul-yaqin. I will insha-Allah, explain these teachings of Tawhid in great detail in this chapter.

2. "The all truth" and a universal perspective of reality, which is the same for all the diversities in any one relationship of Tawhid. For example, in the relationship between the seen and unseen both of it have to intersect with one another. In other words, both have to agree that God exists and that He has no shape or form, partners, sons and daughters. Similarly, in the relationship between the secular and religious both sides have to agree that they will develop

36

according to science, reason, history, experience, etc. For example, according to the Qur'an, it is wrong to believe in saints, taqleed (blind following of religion), priesthood, etc, in this relationship. Hence, in this relationship, an Aalim is a scholar, not a priest, and a musjid is not only a place of worship but also the Assembly of the Ummah, where the political aspirations of the ummah are accomplished, according to the true teachings and practices of the Holy Qur'an and Sunnah.

3. Peace within ones self, family, community, nation and international community, which are the prime objectives of Islam. Therefore, all teachings and practices of peace have to be supported by a very comprehensive knowledge and understanding of unity. In Islam, we are gifted with the divine teachings and practices of Tawhid. If we are willing to accept these in every aspect of our lives, we will experience eternal peace.

Although all nations teach peace and unity, none of them have been able to successfully intersect the seen and unseen and the secular and religious, except Islam. World history is witness to this fact. For example, some of the western historians had the following things to say about Islam and the Prophet (SAW):

Philosopher, orator, apostle, legislator, warrior, conqueror of ideas, restorer of rational dogmas, a cult without images; the founder of twenty terrestrial empires and one spiritual empire, that is Muhammad. As regards all standards by which human greatness may be measured, we may well ask, is there any man greater than he?"
Lamartine, Histoire de la Turquie, Paris 1854, Vol ii, pp. 276-77.

"It is not the propagation but the permanency of his religion that deserves our wonder; the same pure and perfect impression which he engraved at Mecca and Medina is preserved, after the revolutions of twelve centuries by the Indian, the African and the Turkish proselytes of the Koran . . . . The Mohammedans have uniformly withstood the temptation of reducing the object of their faith and devotion to a level with the senses and imaginations of man.

'I believe in One God and Mahomet the Apostle of God', is the simple and invariable profession of Islam. The intellectual image of the Deity has never been degraded by any visible idol; the honors of the prophet have never transgressed the measure of human virtue; and his living precepts have restrained the gratitude of his disciples within the bounds of reason and religion."

Edward Gibbon and Simon Ocklay, History of the Saracen Empire, London 1870, p. 54.

"He was Caesar and Pope in one; but he was Pope without Pope's pretensions, Caesar without the legion of Caesar; without a standing army, without a bodyguard, without a palace, without a fixed revenue; if ever any man had the right to say that he ruled by the right divine, it was Mohammed, for he had all the power without its instruments and without its supports."

Bosworth Smith, Mohammed and Mohammedanism, London 1874, p. 92.

"My choice of Muhammad to lead the list of the world's most influential persons may surprise some readers and may be questioned by others, but he was the only man in history who was supremely successful on the religious and secular level."

Michael H Hart, The 100: A Ranking of the Most Influential Persons in History, New York: Hart Publishing Company, Inc. 1978, p. 33.

The above citations about the Prophet Muhammad (SAW) and Islam are not based on the teachings and practices of the Hadith or Islamic history. They are based on the teachings and practices of world history. Therefore, when we study some of the reasons western historians give for the success of Islam and the Prophet (SAW) in world history, it reflects the teachings and practices of the Qur'an and not the Hadith and how these establish the most intricate balance between the secular and religious. We have to distinguish these universal facts about the Prophet (SAW) and the Qur'an. And, point to some key issues of our lives, which we cannot take for granted. Hence, some of these are as follows:

1. It is obvious that the Prophet (SAW) could not be "the founder of twenty terrestrial empires and one spiritual empire" if he followed the Hadith and not the Qur'an. For example, the Hadith does not tolerate the different identities, cultures, customs, languages, dressings, traditions, etc, and sights and sounds of the different terrestrial empires within Islam. It expects all Muslims of different Islamic terrestrial empires to have the same identity, culture, custom, language, dressing, tradition, etc., that the Prophet (SAW) experienced during his time as his Sunnah. This is not only a total misconception of the true knowledge and understanding of the Holy Qur'an. But it is also a complete distortion of the true definition of the Sunnah. It is not natural to conquer a country and ask that country to change its identity, culture, custom, language, dressing, tradition, etc. No conquering nation has achieved this, neither the colonialists Christians nor the Muslims. Hence, each country has its own unique sight and sound, culture, custom, tradition, identity, sovereignty, etc.

2. If the Prophet (SAW) "was Caesar and Pope in one" then the Prophet (SAW) could have never become Caesar by using the Hadith and Pope by using the Qur'an. It would be like establishing a political base on a religious base that was totally hostile to the diversity of language, custom, identity, dressing, culture, tradition and all secular and scientific development of this world, by stating that it was western and worldly and will not help in the akhirah. Thus, in Islam, Caesar can only become Pope and vice versa if he is allowed to work according to the universal teachings and practices of the Holy Qur'an, and not according to the fundamentalists and extremists teachings and practices of the Hadith.

3. If the Prophet (SAW) and Islam succeeded by "conquering ideas and restoring rational dogmas" then it is hardly likely that the Prophet (SAW) and Islam had anything to do with Hadith, which is extremely religious and fundamentalist. Whereas its possible they were greatly influenced by the Holy Qur'an, because the Holy Qur'an is highly revolutionary, dynamic and appeals to the universal perspective of reality, found in world history and not in Islamic history based on the Hadith.

In addition to the above, in recent world events, other important facts have also emerged, which encourage us to promote a very post modern concept of Islam like I have done in this book, according to the divine teachings and practices of Tawhid. Some of these are:

1. Neither scientists nor religious people can prove or disprove the existence of God. Therefore, the Islam promulgated by the Qur'an is more likely to succeed in the modern and post modern era than the Islam that is promulgated by the Hadith.
2. The majority of religious people in the "Rainbow Nation" of South Africa reject the secular extremes of their new constitution, which is the best secular constitution in history, because it permits gay marriages, abortion, prostitution, etc.
3. The majority of the religious and secular people of this world reject both secular and religious extremism and fundamentalism, be it Islamic or otherwise.

Therefore, according to world history and recent world events, Muslims are sitting in a very pretty position to establish a new world order based on the true teachings and practices of the Holy Qur'an, because it is the only Book of God in history that can establish the most intricate balance between the secular and the religious, and solve all problems of diversity that confront it. If it were not so then how else could the Prophet (SAW) and early Muslims become so successful in world history? Therefore, it is fundamental for all Muslims to have a very pure knowledge of the Qur'an and Sunnah, which is completely free of Hadith and the kitabs (religious books) of their ulama and saints.

Nevertheless, before explaining some of the pure teachings and practices of the Holy Qur'an and Sunnah that intersect the secular and religious compartments of the Islamic way of life, it is important to know how different people handle these compartments in their daily lives and what are the Islamic perspective in the matter. For example, some people neglect the secular at the expense of their religion and others vice versa. This can be diagrammatically illustrated as follows:

GROUP 1: THE SKEWED DEVELOPMENT OF SECULAR AND RELIGIOUS:

Case 1.

SECULAR   RELIGIOUS

Where secular aspect of our life grows at the expense and neglect of our religion.

Case 2.

SECULAR   RELIGIOUS

Where religious aspect of our life grows at the expense and neglect of the secular.

In addition to the above, there are other people in this world who care for both the secular and religious developments of their lives. Although, they do not have true Islamic knowledge that combines the true teachings of the secular and religious to form the Islamic way of life, they manage to develop both, in the most suitable manner that is available to them. They usually render unto Caesar what is Caesar's and unto God what is God's. Hence, they separate the affairs of the church and state, and the boundaries of science, politics and religion, to make them separate and exclusive.

At times they are very hypocritical. For example, they will usually claim in the church or the mosque that it is wrong to believe in evolution but at their workplace or in the school they will teach evolution. Likewise, they use the religious method of taqleed, sainthood, priesthood, silsilas and khanqahs to promote and practice their religion, but use all secular method of ilm-ul-yaqin, ayn-ul-yaqin and haqq-ul-yaqin to promote and develop the secular aspects of their lives. We call this the parallel development of secular and religious. Diagrammatically, this can be represented as follows:

GROUP 2: PARALLEL DEVELOPMENT OF SECULAR AND RELIGIOUS:

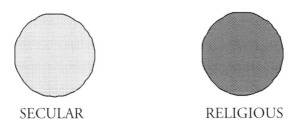

SECULAR   RELIGIOUS

Where the secular and the religious grow side by side in contradiction of their realities, rendering unto Caesar what is Caesar's and unto God what is God's. For example, one usually states that we should not bring our religion into our business or vice versa. Or where one usually separates the boundaries of science, religion and politics and makes them separate and exclusive.

The Holy Qur'an does not approve of any of the above practices of the secular and religious. It does not want us to develop in such a manner that we neglect the truth in either the secular or the religious aspects of our life. Likewise, the Holy Qur'an does not want us to separate the boundaries of science, politics and religion and make them separate and exclusive. It wants us to practice a way life that is as much secular as it is religious both inside and outside the mosque without any confusion.

Therefore, the Islamic way of life is a complete fusion of the secular and the religious except for that part of the secular, which does not believe in the existence of God, and that part of religion that is incompatible with the secular or outside of what is written in the Qur'an. Diagrammatically, this is represented as follows:

GROUP 3: THE ISLAMIC DEVELOPMENT OF THE SECULAR AND RELIGIOUS:

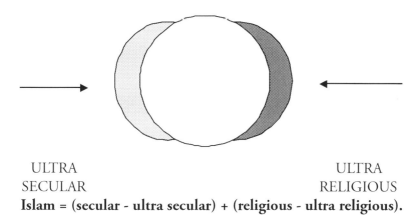

ULTRA SECULAR   ULTRA RELIGIOUS

Islam = (secular - ultra secular) + (religious - ultra religious).

Thus, the Islamic system of life is unique. The advantage of this system of life is that, it frees us from a very ritualistic type of a religion based on mysticisms and myths, which does not only create a rift between our faith in God and the secular progress and developments of our lives, but also makes us become irrational and un-intelligent in religion. For example, we perform salaah, give zakaat, make haj, etc, not to build our nation but for the sawaab of the akhirah. Hence, it feels that if it were not for the sawaab of the akhirah a Muslim might not even give you a cup of water.

Therefore, it is essential that if we wish to secure a very intricate balance between the secular and the religious, we stick to a religious belief and practice that are contained only in the Holy Qur'an, no more no less, and secular beliefs and practices, which can rationalize and intellectualize such beliefs and practices without restricting its own beliefs and practices, which do not only not deny the existence of God but also all the other injunctions of the Qur'an.

Hence, in Islam, it is not bid'ah (innovation) to use a car or an aeroplane for transportation, microphone in the mosque and to do astronomical calculations to determine the birth of the moon for the day of Ramadhan and Eid, or to establish the lunar calendar. Likewise, going to secular schools and developing our lives according to secular education is an integral part of the Islamic way of life and not un-Islamic, worldly, western and Christian. And, in the same way, it is not against Islam to play modern sports like tennis, soccer, cricket, etc, or play music, etc, within Tawhidi limits, by discarding the negative and enhancing the positive, within and between them.

In order to establish a very intricate balance of the secular and religious aspects of our lives, it is not only essential to limit all our religious teachings and practices of Islam to that of the Qur'an but also to give a secular meaning to these religious instructions that are compatible with our secular way of our lives. For example, we should not perform our salaah, give zakaat, make haj, etc, for the sawaab of the akhirah but we should do it for the love of Allah (SWT), the Prophets (peace be upon them), and all of humanity, as a means to an end to our materialistic way of life. Thus, we should use our salaah to spread democracy and the sovereignty of God like it is explained in this book; the zakaat to alleviate poverty and haj to unite the ummah on the international front and so on.

Therefore, the very intricate balance between the secular and the religious in Islam is not something that is shallow and superficial. Its very involved. For example, in addition to the above, it does not allow priesthood and sainthood and many other beliefs and practices of religion such as taqleed, aqeeda, silsilas and khanqahs, which divides the Muslim ummah into the different religious sects and madhabs. It is also against all jamiats of the ulama and ulooms that spread religion in such an un-Islamic manner or any other religious beliefs and practices like urs, forty days and one year ceremonies for the dead, etc.

In addition to the above, another reason why it is important to perceive the reality of the secular and religious is because God created us on the eternal plane and wants us to live in an eternal abode. Therefore, He has put us on this eternal journey to become aware of the eternal reality that does not separate the boundaries of science, religion and politics and make them separate and exclusive. Hence, according to the true teachings of the Holy Qur'an we are supposed to become aware of the fact that the ultra secular and the ultra religious is the false teaching and practice of this world and does not exist on the eternal plane. Unless we come to such a realization of our life how are we expected to qualify to live on the eternal plane in the akhirah?

This is the reason why I have stated time and again in this and my previous book, that there are very little rituals on the eternal plane, and that, whatever rituals, that we practice on this earth are a means to an end and not an end in themselves. What will go with us on the eternal plane will be the true knowledge of the Qur'an, and not our false perception of religion. Therefore, adding any more rituals like urs, forty days and four months with the jamaat or practicing the fabricated teachings of the Hadith, etc, does not improve our spirituality, but makes things worse for the eternal understanding and practice of Islam.

Thus, in order to establish the reality of both the secular and religious on the eternal level, the Qur'an tells us what is right and wrong in both the secular and religious aspects of our lives. Mathematically, this is written as follows:

Islam = (secular + religious) - (ultra secular + ultra religious).

In terms of the above, the core teachings and practices of the secular and religious systems of our lives on the earthly plane are more or less as follows:

THE SECULAR SYSTEM:

1. In this system of life, neither the creationists nor the evolutionists can prove the existence of God.
2. It's a system of life that educates and develops us according to the teachings of the ilm-ul-yagin (certainly of knowledge by interference or reasoning), ayn-ul-yagin (certainly knowledge by seeing and observing) and haqq-ul-yaqin (absolute knowledge like this is a book, etc.).
3. It's a system of life that encourages us to teach and learn.
4. Has schools and universities, learners (students), teachers and professors.

5. Has a house of parliament representing all the people in all compartments of their lives according to the teachings of democracy and majority rule.

THE RELIGIOUS SYSTEM:

1. It's a system of life that believes in God without the proof of the existence of God.
2. It's a system of life that educates and develops us according to the teachings of taqleed (narrations of spiritual leaders, saints or blind faith).
3. It's a system of life that depends very heavily in preaching and following, and not teaching and learning.
4. Has a mosque (a church), a madressah (a religious school), silsila and a khanqah to propagate the teachings and practices of their religion, sect, madhab, etc.
5. Has ulama (religious teachers) in the form of priests, bishops and saints.
6. Has a Vatican, National Ulama council, Maha Saba, etc., for different sects and schools of thought. Unlike the secular system, they do not promote or propagate the shurah (mutual consultation) and the ijma (consensus) of the majority of their people, followers or adherents to develop their aqidah or their Sharia. They only propagate and promote the shura and the ijma (consensus) of the ulama (priests and saints) of their sects and schools of thought to dictate their aqidah and sharia.

In the context of the above, the Islamic system of life intersects the secular and religious as follows:

THE ISLAMIC SYSTEM:

1. It is a system of life that is based on scientific and religious proof of the existence of God.
2. It is a system of life that educates and develops the ummah according to the teachings and practices of ilm-ul-yaqin, ayn-ul-yaqin and haqq-ul-yaqin.

3. It is a system of life that favors the secular system of teaching and learning.

4. It has schools and universities similar to the secular system that teach science and haqq (eternal truth).

5. It has learners (students) and teachers who are scholars in the real sense of the word, not priests, who are mistaken for scholars (ulama).

6. It has an Assembly of the Ummah representing the shurah and ijma of the majority of the Muslims, and not that of the ulama of the different schools of thought.

Thus, the Islamic system intersects a very large part of the secular system of life and does not approve of any of the ultra religious teachings like sainthood, priesthood, taqleed (the blind following of religion), etc. Therefore, unlike other religions and outright secular systems, Islam represents both except for the ultra secular and ultra religious. For example, the mosque is not only a place of worship. It is also the Assembly of the Ummah, where all who stand shoulder to shoulder in salaah, make shurah by mutual consultation and ijma (consensus) of the majority on all matters of shariah and Sunnah to cement their brotherhood. This means that all the affairs of their religion are made to agree and collaborate with the secular and vice versa.

Thus, standing shoulder to shoulder together in a religious manner in salaah and not having an Assembly of the ummah does not serve the purpose of Islam because it is easier to stand shoulder to shoulder together with your employee in salaah, but it is not easy to sit and make shurah and ijma on shariah, that make him equal to you and a brother, sharing universal viewpoints in both the secular and religious. Thus, the salaah without the Assembly of the Ummah only serves a religious purpose, which might be some what political but definitely not Islamic. Likewise, the trustee of the mosque is not only the trustee of a place of worship. He is also the political and secular leader of the community living in the vicinity of the mosque, who also has to take care of the Assembly of the Ummah, and ensure the community is functioning properly in an organized manner, in both secular and religious levels of their lives according to the divine teachings and practices of Tawhid.

Similarly, in the true Islamic system, an Aalim is a scholar who follows the secular method of teaching and learning, and not the religious method of taqleed, saints and priesthood. Therefore, the present day ulama and muftis are not scholars, but priests, who do not follow the Islamic system of teaching and learning. They follow the religious methods of preaching and following, according to the religious methods of taqleed, sainthood, priesthood, sects, madhabs, silsilas and khanqahs, which are totally contrary to the true teachings and practices of the Holy Qur'an. Hence, it will be foolish and incorrect, under the circumstances to call such an Aalim a scholar. Usually, intelligent Muslims who are aware of the true teachings of Islam call them mullahs (priests).

Let's take a business question to prove their priesthood mentality. In a business program on Radio Islam a mullah who is apparently an expert on a so-called Islamic business transactions was asked if a partner who is working in the business is entitled to a salary. The mullah answers, "No, because the partner is getting his share of the profits and therefore, it is not proper for him to take a salary". Some months later when he was put under pressure, he changed his mind about such a contract of a partnership. He said that the working partner should not take a salary but should ask the other partners to increase his or her share holdings in the business according to his or her salary. Surely, such an Aalim is not only ignorant about business, but also ignorant about Islam. Reaching compatibility between secular and religion is very important aspect of Islam. It's a basis for the true teachings and practices of Islam. What if such a partner dies or sells his or her share in the business? Will he or she be then entitled to benefit by the extra share holding which he or she is now not working for? And, once share holdings are signed on the dotted lines of a contract, then who will convince who that it is not exactly like that?

Hence, the nature of the Islamic system is such that a person is more likely to be correct in almost all of his or her actions, if he or she is secular and scientific than, if he or she is religious, because the common ground between the secular and religious in Islam is more secular than religious. Probably, this is a very bold statement, but it seems that in all matters of Islam, which does not find a common ground with the secular and scientific aspects of our lives, is un-Islamic, unless the Holy Qur'an makes an exception of such an act. Therefore, it was in this context of the Islamic way of life, that I stated that the secular courts and government of South Africa were in a better position to handle the Muslim Marriage Bill than the present Muslim religious institutions like the jamiats of ulama.

All teachings and practices of Islam are universal. In other words, they apply to both, the secular and religious compartments of lives, and also to all people of all cultures, customs and traditions, maintaining their diversity according to all the injunctions of the Qur'an. Thus, the Sunnah, which is the exact practice of the Qur'an, for a particular time and place, does not only apply to the religious compartment of our life, but it also applies to the secular compartment and all cultures, customs and traditions in their pure forms. This then means that keeping a beard, wearing a kurtha, etc, is not Sunnah (exact practice of Qur'an in its global perspective), but the Arab culture, custom and tradition of the time of the Peophet (SAW), which we are not compelled to follow. Likewise, this did not mean that because the Prophet (SAW) did not use the microphone in the mosque or do astronomical calculations to determine the birth of the moon to establish the lunar calendar that it is against the Sunnah of the Prophet (SAW) to do so.

Similarly, the Islamic teachings and practices of Tawhid are universal. They include all teachings and practices of unity that are found within and between the secular and religious compartments of our lives. For example, in a comprehensive Arabic/English dictionary, we find all the secular and religious teachings of unity and universality. To separate them into secular and religious is totally against Islam, because in Islam, we don't believe in the dichotomy of the secular and religious. If such a difference occurs in a language dictionary then it man made and has nothing to do with Islam. Therefore, when we explain Tawhid in the true Islamic perspective or spirit, it should always reflect haqq (truth), which none of the people, both in the secular and religious world should be able to deny, like I have done in the culture, political and science debates in the mass media. If we don't, it will not be Islamic or universal.

Insha-Allah (if God willing), I will try to complete this fusion of the secular and religious in the next few chapters to give a better insight into the true teachings and practices of Islam, which concerns the knowledge of man and the guidance of God.

CHAPTER 4

Islam Is Neither A Religion Nor A 7ᵗʰ Century Way Of Life.

When the Qur'an was revealed to the Prophet (SAW), people of this world had already developed a way of life according to their own knowledge of science, politics, religion, etc. For example, the Greeks, Egyptians and Romans were highly advanced in the knowledge of their ways of life. Today, many people of this world are still using some of their knowledge, for example, Roman laws, numerals, etc. Therefore, if there is any difference between ancient and modern, then it is more cosmetic than reality.

Naturally, when the Qur'an was revealed to the Prophet (SAW), people of this world did not wish to know from God, how to develop different knowledge of the different compartments or cultures, customs and traditions of their lives. They wished to know what was right and wrong in whatever they were saying and doing in the different compartments of their lives, because they disagreed with one another in almost every issue of their life within the diversity of their existence, and were confused with all the knowledge they had acquired in this world.

Some people, for example, were saying that God did not exist while others said He existed. Likewise some people said that there were many gods and others said that Jesus (PBUH) was God and Son of God and so on. All they did when the Qur'an was revealed to them, was to seek guidance from the Qur'an on the matter. For example, concerning the existence of God, they accepted the arbitration of the Qur'an that there was only one God, and He did not have sons, daughters and/or partners. Hence, the Word of God was used to settle their differences and not to give them any more knowledge than they already had.

In this book, I have explained the worldview teachings and practices of Tawhid (unity and universalism), not to add to the knowledge of this world, but to explain the meaning and message of all the injunctions of the Qur'an in a different way. If the majority of the Muslims of this world did not deviate from the true teachings and practices of the Qur'an and Sunnah and did not divide the ummah into so many different sects, madhabs, silsilas and khanqahs, I would not have had any reason to explain the worldview teachings and practices of Tawhid to explain the Qur'an and Sunnah. The injunctions of the Qur'an would have been adequate to explain the truth from falsehood in every human knowledge and experience. But, since no other person or book could explain the Qur'an and Sunnah in its true form, I used the Qur'an to explain the Qur'an and Sunnah, namely the Shariah.

Therefore, in every aspect of life wherein the people of this world differed, the Qur'an became their "Life Guide", nothing more, nothing less. For example, some people disputed that polygamy was wrong. But the Qur'an clearly stated that we were allowed to have up to four wives, provided we could treat them equally, financially and otherwise. Likewise, some people were of the opinion that it was wrong to eat meat or inhuman to slaughter an animal for food, clothing, etc. This type of criticism did not deter them because the Qur'an made it very clear that God created certain animals for food and because of this it was not wrong to slaughter certain animals for food.

Hence, all knowledge in this world is human and all guidance is from God. Some Muslims might not like what I am saying because the majority of them believe that all knowledge, good and bad, is from God, mainly because God taught Adam (AS) the names of the different creations, and if He did not, Adam (AS) would not have known. But, the reality of the situation is that, when God placed man on the planet earth, He did not give him a house, car, stove, fridge, etc. He just gave him a brain, with all the natural faculties of senses and natural resources. Man used his brain how to read, write and educate himself in every field of life in a very perverted manner. God corrected this perverted knowledge with revealed guidance.

Hence, the Qur'an separates the truth from falsehood in human knowledge and experience. Diagrammatically, this can be represented as follows:

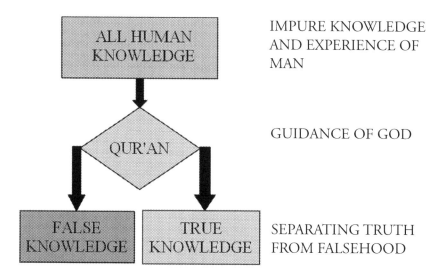

**QUR'AN SEPARATES TRUTH FROM FALSEHOOD
IN HUMAN KNOWLEDGE**

According to the above diagram, it is absolutely clear that in any one issue of our life, we are never subjected to the ilm of God but are always subjected to the ilm of man and the guidance of God. For example, in this knowledge and experience of man, God did not create the idea and concept of the secular and religious. We created it because it was natural to our way of life and understanding under the duress of reason and science that we should separate the secular from the religious. All Allah (SWT) did according to the Qur'an and Sunnah of the Prophet (SAW) was to tell us, purely out of His mercy, what was haqq (truth) and batil (falsehood) in both secular and the religious aspects of our lives, and how to intersect these to establish the truth between them on the eternal plane.

It was because of this guidance of God that man found a way to understand what was right and wrong with his own knowledge and experience of life. For example, we learnt that atheism and evolution was wrong, and that Islam was not a religion, but a way of life. And that we must not believe in anything in religion that was incompatible with science, reason, history, business, politics, etc, according to the injunctions of Qur'an. Likewise, we began to learn more about the balances between the seen and unseen, secular and religious, individual and the community, and so on, and how to establish a proper nation building program with God's guidance.

Recently, one Aalim was involved in a similar type of a debate. He said that one night during the time of Prophet (SAW) it rained heavily. The next morning some Sahabi (RA) were discussing how rain was made according to their knowledge of science. Some Sahabis felt that the discussion was futile because it was God Who produced the rain and it had nothing to do with science. To this, he said the Prophet (SAW) reacted by replying that those who believed that God produced the rain had imaan and those who disputed it lacked imaan.

We agree that God created the rain but it is also true that God used the knowledge of science to create rain, and man used the knowledge of God's creative powers to understand how rain was made. Today, man is also making safe drinking water using the AirQua technique, which is no different in principle in the way in which God used science to make rain. Therefore, the bottom line is that God created this entire creation from a primeval matter that operated according to the laws of physics and mathematics, and in order for us to understand His creation, the Qur'an assures us that He used science wherever it was possible to do so.

Thus, science is the common denominator in understanding God's creation and the knowledge of man. It could not be otherwise. Therefore, it is wrong to state that God did not create rain according to the knowledge of science and those who believe that He did do so did not have imaan. Refer to the chapter on "The Qur'an and Science" for more information on God, His creation and the knowledge of man. Therefore, in this chapter and this book, it is not uncommon for us to question the authenticity of many of the narrations of the ulama based on the Hadith, especially in the name of God and the Prophet (SAW).

The following diagrams illustrate how God used science to make rain, and how man used science, to make safe drinking water from air:

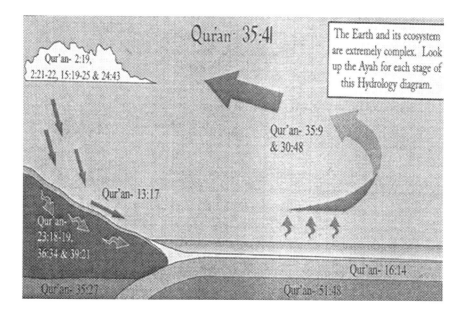

Therefore, when we witness the true relationship between the knowledge and experience of man, and the guidance of God, certain important principles of Islam are established. Some of these Islamic principles are as follows:

1. We become "the friends of Allah (SWT)" when we accept the pure teachings and practices of human life according to the guidance of God, and also trustworthy Muslims among the ummah of the Prophet (SAW).

2. Since the entire knowledge and experience of man is concerned with both the secular and religious aspects of our lives, it does not give either of these the right to dictate what are the pure teachings and practices our lives. Only the guidance of God decides which compartment of our life is the natural, dominant power and force of human life.

3. God's guidance is absolute haqq (truth). It is not associated with either the secular or religious aspects of our lives. Therefore, it can be implemented outside and inside the mosque, but, only according to the shurah and ijma of the Muslim majority. God wants us to acquire knowledge by our own experience and intelligence and not to be forced to do so. Even accepting the

guidance of God should come from within us, and not to be forced upon us.

4. The Holy Qur'an is not responsible for developing man's knowledge about his existence, which is evolutionary and independent. Therefore, we are encouraged to acquire knowledge from the cradle to the grave or be it in China according to the guidance of the Holy Qur'an and shurah and ijma of ummah. Those who state that these are weak hadith, discredit the whole science of Hadith. It's for this reason and many others that we do not trust the book of Hadith as an explanation of the Qur'an and Sunnah.

5. Finally, knowledge cannot be Islamized, because all knowledge of man found in this planet is human. For example, the theorem of Pythagoras cannot be Islamized. All that the guidance of God does to human knowledge is that it changes its perverted reality, which is masked with falsehood, to the genuine reality of life according to haqq (truth) found in the guidance of the Qur'an. For example, Islamic reality does not believe in priesthood or blind following of religion, yet believes in God, revealed guidance, Prophets, etc.

Thus, all of man's knowledge and experience in this world is not only impure but it is also man-made and has nothing to do with God except for the guidance of God that makes it pure. Therefore, in order to examine these teachings and practices of Islam according to the guidance of the Qur'an, let us first examine the Oxford dictionary meaning of religion, which is actually human knowledge and notion of religion and has nothing to do with God. It is as follows:

1. Monastic condition, being monk or nun, (enter into, be in, ~); (rare) a monastic order.
2. (rare). Practice of sacred rites.
3. One of the prevalent systems of faith & worship (the Christian, Mohammedan, ~; established ~, that of established CHURCH; NATURAL, REVEALED, ~; all ~s are the same to him).
4. Human recognition of superhuman controlling power and esp. of a personal God entitled to obedience, effect of such recognition on conduct & mental attitude, (get ~, Vulg. Or joc., be converted to such belief).

5. Action that one is bound to do (make a ~ of doing). Hence ~LESS.

In the above dictionary meaning of religion, there are some core teachings and practices of religion that are generally associated with religion in the western Christian world. These are as follows:

1. It is a **monastic order**, where monks and nuns do not marry. Likewise, it supports a system of life that divorces itself from all the worldly activities of our lives, like business, politics, sports, etc.
2. It is **limited to the teachings of "faith and worship"**. Hence, although it is a system of life that believes in God and revealed knowledge of God, it does not question what it believes.
3. Unlike in Islam, **God, His revealed knowledge and His Prophets are associated only with religion** and not with the secular or the other realities of our existence.

In addition to the above, there are some other core teachings and practices of religion that are hidden by the above dictionary meaning of religion. These are as follows:

1. A great part of the teachings and practices of all religions are based on **blind faith or taqleed**. Hence, religious people usually accuse secular people of having a weak imaan (faith) for questioning their belief or for asking for proofs. This is exactly the opposite of what happens in our secular way of life where we put our neck on the block for what we can prove. Therefore, in the secular aspects of our lives the highest form of faith is on those things that we can prove and in religion the highest form of faith is to believe on those things for which we have no proof.
2. In the secular system we usually teach and learn according to the secular system of ilm-ul-yaqin, ayn-ul-yaqin and haqq-ul-yaqin. In religion they usually **preach and follow** according to the religious method of taqleed (blind faith). Hence, in religion they rely very heavily on religious teachers or priests, saints, silsilas and khanqahs, to teach religion according to the religious method of taqleed. They contradict almost every teaching method of the secular system based on ilm-ul-yaqin, ayn-ul-yaqin and haqq-ul-yaqin.

3. In religion **almost all the teachings of all sects or denominations within each religion are different.** This is mainly due to teaching of blind faith. Scientists who have studied these differences say that they all contradict one another to such an extent that not all of them can be right but all of them can be wrong. In the secular system such differences and contradictions do not occur on such a large scale that all of them can be wrong because they are able to prove what they believe. Even if they differ they do not have different schools, universities, house of parliament, etc., for different thoughts, ideas and beliefs.

4. **In religion, the shurah and ijma of the ulama is more important than the shurah and ijma of the ummah.** Therefore, in religion a group of religious leaders who sit in the Vatican, the council of churches, the Maha Saba or the jamiats of different religions and sects decide what are the true teachings and practices of their religions and sects. In the secular system, the people decide.

Thus, it is very clear from the above dictionary meaning of religion that all the core teachings and practices of religion are absolutely contrary to the true teachings and practices of the Holy Qur'an, except for the fact that Islam also believes in God, His Revealed knowledge and His Prophets but in a very different manner. For example, all religions believe in God, His Revealed knowledge and His Prophets but not all religions establish a rational way of life that combines religion with the secular. They establish a tribal religion of a particular culture, custom and tradition suitable for their nation and whims.

Islam is not like that. Islam does not use God, His Revealed knowledge and His Prophets to establish any religion or a particular way of life with a particular sign, symbol, dressing, culture, language, custom, tradition, political affiliation, etc. It uses God His Revealed knowledge and His Prophets to provide guidance to all the people of this world of all signs, culture, custom, tradition and compartments of our lives, telling them what is good, bad, truth and falsehood in their way of life. Hence, Islam is a LIFE GUIDE, "enjoining good and forbidding evil", to all people of all cultures, customs, traditions and compartments, with time and space.

Similarly, in the West, the secular was born out of the contradiction of its religion. It did not come into existence independent of the contradictions. To confirm this let's look at the same Oxford dictionary meaning of the secular in conjunction to the above meaning of religion, which is as follows:

1. Lasting or going on for ages or an indefinitely long time (opp. periodical, cyclic; ~ change, going on slowly but persistently; ~ cooling or refrigeration, that of the earth from fluid state; ~ acceleration, slow increase in motion of heavenly body; ~ fame, enduring; the ~ rivalry between France & England, Church & State, etc.).

2. Concerned with the affairs of this world, worldly, not sacred, not monastic, not ecclesiastical, temporal, profane, lay, (~ affairs, education, music; the ~ clergy, parish, priests, etc., opp. regular; the ~ arm, hist., civil jurisdiction to which criminal was transferred by ecclesiastical courts for severer punishment); skeptical of religious truth or opposed to religious education etc., whence ~ism, ~ist, etc.

According to the above dictionary meaning of the secular, there are some very important core teachings and practices of the secular that are totally opposed to religion, which is somewhat responsible for establishing this relationship between the secular and religious. These are as follows:

1. **It is "worldly".** In other words, it is that part of our life that deals with the material, political, business and other aspects of our lives that are not concerned with religion in the non-Muslim world.

2. **It is "skeptical of religious truths or opposed to religious education".**

Thus, when we look at the whole concept and idea of the secular and religious according to the teachings and practices of the western and Christian world, we observe that it was a Western Christian idea to separate the boundaries of science, religion and politics and make everything in their lives that did not concern their religion to be secular. For example, according to the core teachings and practices of their religion, they separate the affairs of the state and the church and render unto Caesar what is Caesar's and unto God what is God's.

It was never the guidance of God to do so. In addition to this, contrary to the true word of God, they do not reason in matters of faith. The majority of the Muslims are also doing the same thing not because it is Islamic to do so but because they are ignorant of the truth. For example, when we tell them that the 7th century Islam of the Hadith is fundamentalist and extremist, they ostracize and condemn us as munafiks instead of reasoning or rationalizing with us to commit themselves to the truth.

Thus, according to the above dictionary meaning of the secular, another very important reason why the Christians have separated the secular from their religion is because the secular is "skeptical about their religious truths and is opposed to their religious education". This does not make sense because all the dogmas and doctrines of the Christian Church that are based on the assumption that Jesus is God and the Son of God are not religious truth according to Islam. Then how can the secular be secular when it is opposed to religious truths that are not religious truths?

As far as we are concerned, this whole idea and concept of the secular and religious is western and Christian and has nothing to do with Islam or haqq (eternal truth about our creation). It is an impure knowledge and understanding of this world. We should therefore not associate our God with the secular or the religious. And should always consider Him to be our Guide in all the affairs of our life, which is not separated into the secular and religious.

In the true teachings and practices of Islam, if we consider the fact that Islam is not a religion but a way of life then, we should refrain from saying or doing some of the things we say and do in religion. For example, we should not say or do the following:

1. Refrain from using religious schools and institutions like ulooms and jamiats, that promote the religious teachings and practices of their sects, madhabs and schools of thought. Instead unify the application and understanding of the Holy Qur'an and Sunnah in all the compartments of our lives, according to the shurah and ijma of the ummah in the assembly of the ummah, which we are required to establish in the local mosque and network these region-by-region, area by area and province by province.

2. Stop dividing the ummah into religious sects, madhabs, silsilas and khanqahs according to blind faith. Instead, we should unite the ummah according to the simple injunctions of the Holy Qur'an in all the aspects of our lives, according to the worldview teachings and practices of peace and Tawhid, in a very skilful, logical and rational manner.

3. Not to perform our salah, give zakaat, perform haj, recite (read) Qur'an, etc, for sawaab of the akhirah, which defeats the object of Islam. But, perfect these acts to create a dynamic and a well-balanced society in all compartments of our lives. And, use them as nation building programs like it is explained in this book.

4. Refrain from dividing the progress and development of our life in this world into secular and religious. We must continue to progress and develop in our lives according to human knowledge and experience, and seek the guidance of God in every compartment and level of our lives, according to the true teachings and practices of the Holy Qur'an, Sunnah and the shurah and ijma of the ummah.

5. We must not limit the teachings and practices of Islam to the time of the Prophet (SAW) or to the Arab culture and custom of his time according to the religious teachings and practices of Hadith. The Quranic injunctions are haqq (eternal truths), and these do not change with time and place. Hence, they are the same for all cultures, customs, traditions and compartments of our lives, over all time and place.

Thus, it is our duty to inform the Muslim ummah that although we also love our Indo-Paki culture, custom and tradition, it is our duty to tell our daughters, wives and sisters that it is not religion but tradition to wear the scarf on the head or to cover their faces in public, because when their cousins come from America or England, they must not feel that their cousins are inferior Muslims to them, because their cousins do not wear the headscarf or cover their faces in public. If we do not teach our daughters, wives and sisters what are the true teachings and practices of Islam then pride will overcome them and they will feel "holier than thou" and show no respect for other people's culture, custom and tradition and their age. In other words, it is essential that they know what is written in the Qur'an and know what Shariah is.

For example, one young woman came to our shop to buy sausages. She wanted to know if we had a SANNAH certificate to prove if the sausages were halaal (khosher). An elderly woman standing next to her in the queue explained that the people who manufactured the product according to the label on the product were well known butchers in our town and the owners of the shop were well known Muslims in the town who would not dare sell any haraam products. The young woman turned around and told her, "You shut up. You don't even look like a Muslim" because the elderly woman did not have a scarf on her head. We felt sorry for the young woman, not because she did not buy the sausages or did not ask the older woman for forgiveness for not showing respect to her, but because she would leave this world without knowing what is haqq and batil about her dressing and that of the elderly woman.

For Allah's sake (Muslim brother and sisters), come to your senses. Do not feel "holier than thou" if you keep a beard, wear a kurtha, etc., or if you wear the hijab or cover your face in public. Any stupid person can do that. If it is your culture, custom and tradition to do so, you have the right to do so but you have no right to say that it is religion to do so, or distort the truth and destroy the true definition of the Sunnah. And confuse the ummah, mislead them or even reject them for your misunderstanding of Islam and divide your brotherhood with them.

Therefore, in Islam, like we preserve the diversity of all the signs, symbols, dressings, languages, customs, cultures, traditions and compartments of our lives according to the injunctions of the Holy Qur'an and Sunnah in their pure forms, we should preserve the diversity of all our human experience and knowledge in their pure forms according to the injunctions of the Holy Qur'an and Sunnah. From this point of view, we should respect all human knowledge and experience in this world be it in China unless the true teachings and practices of Islam reject it according to the shurah and ijma of the ummah.

In conclusion, it is my contention that according to the divine teachings and practices of Tawhid, Islam is neither a religion nor a particular way of life with a particular sign, symbol, dressing, language, culture, custom, tradition, etc. In it, each nation or nationality is supposed to have it's own unique sign, symbol, dressing, language, culture, custom, tradition, etc., according to the true knowledge of haqq and the diversity of their creation. Likewise, we are forbidden to interfere with the diversity of our politics, business, science, education, etc, with time and space.

We are required to find universal solutions to all our problems in all dimensions and levels of our lives, according to the true teachings and practices of the Holy Qur'an, Sunnah and shurah and ijma of the ummah. Therefore, in Islam, like we do not have an Islamic sign, symbol, dressing, language, custom, culture, tradition, etc., we are not supposed to have Islamic politics, science, education, commerce, business, medicine, etc. We are supposed to acknowledge pure knowledge and experience from the impure, over all time and place according to haqq, and if we deviate from haqq, we will suffer the consequences.

CHAPTER 5

In Search Of 'The Straight Way'

Usually, in any religion, it's very difficult to convince anybody "What is the straight way". Religion is like that. It is based on blind faith, for example, if we tell the Christians that Jesus is not God and Son of God, they will not believe us. Likewise, if we tell the Hindus that it is wrong to worship idols and attach partners to God, they will not believe us. This did not mean that all the Muslims will agree with us when we tell them what is written in the Holy Qur'an.

The so-called Sunnis or Bareilly's will not believe us if we told them that according to the Qur'an, the Prophet (SAW) was an ordinary person, who was a universal example for all of mankind. And, that they must not believe in saints and venerate the graves of saints, because it is against the true teachings and practices of the Holy Qur'an to do so. Similarly, the Wahabi's will not believe us if we told them that according to the Qur'an, it is wrong to state that it is Sunnah to keep a beard, wear kurtha, kneel and drink water, etc., and force Muslim women to cover their faces or their heads in public.

Nowadays, not only religious people believe what their worldly masters want them to believe, but scientists also do the same thing. Today, a great deal of science, which is of national interest, is commercialized and politicized. For example, the doctor of the nation in the United States of America, who worked for the Bush administration for two terms, stated that he was "gagged" by the President on some vital issues of national interest like global warming and stem cell research.

Similarly, some scientists who stated that global warming was a scam by the developed nations to undermine the industrial growth of the developing nations, were given a bad name and discarded by their colleagues. Thus, nowadays, in all compartments of your life, whether it is politics, science, business or religion, you have to say and do what your worldly masters want you to say and do, otherwise you will be ostracized and discarded by your own people. Therefore, in this kind of a confusion and chaos, how do you convince anybody? "What is the straight way?"

A similar type of problem was experienced recently here in South Africa when we were involved in a cultural debate. Everybody was criticizing and condemning everybody else's culture. Some people were very unhappy with the African culture when Tony Yengeni, an MP, stabbed the bull with a spear in a cleansing ceremony, after he was released from jail for defrauding the state, saying that it was inhuman and cruelty to animal. Likewise, some individuals objected to the behavior of some Black African taxi drivers who raped a Black African woman for wearing a mini skirt, which they said was against their culture. Similarly, President Zuma was criticized for having four wives, being Western at work and African and traditionalist at home.

In this debate, the Muslims also came under severe criticism for compelling Muslim women to cover their faces in public, etc., and not allowing them to go to school, work, drive a car, etc., like in Saudi Arabia and Afghanistan under the Taliban. There were many other complaints against the Muslims such as they encouraged polygamy, were against freedom of speech and expression and homosexuality, etc, and were also scrutinized for their method of divorce, etc.

Naturally, some well known Black African professionals did not like what some of the White people had to say about their culture. As it is, we were experiencing a lot of racial tension in our country between the Black and White people of our country at that time. Therefore, when some Black people told the Whites to "Go to hell", it was very intimidating. Thus, in order to bring about some sanity to the debate, Max du Preez, a well-respected journalist wrote an article in The Star, that stated that in order to keep the peace we should respect the cultures of all people, immaterial of the fact whether we liked it or not.

Although, I appreciated du Preez's article under the circumstances, I did not agree with some of the things that he said in the name of Islam, because they were completely contrary to the true teachings and practices of the Holy Qur'an. I felt that it was my duty to preserve the true teachings and practices of the Holy Qur'an not only for the Muslim ummah on this issue, but also for all people with diverse cultures in our country. Therefore, my reply to du Preez was as follows:

"I appreciate Max du Preez's article, 'You don't have to like a culture to respect it' (The Star, January 17), but I am very reluctant to accept it.

For example, it is very difficult for me to respect his 'Muslim friends' who compel women to cover their faces in public according to the Wahabi sect when such teachings not only contradict the true teachings of the Holy Qur'an but also destroy the universal image of Islam.

I am duty bound to my Creator to protect and preserve the true teachings and practices of God's word in the Holy Qur'an. For example, if I did not have the Qur'an, how would I know that Muslims are permitted to slaughter certain animals for food?

Hence, I respect all the people of this world who do not eat meat or eat meat but I do not respect those who insist it is wrong for me to take the life of an animal for food.

Likewise, I am against all Muslims, who insist that it is religion to keep a beard, kneel and drink water, etc., or compel Muslim women to cover their faces in public. Such teachings are not in the Qur'an. If some Muslims of a certain tribe wish to do so because it is their custom, culture and tradition to do so, then they have the right to do so but it is wrong for them to insist that it is religion.

Islam is a universal system of life. It embraces all customs, traditions, cultures and compartments of our lives, which do not contradict the true knowledge of the Qur'an.

So what if Zuma has four wives? Such behavior does not contradict the Qur'an. Likewise, so what if Zuma is Western at work and African and traditionalist at home?

I wish all the people of this world could come together and use the true word of God to solve all the problems of our diversities and preserve our brotherhood."

The editor of The Star newspaper supported my viewpoint in the culture debate with the following caption and photo of the Qur'an::

- The Star Newspaper, Johannesburg, South Africa

Some Muslims did not like my letter in The Star. For example, one Muslim businessman stated that there was no real merit in what I had to say in the letter, stating that The Star had only printed it because I collaborated with the West on the issue of the hijab, which was used by the West to ridicule Islam. I expected the Muslim brother to say this because he was a fundamentalist. He failed to understand that in this culture debate, I was not only talking to Muslims, but all people with the different cultural backgrounds of this world, and that the editor of The Star newspaper was challenging not only the Muslims, but all people to take up the challenge that the Holy Qur'an was a LIFE GUIDE or give an alternative.

This Muslim brother, was not uneducated. He was a university graduate of science. If I could not convince him what were the true teachings and practices of the Qur'an and Sunnah, what chance did I have to convince 90% of the Muslims of this world who did not have even a matric certificate to accept my arguments in the culture debate? Under the circumstance, there was no ways I could convince an Aalim who was a priest.

Unfortunately, nobody could take up the challenge, not even an atheist, except a fundamentalist Muslim who did not like what I said about Wahabism in the debate. As expected a Wahabi mufti from Durban wrote a letter to the editor, claiming that he did not agree with my letter to Max du Preez. His letter was entitled, "Views on Islam are way off the mark", which reads as follows:

"I refer to two highly offensive letters published in The Star on January 30 2008. The letters are from AK Sayed and K Muller.

AK Sayed implies he's knowledgeable in Islamic law. If this is correct, then the misrepresentations are intentional.

The correct position is the following:

- It is obligatory on a Muslim man to keep a beard of the length of his clenched fist, measured from his chin.
- It is also the practice of our Prophet Muhammad, which Muslims are obliged to follow, to sit when drinking water.
- The position relating to the acceptable dress code for women in the Holy Qur'an, where God commands that your wives, your daughters . . . shall let down their garments over themselves, i.e. comply with the requirements of hijab.

AK Sayed should tread cautiously, as the misrepresentations he perpetuates are material, gross and misleading.

K Muller's letter is nothing but clichés of unwarranted attacks on established principles of Shariah. A true Muslim is desirous of complying with his/her obligations in terms of Shariah. Non-compliance compromises one's faith. Would you rather your daughter prancing around in a bikini, attracting negative gazes, than being clad in a manner acceptable to God?

AK Sayed and K Muller are misguided and I pray that they correct their courses before they self-destruct."

I was totally unimpressed with the mufti's reply. My reply to the mufti was published in The Star on the 1st of April, 2008. It was titled "**Qur'an is to be understood in the context of all cultures**" and conveyed the following message of the Qur'an:

"I wish to thank Mufti E Desai for his letter entitled, 'Views on Islam are way of the mark', (The Star, March 19). At least he has done the decent thing by writing to the press instead of inciting his congregation, like a well-known mufti did the previous Friday in my mosque.

Unfortunately, the problem with Desai is that he does not understand some of the most basic teachings of Islam. For example, he fails to understand that according to the divine teachings of Tawhid (unity and universalism), all the Prophets of God were given strict instructions not to say or do anything in their religion that was not revealed to them.

In surah 10 verse 15 and 16, the Prophet Muhammad was instructed to do the same. He did not state that keeping a beard, wearing the kurtha, kneeling and drinking water, etc, was obligatory like the mufti states in his letter, because these things were not revealed to him in the Holy Qur'an.

Likewise, in surah 33 verse 59 and surah 24 verse 31, the Qur'an does not restrict a woman from driving a car, going to school, working with men, etc. The only restriction on her is to cover her chest or bosom (jayb), not her hair (sha'r) or her head (ra's) like our mothers and grandmothers did, in a society where both men and women are commanded to 'lower their gaze'.

According to the divine teachings of Tawhid, it is critical for all Muslims to understand the message of the Holy Qur'an in the context of all the cultures, customs, traditions and compartments of our lives and not only in the Arab culture and custom of the time of the Prophet.

The most important reason why God wanted all the Prophets to preserve the true word of God was because He wanted to prove to all the people of this world that their God is one God and He provides the same guidance to all of us, so that we may recognize 'the all truth' of our creation.

When religious leaders like mufti Desai add words to the word of God and distort the true meaning and message of the word of God, they become another problem of diversity and not a solution thereof.

All I did in my letter of January 30 was to conclude that human knowledge was not good enough to solve the problem of diversity and that we should all, Muslims and non-Muslims of all sects and denominations, come together to use the true word of God to solve all the problems of our diversity and preserve our brotherhood."

The above letter was published in The Star on the 1st of April 2008, with a picture of a mosque with the following caption:.

UNITED: People pray at a mosque in Lahore. All religions need to come together to use the word of God for good, says the writer. **PICTURE: REUTERS**

- The Star Newspaper, Johannesburg, South Africa

In addition to the above, I would like to state that the word "Hijab" appears approximately seven times in the Holy Qur'an, five times as "Hijab" and twice as "Hijaban". See surah 7:46, 33:53, 38:32, 41:5, 42:51, 17:45 & 19:17. None of these "Hijab" words are used in the Qur'an with reference to what the traditional Muslims call today as the dress code for the Muslim women. Hijab in the Qur'an has nothing to do with the Muslim women's dress code. Therefore, the Qur'an did not compel Muslim women to "comply with the requirements of the hijab" in the form of a dress code. For more information on this subject, please compare verse 33:53, which applies to the wives of the Prophet (SAW) with verse 24:31, which applies to all believing women. Also read Yusuf Ali's note 3760.

Thus, in the culture debate I made many important findings, which both Muslims and non-Muslims could not deny. Some of these are:

1. Human knowledge was not good enough to solve the problems of our diversity, and that we relied very heavily on the guidance of God, in the Holy Qur'an to do so.
2. The Qur'an cannot be challenged by any nation, and it was a universal solution to all the problems of our diversity (in our multi-cultural society).
3. The Muslims were divided into two distinct groups. Those that believed in the universal teachings and practices of the Holy Qur'an and those that believed in the fundamentalist teachings and practices of the Hadith.
4. There was no place for religious fundamentalism and religious extremism in Islam. Mufti Desai's letter was threatening when he used words like "self-destruct", and some of the ulama definitely used the mosque to incite the congregation against fellow Muslims instead of approaching them in a civil manner and solving their differences with them.
5. I felt free to intellectualize the Qur'an in a very universal manner in the mass media but not the Hadith. It was easier to teach and learn the knowledge of the Qur'an but not to preach and follow the knowledge of the Hadith. I could see this difference very clearly in Mufti Desai's letter and my reply to him.
6. In this debate I could prove beyond any doubt that Muslims did not have to be followers in any world event anymore. They could become leaders once again, if they used the Qur'an correctly.

In the above debate, the strength of Islam was not only centered around the simple injunctions of the Holy Qur'an, which could solve only the simple problems of diversity within and between all cultures, customs, traditions and compartments of our lives but it could also solve all the problems of diversity that formed an intricate balance between seen and unseen, secular and religious, individual and community, national and international, this world and akhirah and so on in their abstract form. For example, I used the worldview teachings and practices of Tawhid (unity and universality) to explain that all the Prophets of God were given strict instructions by God not to say or do anything in their religion that was not revealed to them in order to prove to all people of this world that their God was one God and He provided the same guidance to all of us so that we may recognize "the all truth" of our creation, over all time and place.

Thus, my experience in writing to the mass media gave me deep insight to the fact that all the people of this world had a relationship with either the DUNYA (worldly) or the AKHIRAH (herafter) or both, sometimes in a very positive manner and sometimes in a very negative manner. Sometimes these relationships were very balanced and at other times very skewed. For example, some people find a fair balance between the DUNYA and the AKHIRAH and sometimes they divorce themselves from the DUNYA and take more care about the AKHIRAH and sometimes vice versa.

Mathematically, we can represent all the different attitudes of the different people of this world with different lines on our graph paper. For example, if we represent all the issues of the DUNYA (worldly) on the Y-axis and all the issues of the AKHIRAH or religion on the X-axis, then the different people of the different religion and ways of life of this world will represent different lines in the different quadrants of our graph paper. For example, take a person from Europe, who is a Christian and a scientist. When he or she is involved with the affairs of the DUNYA, he or she will be standing on the Y-axis in the first quadrant of our graph paper or very close to the Y-axis in the first quadrant.

Likewise, if he or she is involved with the affairs of the AKHIRAH or religion, he or she will be standing on the X-axis in the first quadrant or very close to it but not on the line that dissects or bisects the first quadrant because he or she does not have the true knowledge and understanding of life that represents the exact balance between the DUNYA and the AKHIRAH in such a fashion where they can intersect all the affairs of this world with their religion. This is because they usually render unto Caesar what is Caesar's and unto God what is God's or separate the affairs of the church and the state. These people are different from those people in their communities who do not believe in God, religion and the akhirah or the communists who represent only the positive values of the Y-axis in the second quadrant because all their values of religion and the akhirah are totally negative like the values of the X-axis in the second quadrant of the graph.

Unfortunately, compared with the people of the West who are mostly Christians, communists and atheist, the majority of Muslims who state that secular education and our secular way of life in this world is western, Christian, temporary and worldly and will not help in the AKHIRAH have lost their legitimate place in the first quadrant of our graph. They now represent both the DUNYA and the AKHIRAH in the fourth quadrant of our graph where almost all their values of the DUNYA relative to their religion or the AKHIRAH are negative. At least the Christian have secured the positive values of the DUNYA by separating the secular from the religious and by rendering unto Caesar what is Caesar's and unto God what is God's. Muslims have even failed to do that.

Thus, in every situation of life, where there is a relationship between one or two issues, the general formula of the straight line is as follows:

$$Y = MX + C.$$

In the above formula, the line that dissects or bisects the first quadrant or the line that represents both the DUNYA and AKHIRAH without any bias for the dunya or the akhirah, or "the straight way", is Y=X, where the value of M=1 and C=0.

On the graph paper, it is represented as follows:

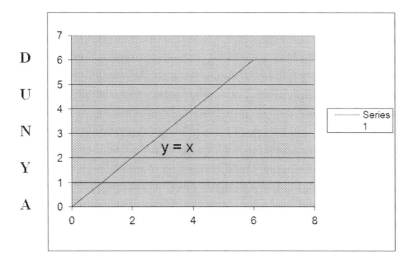

A   K   H   I   R   A   H
The graph of "the straight way", where y=x.

The above graph represents the graph of "the straight way", where both the values of X and Y are positive and equal because they are in the first quadrant of the graph, and they dissect or bisect the first quadrant of the graph. Therefore, on this line, if we represent the DUNYA on the Y-axis and the AKHIRAH on the X-axis, then both the DUNYA and the AKHIRAH will represent all the positive issues of our life in all the compartments of our life without any bias either for the DUNYA or the AKHIRAH. For example, if there was a line slightly above this line it will be partial to the DUNYA and any line slightly below this would be partial to the AKHIRAH.

Take for example, the recitation of the Holy Qur'an. If we recited it in Arabic only, for sawaab of the akhirah, without knowing the meaning and applying it in our lives to build our nation, then we would not be representing the line y=x but a line below it, which is bias to the DUNYA and impartial to the AKHIRAH. Likewise, if we were like some of the western people who were reading the Holy Qur'an to denigrate Islam or like some Muslims who state that it is outdated, we would be impartial to the DUNYA and bias towards the AKHIRAH.

Thus, a good Muslim will not read the Holy Qur'an only for the sawaab (blessings) of the akhirah, or to cause mischief, or to read faal (fortune), or to make taweez (amulet, talisman) for shifa (cure illness) and protection against evil, accident, etc, or even to establish a religion and a way of life that divides humanity, and is a major cause for war. He or she will read the Holy Qur'an to establish guidance, "the all truth", peace and one reality of this entire universe, like we did in the culture debate. By all means recite the Holy Qur'an in the Arabic language but at least try to understand what is written in it so that we can unify the true teachings and practices of the Holy Qur'an and Sunnah, to unify not only the Muslim ummah, but all the people of this world, for their progress and development for the good in this world.

The above teachings and practices of Islam do not only apply to the recitations of the Holy Qur'an, but also apply to all the teachings and practices of Islam. For example, in the previous chapter, we stated that Muslims who performed the jamaat salaah (five daily congregational pryer) only for the sawaab (blessings) of the akhirah were defeating the whole object of the jamaat salaah, because if the jamaat salaah did not wipe out the race or class differences or even religious differences in our society, and built our nation by consensus of the majority, then such a jamaat salaah was incapable of achieving the sawaab of the akhirah.

Therefore, in order to give a greater meaning to the salaah, the Prophet (SAW) did not only make the king and pauper, rich and poor, bosses and workers, etc., stand shoulder to shoulder together, but he also made them to talk to one another in the Assembly of the Ummah on how to establish the shariah and live together as one brotherhood of the ummah. Hence, it is easy to stand shoulder to shoulder together in salaah and thereafter to go out on your own way but it is not so easy to sit down together with people of other races, class, etc., and establish rules of shariah that makes them your brothers and sisters in every respect and in every compartment of your lives.

Therefore, it is for this reason that it feels that if we do not attach the Assembly of the Ummah to our daily salaah and humble ourselves with all of humanity in their shortcomings; we are wasting our time performing such a jamaat salaah. Likewise, we are also unhappy when zakaat and hajj are performed in the same way, only for the sawaab of akhirah. We wish the Muslims would see the point that Islam is a universal system of life, and that it represents the DUNYA as much as it represents the AKHIRAH, in every issue of our life.

The Muslims have many lessons to learn from the mathematical model of "the straightway". The first thing is that they must learn that even if we choose a line to represent "the straightway" on the graph, we cannot just do it on blind faith. We have to be rational and intellectual about it. Therefore, when the doctors, lawyers and so-called muftis in our communities choose their madhabs and sects, based on blind faith, and refuse to hear the voices of reason, that their teachings and practices of their sects and madhabs are totally contrary to the true teachings and practices of the Holy Qur'an and Sunnah, I am very disappointed with them. They are the ones who should be telling the ummah that Islam is much more complicated than just choosing any one sect, madhab, silsila and khanqah on blind faith, and that we should be more objective about what we say and do in Islam, because it is totally against blind faith of religion and priesthood.

In the above diagram, the graph of $y = x$ does not only represent the relationship between the DUNYA and AKHIRAH. It also represents all other teachings and practices of Tawhid that bring about a very intricate balance between the seen and unseen, secular and religious, individual and community, national and international and so on. In the previous chapters, we spoke a great deal about the balance between the secular and religious and how it has assisted us in understanding the universal teachings and practices of Islam and given us the freedom to progress in the secular compartment of our life without the fear of violating any of the laws of our faith. In this relationship between the SECULAR and RELIGIOUS all a person has to do is apply the Qur'an and Sunnah to the secular knowledge and experience of man, and he or she will have no problem fulfilling all the requirements of their religion.

Another very important teaching and practice of Tawhid that the majority of Muslims neglect is the balance between the individual and the community. The most important lesson of this teaching and practice is that, if we are not doing well as a community, then it is a fair reflection or a positive reflection that we are not doing well as individuals. For example, as individuals we earn well and live a very fundamentalist Islamic way of life with which we are satisfied but as a community in our worldly way of life in science, technology, secular education, etc., we are lagging behind and no comparison to the rest of the non-Muslim world.

In my previous book, "An Islamic Revolution for Peace and Unity", I stated that if we put together all the economies of the 56 Muslim countries, it would not equal half the economy of Germany, which was then only the third largest economy in the world at that time. Nowadays, even China and India have overtaken the economy of Germany. Thus, in Islam, the nation demands a certain level of commitment and sacrifice from the individual, according to the Qur'an, in every sphere of our life. Therefore, feeling satisfied with the fundamentalist teachings and practices of your sects and not worrying about the present state of the ummah or doing anything about it is totally misleading.

In terms of the strategy and the progress and development of this world, we need to send our children to the schools and teach them according to the guidance of God, that they need to progress in every dimension of their lives, not only in religion but also in science, politics, business, etc. Unfortunately, in this book, I will not be able to tell the Muslim ummah what are all the Islamic requirements to establish the correct balance between the individuals and the community because an ideal Islamic society does not exist at this moment in our history according to the true teachings and practices of the Qur'an and Sunnah. But, we are certain that some of the teachings and practices of the Holy Qur'an and Sunnah that are important from this point of view are as follows:

1. The mosque should be made the nucleus of our development and center of all our activities, whether it is science, politics, business, welfare, religion, or otherwise.
2. The Muslims representing all households around the musjid should commit themselves to the shurah and ijma of the ummah, to establish the true teachings and practices of the Holy Qur'an and Sunnah.
3. The leadership and executive running the affairs of the ummah has to be selected and elected by the majority of Muslims at local,

regional and national levels. It does not necessarily have to include the ulama.

4. When we have selected and elected our leadership and executive, we should show sincere allegiance to them.

5. All salaried positions in the ummah should be filled according to experience and qualification with total disregard for color, race, class and sex.

6. All Muslim children that pass matric with merit should be supported financially to become professors in their field of work. If we do not do so then it is obvious that we will not have the best brains to run all the affairs of the ummah.

Thus, in conclusion, I sincerely hope that the ummah will implement all the teachings and practices of Islam, in a similar manner according to the world-view teachings and practices of Tawhid.

CHAPTER 6

The Universal Prayer

The seven verses of the universal prayer (surah Fatiha) are as follows:

1. Praise be to God, Lord of the worlds,
2. The Beneficent, the Merciful,
3. Owner of the Day of Judgment,
4. Thee (alone) we worship, Thee (alone) we ask for help,
5. Show us the straight path,
6. The path of those whom thou hast favored,
7. Not (the path) of those who earn Thine anger, or of those who go astray.

Surah Fatiha is the opening chapter of the Holy Qur'an. Actually, surah means **step** and Fatiha means **opening chapter.** Hence, surah Fatiha is not only the first step and opening chapter of "the Last Book" of God, but it is also the first step and opening chapter in the life of a Muslim. For example, when we recite surah Fatiha, we are confronted with two very important issues of our lives, which are as follows:

1. That Allah (SWT) is the Lord of the worlds, the Master of the Day of Judgment, the Benefactor and the Most Merciful.
2. That only He has pure knowledge and true understanding of "the straight way".

Thus, surah Fatiha makes the most important statement of our life. It states very clearly that our human knowledge is not good enough to solve any of the problems of our diversity, and that we require a neutral source outside of our human knowledge and experience to do this. Who can be better than the Lord of the worlds and the Master of the Day of Judgment, The Most High, The Supreme, The All Knower, The Creator?

The fact that surah Fatiha associates the teaching and learning of "the straight way" with the Almighty, its' irresistible, and not to accept it under the circumstances would be foolish. Furthermore, in the context of our diversity and our uncertainty about the truth, it is not only conclusive that only God knows what is "the straightway" but also that only His guidance would be acceptable to the majority of human beings as a natural and universal solution to all the problems of our diversity, deviation and division.

Another very important fact to consider about surah Fatiha is that although it is not the first wahy (revelation of the Qur'an) that was given to the Prophet (SAW), he and his companions considered it to be the first chapter of the Qur'an and in the life of a Muslim. Therefore, in every rakaat of their salaah they recited surah Fatiha to signify their submission to the will of God, by rukhu and sujood. And when we consider that it is recited for more than forty times a day in the life of a Muslim, we can imagine how important this surah is in understanding Islam and grasping the preconditions of the kalima.

In Islam, the Word of God is meant to establish **truth** and **justice**, with the wisdom and knowledge of God. This is the same as establishing **peace** in all the diversities of the universe, and **peace** we know is a product of **unity** and **diversity**. Mathematically, this can be written down as follows:

$$\textbf{God's Word} = \textbf{truth} + \textbf{justice}$$
$$= \textbf{peace}$$
$$= \textbf{unity} + \textbf{diversity}$$

In surah Fatiha, we take the pledge that in view of the differences of opinion we experience in this world, we will not, from this day onwards, listen to any mufti, saint or Aalim or find out from any Hadith or kitab of any saint or molvie what is "the straight way", because up until now we have listened to them, and have come to the conclusion, that they have no knowledge of what is "the straight way". Their main fault is that they failed to unite themselves and the ummah and provide clear direction and leadership to the followers of the Qur'an and Sunnah. I have demonstrated this fact in many different ways in this and my previous book.

Furthemore, it is important to note that Islam is not a religion but a way of life. And that, all the teachings and practices of "the straightway" do not only apply to all the religious problems of diversity, but to the problems of diversity in every compartment of our lives, be it science, politics, or otherwise. For example, in science, we can argue by the Intelligence Design theory that God exists, and that all species of creation were created from primeval matter and not from the origin of the previous species and so on and so forth. For more information on this subject, please refer to the chapter on "Qur'an and Science". Therefore, in any problem our diversity, in any aspect of our life, of culture, custom, tradition or compartment of life, we should not turn to anybody except God, and ask Him, "What is the straightway?".

Unfortunately, when we are born as Muslims, we are not taught how to use surah Fatiha to establish "the all truth" in every issue of our life. We are taught to use it as a ritual of dua and salaah. If I did not find the ummah in such state of division and contradiction in all the issues of the Qur'an and Sunnah, I would never have known that my recitation of surah Fatiha was more than just a ritual. And that, I had to use it to turn my face away from all my Muslim brothers and sisters and ask Allah (SWT) what is "the straightway" in every issue of my life. Ever since then, the surah Fatiha did not only inspire me to explain "the all truth" of the Qur'an to non-Muslims, but also to Muslims, in the most universal manner, making it irresistible to all, even myself.

Thus, the most important purpose of "the straightway" in surah Fatiha is not only to establish "the all truth" in every situation of our life, but also to establish true reality based on haqq, where the boundaries between science, politics and religion do not exist. For example, in Islam, there is no priesthood, yet the majority of the Muslims accept priesthood by accepting taqleed, aqidah, sects, madhabs, silsilas, khanqahs, sainthood, etc. When they are told this is wrong, they ostracize us by stating that we don't have imaan. Similarly, they believe in an Islamic sign, symbol, sight, sound, dressing, socio-economical, political and scientific association, which is totally contrary to Islamic reality based on diversity and haqq.

Therefore, in surah Fatiha, when we ask Allah (SWT), who are those people on whom He has bestowed His grace and on whom He has shown

His anger or are gone astray, He gives us all the answers to these questions in great detail in all the other chapters of the Holy Qur'an. And when we read the Holy Qur'an in great detail, we find that on most occasions the people on whom Allah (SWT) has shown His grace are the Prophets, like Abraham, Moses, Jacob, David, Jesus and Prophet Muhammad (peace be upon them). And on most occasions, the people on whom He has shown His anger are those who have defied the Prophets and fought against them or did not agree with the true word of God. In other words, the bad people are people like Pharaoh, Nimrod, the people of Ad and Thamud and so on.

According to the divine teachings and practices of Tawhid in Islam, it is very important that when we try to distinguish who are the good people whose path Allah (SWT) has approved, and the bad people whose path Allah (SWT) has disapproved, we should not look at their appearance, their worldly status, wealth or qualifications. This is totally against Islamic reality based on haqq. For example, when we compare Abu Jah'l with the Prophet (SAW), we cannot state that because Abu Jah'l went to school and knew how to read and write Arabic, or because he was wealthy or because he had bigger following or more influential in Arab community of his time, that he was right that the Prophet (SAW) was wrong.

Besides, both the Prophet (SAW) and Abu Jah'l, kept a beard, wore a kurtha, used the camel for transportation, etc. Similarly, all Prophets were either rich or poor and all bad people (non-believers) were also either rich or poor and in appearance they looked very similar. Thus, a person's appearance, wealth, status, qualifications, etc., had nothing to do with whether a person was telling the truth or not or had knowledge of "the straight way". In Islam, even if a person was regular in salaah was not reason enough to believe that such a person was a credible person with the true knowledge of Islam or good witness in an Islamic court of law.

Therefore, if you are a person who keeps a fist-length beard, wears a kurtha, etc, for example, and is a doctor, lawyer or a businessman or woman who wears the hijab, you should never think that if a person does not dress like you or is not as highly qualified like you in society, or as wealthy as you are, that he or she is not knowledgeable about Islam or inferior Muslim in any way. We do not know whom God has bestowed with true knowledge in times of need. After I published my first book, some fundamentalists told me that because I did not dress according to what they called Sunnah it was not worth buying my book, because I could not offer them any true knowledge or guidance. It is sad that they associated the truth with my dressing. Can there be more foolish people in this world than such people who call themselves the most knowledgeable Muslims and the only correct sect?

I have no doubt that the very first step to recognize the truth is to establish what God has to say to the Prophets in the Holy Qur'an and how they interacted with the wrong doers (non-believers) and how the non-believers behaved with the Prophets. The wrong doers always told the Prophets that they found it very difficult to believe that all their ulama of the past and present were wrong and what an ordinary person like a Prophet was saying is the truth. On many occasions we hear some of the present day ulama and their followers say exactly the same thing when the modernists question them about the true teachings and practices of the Holy Qur'an and Sunnah. Therefore, when we enact the Qur'an, we are able to say straight away, who are the wrong doers in the Muslim world and what are the true teachings and practices of Islam.

Unfortunately, majority of Muslims do not see the different teachings and practices of different Prophets as the different teachings and practices of different compartments of our lives. But, see it as the different teachings and practices of different religions at different times of history. This is wrong, because the truth does not change with time and place or the different compartments of our lives. For example, some Prophets were kings and rulers of their time. They showed us how to conduct ourselves as kings and rulers of our time, and how we should treat and interact with the majority of our people or how we should rule with justice, transparency and accountability. Other were peasants and they taught us how to conduct ourselves with our rulers who were oppressive and unjust.

Just like this there were many other Prophets who fought the injustices, oppressions and falsehood of the different people of the different compartment of our lives as shepherds, business people, carpenters, governors, scientists, religious leaders, etc. The purpose of all these teachings and practices of Holy Qur'an is to make all the teachings and practices of all the compartments of our lives universal so that they may be compatible with one another in the different spheres of our lives. Muslims, are most unfortunate that they do not see this point and do not use the guidance of the Holy Qur'an to intersect these. Hence, the greatest blasphemy in Islam is to replace the pure guidance of the Qur'an with the fundamentalists and religious knowledge and understanding of the Hadith or those of the ulama of the different sects, madhabs, silsilas and khanqahs.

The Prophet (SAW) is the universal Prophet. We should not look beyond him in world history and the true teachings and practices of the Holy Qur'an for universal knowledge and understanding of Islam. Firstly, he combined all true teachings and practices of all the religions according to the true teachings and practices of the Holy Qur'an. Refer to the chapter entitled, "The Vision and Mission of Prophet Abraham (PBUH)" for further information on this subject. Secondly, in doing so, he combined all true teachings and practices of all compartments of our life, establishing a very intricate balance and equilibrium within and between the seen and unseen, secular and religious, individual and community, national and international, this world and the akhirah and so on.

Thirdly, he made sure that in the context of the diversity we experience in this world, he did not deviate from the word of God but told us everything that was revealed to him exactly like God wanted him to tell it. He knew that in the context of diversity only the purity of God's word was the solution to all kinds of defects in human knowledge. The accuracy with which he told God's word was commanded to him in both the Bible and the Holy Qur'an. If we really wish to follow his Sunnah according to the true words of God in the Holy Qur'an, then we are also requested not to follow the words of any Aalim, saint, mufti, uloom, jamiat or Hadith that contradicts the true teachings and practices of the Holy Qur'an. Nothing else is important in Islam than God's pure word and pure Sunnah of the Prophet (SAW), which is the exact practice of the Holy Qur'an in its global perspective.

In the context of the diversity that exists in our lives today, it is important to use the following strategy to establish the true teachings and practices of Islam:

1. The Qur'an.
2. The worldview teachings and practices of Tawhid found in the true teachings and practices of the Holy Qur'an because these are the only teachings and practices of the Holy Qur'an that establish the precise knowledge of it in context of peace and diversity, which are the prime objectives of Islam.
3. The teachings and practices of some of the rituals like the salaah and the haj, which collaborates with the true teachings and practices of the Holy Qur'an.
4. Teachings and practices of some of the documents like the articles of faith, last sermon, etc., that reflects the true teachings and practices of the Holy Qur'an.
5. The writings of all Western historians that states why Prophet Muhammad (SAW) is the greatest personality in world history.
6. All world events such as the Charter of the United Nations, the constitution of the new South Africa, etc., which teaches peace and unity according to the worldview teachings and practices of Tawheed.

Note: In the context of the diversity that we experience in this world, I do not claim that whatever I am saying in this chapter is "the absolute truth". I might be wrong because in the diversity of our situation I don't have the right to claim what is right and what is wrong. Only the majority of the Muslims who are regular in salaah have the right to do this by shurah and ijma of the ummah in the Assembly of the Ummah, after great deliberation and scrutiny of my work.

Thus, in the context of the diversity that we experience in this world, the above teachings and practices of surah Fatiha can be represented as follows:

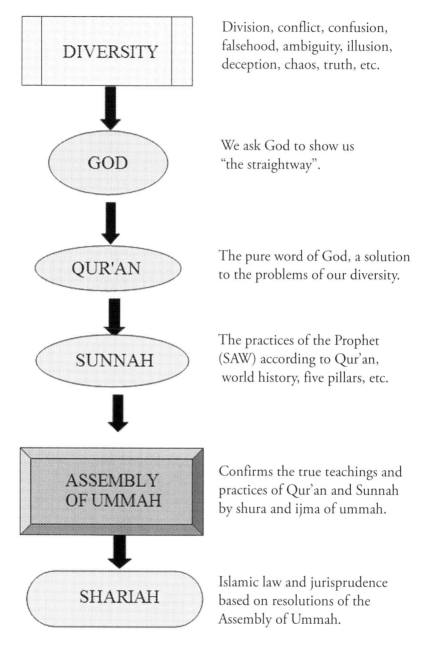

DIVERSITY — Division, conflict, confusion, falsehood, ambiguity, illusion, deception, chaos, truth, etc.

GOD — We ask God to show us "the straightway".

QUR'AN — The pure word of God, a solution to the problems of our diversity.

SUNNAH — The practices of the Prophet (SAW) according to Qur'an, world history, five pillars, etc.

ASSEMBLY OF UMMAH — Confirms the true teachings and practices of Qur'an and Sunnah by shura and ijma of ummah.

SHARIAH — Islamic law and jurisprudence based on resolutions of the Assembly of Ummah.

THE TRUE METHOD OF ESTABLISHING THE TRUE TEACHINGS AND PRACTICES OF ISLAM ACCORDING TO HOLY QURAN AND SUNNAH.

In the above procedure, it is very clear that I have totally ignored the Hadith, ulooms, jamiats of different madhabs and sects, their ulama and saints, their kitabs (religious books), etc., and concentrated only on those teachings and practices of the Prophet (SAW) that reflected the true teachings and practices of the Holy Qur'an according to shurah and ijma of the ummah in the assembly of the ummah. Hence, I rejected all teachings and practices of religion within the ummah except those that are mentioned in the Qur'an because religious teachings and practices are not only based on blind faith, but they also divide the boundaries of science, religion and politics and the brotherhood of the ummah.

In addition to the above, there are other people who can guide us to "the straightway" in our daily life according to the true teachings and practices of the Holy Qur'an and Sunnah. The majority of the scholars of the Holy Qur'an state that these people are the shuhada (martyrs), the sidiqeen (truthful) and the saleheen (pious). But, our problem is how do we recognize them in our society, which is divided into so many different sects, madhabs, silsilas and khanqahs and the majority of them are not familiar with the true teachings and practices of the Holy Qur'an and Sunnah?

Take for example, the so-called Tabligh Jamaat and Sunni Jamaat. Each has their own knowledge and understanding of Islam. And I disagree with both of them. Therefore, when one so-called Sunni brother died in a clash with the so-called Tabligh Jamaat in Azaadville many years ago, can I claim that he was a martyr? The so-called Tabligh Jamaat will say, "No", because he was against the true teachings and practices of the Tabligh Jamaat, and did not represent their cause, which they claimed are the true teachings and practices of the Holy Qur'an and Sunnah.

In other words, they killed him because they felt that he was distorting what they believed was the true teachings and practices of Islam while their teachings and practices of the Holy Qur'an and Sunnah according to this book was not any better. Therefore, nowadays, with such a massive division of the ummah, how can we state who are the real shuhadaa, sidiqeen, saleheen and leaders of the ummah?

The reason why the shuhada, sidiqeen and saleheen or leaders of either the Tabligh Jamaat or the Sunni Jamaat are not the real shuhada, sidiqeen, saleheen and leaders of the Muslim ummah as a whole, is because they are divided, and they do not represent the ummah as a whole or the true teachings and practices of the Holy Qur'an and Sunnah. We have already discussed this issue in great detail in our previous book. Therefore, in order to establish who are our real leaders, shuhada, sidiqeen and saleheen in the Muslim world, it is imperative that we establish the one unified teachings and practices of the Holy Qur'an and Sunnah according to the shurah and ijma of the majority of the Muslims, and unify the ummah so that we do not have any sects, madhabs, silsilas and khanqahs.

I wish the ummah can understand this and make sense of it. It stands to reason that if we have one Allah (SWT), one Qur'an, one Nabi (SAW) and one Kalima then we should have only one knowledge and understanding of the Holy Qur'an and Sunnah, and one Assembly of the Ummah, that decides what are the true teachings and practices of Islam, according to the shurah and ijma of the ummah, and not according to the shurah and ijma of the ulama of any one sect or madhab. Thus, the people who state that the unity of the ummah is impossible are not true Muslims. They have absolutely no idea what are the true teachings and practices of Islam. Yes, if they said that the unity of the ulama of different sects, madhabs, silsilas and khanqahs was impossible, I would agree.

The unity of the ummah is not to be scoffed at. It is an important pillar of Islam in the form of the salaah and assembly of ummah in the mosque after accepting and reciting the kalima (the articles of our faith). It represents the unified opinion of the most accurate and pure word of God, which in the context of diversity is the only solution to problems of diversity, not only amongst the Muslims but the entire world. We demonstrated this fact in the culture debate when the editor of The Star newspaper stated that the Qur'an was the "LIFE GUIDE". Therefore, if we are fragmented with differences of opinion that distort and exaggerate the true word of God like the so-called Tabligh Jamaat and Sunni Jamaat have done, then the ummah is no more a solution to the problem of diversity, but a problem of the problem of diversity.

In the context of diversity, a Muslim who distorts the word of God or deviates from the truth is no better than a non-believer who is already a problem of diversity. When the Prophet (SAW) said that only one sect out of the 73 will enter jannah it's no exaggeration. He was very serious about the matter. No person in the world (Muslims and non-Muslims) except the one sect of Islam, which abides by the pure word of God, will enter jannah unless there is intercession by Allah (SWT) on the matter. (Al-Quran 20:109, 40:18-20). The first to enter jannah will be, those who uphold the true word of God with the greatest of purity. Among them, who can be more pure than the Prophet (SAW)? Even western historian claim that he was the greatest human personality in world history.

This is a true reflection of his purity because he never said one word that was not revealed to him in the Holy Qur'an. In other words, the Prophet (SAW) was the total image of the Holy Qur'an and not vice versa. Otherwise, how could he, an ummi (unlettered), become the greatest person in world history without the very pure teachings and practices of the Holy Qur'an? Hence, Muslims are expected to say and do likewise if they claim that they follow the Sunnah of the Prophet (SAW), and not to follow the Hadith, which states that his Sunnah is what he said and did "outside" of what is written in the Qur'an.

It is weird that Muslims who state that Islam is not a religion, are divided into so many different sects and madhabs like the people of all other religions. How can they elect a leader, sidiqeen, shuhada or saleheen for the whole ummah, when they are divided into so many different sects and madhabs, and contradict the true teachings, and practices of the Holy Qur'an and Sunnah in so many different ways, and they believe that theirs is the only true teachings and practices of Islam? Which sect of which religion will agree that a certain member of a certain sect should become the leader of all sects and madhabs? Where has it happened?

Furthermore, we wish to know how can a religious leader of any sect, who has not seen the inside of the secular school and university, run a modern day country like ours? Look at all the countries of this world. Who are the people who really run these countries? Are they religious educated people or are they secular educated people? In addition to this, we wish that the Muslims could come to grips with the fact that Allah (SWT) does not like a large part of religion that is incompatible with the secular part of our life. In Islam, we do not only reject taqleed and priesthood and a very large part of religious rituals like burning god-lamps, ringing the bell, worshiping idols, etc., but we also reject all kind of divisions and sects according to the true teachings and practices of the Holy Qur'an. This is true Islamic reality.

Today, I am not happy with what I see in the Muslim world. Not only is our brotherhood and humanity divided according to our sects and madhabs, but also all our masajid, sidiqeen, saleheen, shuhada and leadership. What is this? Is this Islam? According to the worldview teachings of Tawhid, every individual is responsible for the present state of the ummah. If they do not wake up and rectify the situation, they will be accountable for it on the Day of Judgment. And, in this world, Allah (SWT) will replace them with a people who will listen to His Word. We can already see it happening in many areas of the Muslim world, where foreigners are dictating how they should run their lives.

In addition to the Prophets, the shuhada, sidiqeen and saleheen are our role models. During the time of the Prophet (SAW), they existed in the form of Hazrat Abbas (RA), Hazrat Abu Bak'r (RA) and Hazrat Omar (RA) respectively. We need to look at their history and ask ourselves why they were held in such high esteem. Some of the reasons we think are as follows:

1. They had an immaculate knowledge and understanding of the Holy Qur'an and Sunnah.
2. They followed the path of the Prophet (SAW) that he followed in world history, and not the path that the majority of the fundamentalists and religious extremists Muslims pursue today.
3. They were prepared to give their life, and all their wealth for the cause of Islam.
4   They did not associate their taqwa with their wealth, name, fame, status, appearance, race, nationality, class, etc. They always associated taqwa with the pure knowledge and practices of the Holy Qur'an and Sunnah. Hazrat Umar (RA) even went further than that. He did not associate our taqwa with our five daily salah,

but with our aklaaq (character) and knowledge and understanding of the Holy Qur'an.

5. They were always humble, compassionate, dedicated, sincere and helpful people.
6. They never dictated shariah, they established it by the shurah and ijma of the ummah.
7. They had sound judgment and they were extremely revolutionary.

Note: Once again, I wish to reiterate that I am not an expert on Islam or the true teachings and practices of the Holy Qur'an and Sunnah. I am totally aware of the fact that I do not consider any teaching or practice of Islam to be true, unless it is sanctioned by the majority of the Muslims in the assembly of the ummah. My intention is solely to inject the ummah with some lateral thinking so that they unify the knowledge of Islam, unify the ummah and put them back on track. I hope that you will take this challenge up and form the assembly of the ummah, at least at the level of your local masjid.

In conclusion to this chapter I wish to advice all our Muslim brothers and sisters not to settle for a shallow knowledge and understanding of the Holy Qur'an and Sunnah. And, not to rely on anybody to explain what are the true teachings and practices of Islam. Investigate it yourselves because in the end your salvation will depends on your knowledge and understanding of the Holy Qur'an and Sunnah. You have no excuse because Allah (SWT) has given you intelligence and told you in the Holy Qur'an in no uncertain terms that certainty of knowledge can only be found by the process of ilm-ul-yaqin, ayn-ul-yaqin and haqq-ul-yaqin.

Therefore, why are you running around and looking for this and that mufti, Aalim, saint or jamiat of the ulama? This is not what Allah (SWT) told you to do in the Holy Qur'an when the ummah is divided into so many sects and madhabs. Remember that in the context of diversity, it is only you and the Assembly of the Ummah that can decide what are the true teachings and practices of the Holy Qur'an and Sunnah, for there is nobody else in between. Even during the time of the Prophet (SAW), he established shariah by the shurah and ijma of ummah.

Hence, our system of life is different from that of the Christians. They have intermediaries between God and the individuals, but we do not. We lift our hands directly to God. Surah Fatiha tells us to do so by telling us to say, "Thee Alone we worship, and Thee Alone we ask for help, show us the straight path".

CHAPTER 7

The Articles Of Our Faith

Some modernists Muslims do not like the idea of calling the kalima our articles of faith. They wish to know, "What articles of faith?" Who invented the idea? Perhaps, they think that we are attaching a religious meaning or perspective to Islam when we speak about the articles of faith, especially when everybody should know that Islam is not a religion and does not have a religious perspective or connotation to any of the teachings and practices of Islam. Hence, they totally reject the idea and a concept of the articles of faith. They say it is un-Islamic to have such articles of faith in the Islamic way of life because every injunction of the Qur'an is an article of our faith.

I also have a similar problem with the articles of faith because I have always believed that Islam was not a religion but a way of life, but I do not reject it outright like some of the modernists Muslims expect me to do because I am sure that the Prophet (SAW) used it in the form of the shahada. Besides, the third and fourth kalima are a very integral part of the tawaaf of the khabaa from time immemorial. I do not have any reason to reject any of the articles of faith because I consider it to be as much secular and political as it is religious. Besides, I have complete faith in God and His Word to solve all the problems of my diversity and deviation, which are based on haqq.

Perhaps, the fault with the kalima is that it has been wrongly translated to mean articles of faith rather than being called some kind of a protocol or memorandum of agreement or declaration or something like that. Perhaps, there is a need to give a more appropriate meaning to the kalima that is suited to a way of life rather than a religion, like saying that it is a universal declaration of our faith in God and His Word, in all the issues of our life, whether it is social, political, business, religion or otherwise.

The big problem with the kalima is that when it is treated as an article of faith, which it is not, it cannot be questioned, and it has to be accepted on blind faith like all the articles of faith in all religions. The modernists and the true believers of Islam do not like this because Islam is not a religion, but a way of life that is based on sound reason, logic, experience, history, diversity, etc, which is opposed to blind faith. This meant that the kalmia is not really an article of faith, but primary articles of our way of life, which places our faith in God and His Word as a solution to all the problems of our diversity and our misunderstanding of the truth.

During the time of the Prophet (SAW), no Jew, Christian or pagan Arab accepted Islam on blind faith. They had a rational, intellectual and logical cause to believe in Islam. Hazrat Omar (RA) was on his way to kill the Prophet (SAW) but on his way he was confronted with some of the pages of the Holy Qur'an, which made sense to him. Hence, he abandoned the idea of killing the Prophet (SAW) and reverted to Islam.

Likewise, many people accepted Islam because it made some sense to their way of life. For example, it was against slavery or the burying alive of their baby girls or some kind of injustices, oppression or racism, etc., that they experienced in their lives that made them to be attracted to Islam. Today, some Christians accept Islam because it rejects TRINITY purely on the basis of reason or it provides them with some scientific clue that is invaluable in their work.

Therefore, the best way to propagate Islam today is not by criticizing and condemning other people's religion but by explaining the worldview teachings and practices of Tawhid, which is at present not only very relevant to the constitution of our country but also to our global community where people can neither prove or disprove the existence of God, like I have demonstrated in the evolution, culture and constitutional debates in this book.

In view of the above, the seven articles of faith are as follows:

1. There is none worthy of worship besides Allah (SWT) and Muhammad (PBUH) is the messenger of Allah (SWT).

2. I bear witness that there is none worthy of worship besides Allah and I bear witness that Muhammad (PBUH) is His servant and messenger.

3. Glory is to Allah (SWT) and all praise is to Allah (SWT). There is none worthy of worship besides Allah (SWT). And Allah (SWT) is the greatest. There is no power and might except from Allah (SWT), The Most High, The Great.

4. There is none worthy of worship besides Allah (SWT). He is alone. He has no partner. His is the kingdom and for Him is all praise. He gives life and causes death. In His hand is all-good. And, He has power over everything.

5. O Allah! I seek protection in You from that I should join any partner with You knowingly. I seek Your forgiveness from that which I do not know. I repent from ignorance. I free myself from disbelief and from joining partners with You and (I free myself from) all sins. I submit to your will. I believe and declare: There is none worthy of worship besides Allah (SWT) and Muhammad (PBUH) is the messenger of Allah (SWT).

6. I believe in Allah (SWT) as He is understood by His names and His attributes (qualities) and I accept all His orders.

7. I believe in Allah (SWT) and His angels and His books and His messengers and the Last Day, and in the predestination of our fate for the good and the bad that we do on this earth and our resurrection.

In summary form, the above articles of faith are as follows:

1. Allah (SWT) is the greatest. There is no power and might above His. He has no partners.

2. Prophet Muhammad (PBUH) is the final Prophet and messenger of Allah (SWT).

3. We believe in Allah (SWT), His angels, His Books, His messengers and the Last Day or life after death.

In a diagrammatic form, the full and final article of our faith is divided as follows:

1. ### **THE UNSEEN FORM:**

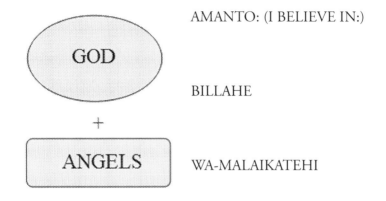

AMANTO: (I BELIEVE IN:)

BILLAHE

WA-MALAIKATEHI

2. ### **THE SEEN FORM:**

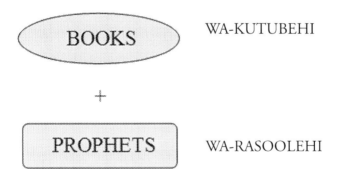

WA-KUTUBEHI

WA-RASOOLEHI

3. **THE HEREAFTER:**

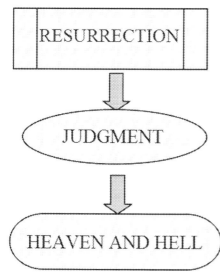

WAL-YOMIL AKHIREH
WAL-KADRI KHAIRAHI
WA-SHARRIHI
MINALLAHE TALA
WAL-BASI BADAL MAUT.

THE LAST DAY, THE
PREDESTINATION OF OUR
FATE FOR THE GOOD AND
BAD THAT WE DO ON THIS
EARTH AND OUR
RESURRECTION.

DIAGRAM REPRESENTING THE PRIMARY ARTICLES OF OUR FAITH

The above articles of faith do not create any challenges for the majority of Muslims who are blind followers of their religion, because it is the nature of all religious people of this world to accept anything that is written in their articles of their faith in a blind manner. This is typical religion because the highest form of faith in religion is not to question the articles of your faith. In the above, if we were to state that it is important for our faith to believe in saints and spiritual mentors, the majority of the Muslims will accept it immaterial of the fact that it is contrary to the true teachings and practices of the Holy Qur'an, to believe in saints and spiritual mentors.

Even without mentioning it in the above articles of faith, the majority of Muslims believe that those Muslims who do not believe in saints and spiritual mentors do not have imaan (faith). But, this is not so with the secular educated Muslims, who do not accept any articles of their faith unless they are sure that it is not against the Qur'an to do so. Therefore, it is important to realize the secular approach to the kalima is obvious because Islam is not a religion, but is a way of life, which is compatible with science, reason, experience, history, etc.

The real challenges of the above articles of faith, therefore, do not come from the fundamentalists Muslims, but it comes from the rational and intellectual people of the secular world, both Muslims and non-Muslims, who question everything they believe, otherwise they will not believe. Islamic challenges lie in answering these questions correctly to win universal acclaim, and not by shunning any secular educated person who questions their beliefs to be person of a lesser faith or a modernist or a secularist.

Let us start with the belief in God, for example. A secular educated person might ask, "Where is the proof of the existence of God?" This is a perfectly legitimate question, and we are not afraid to answer this question purely from the scientific perspective because the majority of the scientists, who believe in evolution, cannot, without reasonable doubt, disprove the existence of God. Therefore, the final conclusion of the evolution and creation debate is that each species of creation was created from primeval matter, and varieties within species, and this too by the grace of God, evolving with time and space.

Similarly, when the secular educated people ask us about the malaiekas (angels) we might tell them that these are powers and forces of nature, which were created by God to perform certain natural functions in God's creation. Just like the powers and forces that keep the planets in a fixed orbit around the sun, etc, without which the universe would collapse. These include the Angel of Death, Archangel Gabriel, etc, (not to be confused with jinns, another form of unseen creation, which procreate and live in a community like ours).

Unfortunately, many modernists and secularists scholars of the Qur'an do not believe that Angels are winged like creations, which Allah (SWT) created as Messengers to perform certain chores in His creation. In their haste to give a modernist and secularist meaning and message of the Qur'an, they overlook certain verses of the Qur'an, which make it clear that Angels are winged like creation, which perform the duties of their Lord. Read surah 35 (Al-Fatir) verse 1 for more information on this subject. This means that although certain people have the privilege to inherit the Qur'an, they exaggerate its meaning and message and "wrong their own souls", (surah 35 verse 32). Hence, the correct path of interpreting the

Qur'an among those that inherit it is "the middle path", like the path of Tawhid that I have explained in this book. This does not mean that I am better than those that have "wronged their souls". The best among us are those that make amal (practice) on the correct interpretation. Besides, it is not within me to believe that my interpretation is correct, unless it is approved by the majority of the Muslims in the Assembly of the Ummah.

In Islam, if we can explain the unseen part of our articles of faith in such a rational, intellectual, scientific and secular manner, convincing people that only Allah (SWT) knows the truth, then we should have absolutely no problem in explaining the seen part of our articles of faith, which include the effects of the Prophet (SAW) and the Qur'an in our lives. Firstly, world history supports the fact that the Prophet (SAW) was the greatest person in history because he was the only person in world history who was "most extremely successful in both the secular and religious levels". Secondly, it is not difficult to convince rational and intellectual people that the Holy Qur'an is the only word of God, which can solve all the problems of our diversity in the most universal manner that no secular educated person can reject or resist it.

Thus, taking into account what we have said so far in this book, it is very easy for us to convince the secular educated person about the Hereafter, which is the last part of the articles of our faith. They might wish to know, "How is it possible for God to resurrect us in the Hereafter after we die, decay and disintegrate according to the natural laws of our existence or the scientific laws of entropy?" We have no problem explaining this because in the first instance they cannot prove or disprove the existence of God. And that like He created this creation, He would have no problem recreating it in its permanent form, after the collapse of the present universe.

In the above articles of faith the word that concern the akhirah, is the word taqdeer, which means preplanned, predestined or predetermined. The fact that this word is associated with the Hereafter in the above articles of faith, it's important to conclude that it is associated with the preplanning of the akhirah and not with the predetermination of our fate in this world from the time we are born until death. According to the laws of entropy we are supposed to die, decay and disintegrate. We are not supposed to become alive again after this world comes to an end. But, the fact that we will be raised up once again in the akhirah is preplanned, predestined or predetermined to judge the good and bad we do in this world.

Unfortunately, the majority of the Muslims, who are influenced by the Indian culture and custom of the subcontinent, think that this word taqdeer applies to their fate in this world, for the good and bad they do in this world. They think that our taqdeer in this world is predetermined or preplanned from the time we are born until we die. They have this Hindu belief that when we are born, everything in our life that will happen to us from the time we are born until we die is predetermined and predestined.

According to them, we have no control over our life in this world for the good and bad we do in this world. If we murdered someone or stole something, for example, we would not be responsible for our action because it was written we would end up murdering someone or stealing something when we were born but we will be punished for it in the akhirah. Likewise, they state that it is not our fault that we did not get married or make a success of our marriage or kill someone or ourselves by our reckless driving, etc., because it was written at our birth that it would happen exactly that way and we cannot do anything about it.

According to the Qur'an, I fail to agree with the majority of Muslims that our taqdeer was written at our birth, like when we are going to be born, to whom, when and where we are going to die, whether our marriage or our unity as an ummah, will fail or succeed, etc. Therefore, I am left with no option but to advice that the Muslim ummah revisit this whole concept of taqdeer and try to understand it in the way that Allah (SWT) wants us to understand it in the Holy Qur'an, and not according to normal teachings and practices of religion, where we are forced to believe, that we have no control over our actions, for the good and bad, we do in this world.

Such a concept of taqdeer does not only make us complacent and irresponsible, but it reduces our efficiency, and makes us backwards in this life. When we refuse to believe that our failure in this world as an ummah (at present moment in history), for example, is not written but is due to certain laws of cause and effects, which we fail to understand or are reluctant to believe, we will never change our condition. Likewise, if we believe that our birth and death is written for a certain time and place and that we cannot control it then why do we take birth control tablets to curb population growth, and take medical treatments to prolong our life span? According to religion, is this not a sin? Furthermore, do you think that God will make us caliph (deputy) of God on earth, to take care of our universe, when we have no control over our own destiny?

Thus, in order to challenge these claims of the fundamentalists and religious extremists, let us take the example of our birth and death. If God had predetermined it to happen on a certain date and time then how come certain people make illegitimate babies by committing zina (adultery or fornication)? Is it not under their control not to commit zina? And if it is under their control not to commit zina and have an illegitimate child, then is it not the case that the birth of any child is determined by the laws of cause and effect and is not taqdeer? Can we commit such a heinous sin as adultery and state in an Islamic court that the court should show leniency to us because it was not in our control to do otherwise? Will an Islamic court accept such a plea of taqdeer and pardon us? Likewise, many married couple preplan to have one or two children like in many of the western countries. What has that to do with taqdeer? Or did Allah (SWT) tell us in the Holy Qur'an that we must have sex with our wives only to make babies and not for pleasure?

Similarly, let us take our death. When we reach old age and, for example, develop a pain in our chest, we seek help from a doctor. He tells us that we have angina and that in order to increase our lifespan we are required to take some aspirins, pressure tablets, etc., perform exercises and avoid eating certain foods. Therefore, is it correct to believe that the time and place of our death is written and yet take the treatment? According to religion, will we not be hypocrites who lack faith? Similarly, if people, break all the rules of our roads when they are driving and kill innocent people in a road accidents, then is that predetermined or would it better if we found causes and rectified our mistakes? Thus, marriages and divorces, births and deaths, progress and development of this world, unity, etc., is not predetermined. We have full control over it within the laws of cause and effect, and "never will Allah (SWT) change our condition unless we change it ourselves with our own soul".

Unfortunately, the majority of Muslims don't recognize the fact that the Will of God functions according to the laws of cause and effect, which were created by Him. Therefore, it was in reply to this question of the Will of God, that I wrote a letter to Muslim Views, which was entitled, "We have the power to change". It was published in the May 2012 issue as follows:

The articles by Ibrahim Oksas and Nazeema Ahmed, "Nabi Yunus' (AS) du'ah: a means for obtaining answer to prayer", (MV, March 2012) refers:

It is true that 'Allah SWT is the Causer of all Causes' but it not true that 'causes have no effect'.

All causes have either a positive or negative effects except those that are not under the control of the creation.

For example, 'Never will Allah change the condition of people unless they change it themselves with their own souls', (Qur'an 8:53, 13:11).

Hence, there are causes for the division and disunity of the ummah. We have to recognize them and rectify them. Some of these are:

In religion, the majority of the Muslims believe in taqlid, aqidah, silsilas, khanqahs, sects, madhabs, sainthood, etc, instead of practicing ilm-ul-yaqin (certainty of knowledge by inference or reasoning), ayn-ul-yaqin (certainty of knowledge by seeing and observing) and haqq-ul-yaqin (absolute knowledge, like this is pen, etc).

Similarly, they believe that the Sunnah of the Prophet (SAW) is something he said and did "outside" of what is written in the Qur'an.

They don't believe that the Sunnah is the pure practice of the Qur'an and has nothing to do with things "outside" of it. Hence, they make Sunnah and bid'ah things that are not Sunnah and bid'ah, and vice versa.

They don't take a universal approach to Islam. For example, the halaal food issue is for all the people of this world. They have made it a Muslim thing by using the 'moon and star' stamp on it.

In the unified field, there is no universal sign, symbol, sound, image, dressing, etc. Even if the ingredients are halaal, no food that invokes a name other than God, like the cross on the 'bun', can be made halaal.

Likewise, there are causes for the high divorce rate in our communities. We need to find those causes and rectify the situation. No amount of du'ah can help us solve the problem.

Therefore, it is very irritating when we ask Muslims for solutions and they say, 'Make du'ah'.

As caliphs (vicegerents of God on earth), we are given the power to change causes which are under our control, not those that are inflicted by Allah SWT unless we seek His mercy, according to the teachings and practices of ilm-ul-yaqin, ayn-ul-yaqin and haqq-ul-yaqin.

Therefore, any amount of recitation of Qur'an, Bismillah, etc, cannot change the laws of cause and effect unless thay bring about the reality of what is written in the Qur'an, in our hearts, minds and souls.

In conclusion, to this chapter, it is important to state that our kalimah (the articles of our way of life) is the first pillar of Islam. The other pillars of Islam are salaah, zakaah, saum and hajj. The main function of these pillars is to establish the unity of our beliefs and practices in order to establish the unity of the ummah. Diagrammatically, this is explained as follows:

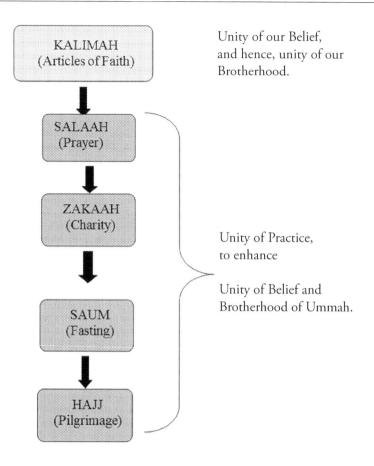

THE BASIC UNITY OF BELIEF AND
PRACTICES OF THE UMMAH.

Salaah, zakaah, saum and hajj are nation building institutions. They should not be used to enhance rituals solely for the sawaab of akhirah. We have discussed this in greater detail in this book.

CHAPTER 8

The Dynamics Of Shariah And Function Of The Shurah

Recently, I wrote a letter to "Muslim Views" of Cape Town stating my position on the very sensitive issue of hijab and niqab. My letter was as follows:

The article by Dr Auwais Rafudeen, "Shaikh Tantawi stirs another hornets' nest", (MV, November2009), is misleading because it does not contain all the facts about the Shaik's remark on the niqab.

According to the Ar-Rasheed (December, 2009), he said, "The niqab is a tradition and has nothing to do with Islam".

I think that the Jamiatul Ulama of the Transvaal, who published the Ar-Rasheed, and Dr Rafudeen, fail to understand Shaikh Tantawi's viewpoints on the hijab and the niqab because they do not understand the Shariah in the global perspective of the Qur'an and the diversity of our creation.

To explain this, let us take, for example, the oneness of the Islamic way of life, where there is no dichotomy of the secular and the religious.

We have no doubt that we cannot maintain this balance if we do not educate and develop ourselves according to the divine teachings of ilm-ul-yaqin (certainty of knowledge by inference or reasoning), ayn-ul-yaqin (certainty of knowledge by seeing and observing) and haqq-ul-yaqin (absolute knowledge, like this is a pen,etc).

Hence, by inference, an Aalim who uses the ultra-religious method of taqleed, aqeeda, silsila, khanqah, sainthood, sects and madhabs to educate and develop the ummah is not a scholar but a priest.

Similarly, an imam is not only a religious leader but also a political leader; the mosque is not only a place of worship but also the Assembly of the Ummah (our house of parliament) at the local level.

It is apparent that Islam is not a religion but a way of life where there is no place for priesthood.

Likewise, it is apparent that Islam does not restrict secular innovations (bid'ah) which does not deny the existence of God but restricts all religious innovations that disturb the balance between the secular and the religious.

Therefore, like Islam embraces the secular and religious, it embraces the customs, cultures and traditions of the world.

It is not an injunction of the Qur'an for a Muslim man to keep a beard, wear a kurtha, or for a Muslim woman to cover her head or the face in public.

To believe that these acts are the Sunnah of the Prophet (SAW) or an act of taqwa (piety) and imaan (faith) is false and misleading.

Also, for the Jamiat to state that the Shaikh is a "secularist", meaning that he is an enemy of Islam, is absurd. A true Muslim is by nature as much secular as he is religious. This is a condition of the Qur'an.

Therefore, to understand the true meaning of secular and religious in the context of Islam, it is important to understand that Islam is not a modern system of life which separates the secular from the religious and makes them separate and exclusive. It is a post-modern system of life, which integrates, assimilates and intersects the cultures, customs and traditions in all aspects of our lives, secular and religious, according to the injunctions of the Qur'an.

In this chapter, I do not wish to give any details of what are the true teachings and practices of the Shariah, and how majority of the ulama have distorted and misunderstood these teachings and practices. I have already done that. What I wish to do in this chapter is to explain the dynamics of those terms of Shariah that make or break it if the majority of Muslims and ulama are ignorant about them. To explain this, let's start by explaining the most indisputable fact about the Shariah, namely that it includes the teachings and practices of both Qur'an and Sunnah. Mathematically, this can be written down as follows:

SHARIAH = QUR'AN + SUNNAH

In the above equation, the whole knowledge and understanding of Shariah is very heavily dependent on the Qur'an, because that is the first term of the equation, which is the source of our guidance, without which the Sunnah cannot exist. Therefore, the most important questions about the

Qur'an are: what is the Qur'an? and, what is the function of the Qur'an in the Islamic way of life?

The answer to the first question is easy. It is the absolute and infallible Word of God. In other words, for 1400 years nobody has added or deleted a word in the text of the Qur'an. It has remained pure just like it was revealed to the Prophet (SAW). The real advantage of this is that it can be used as the only solution to settle any dispute between us. This is an ideal solution for all the problems of our diversities, if all of us are willing to accept it as the only solution to all the disputes of our lives, in any aspect of our creation.

This is exactly where the preconditions of the shahadat play their part. The real purpose of the Qur'an is to fulfill two very important functions of Islam: (i) to achieve PEACE and (ii) to achieve complete SUBMISSION to the will of ONE GOD, and to establish the sovereignty of God on earth, for all of humanity. This mission of the Qur'an can be very clearly observed in the meaning of the Arabic word ISLAM, which was given to us by Allah (SWT) for our way of life. Mathematically, this is represented as follows:

ISLAM = PEACE + SUBMISSION

In addition to this, the PEACE mission in the above equation can also be represented as follows:

PEACE = DIVERSITY + UNITY

In the interpretation of the Qur'an, any Muslim who wishes to achieve the real objectives of Islam in any one aspect of their life has to achieve all four objectives of Islam, namely that of DIVERSITY, UNITY, PEACE and SUBMISSION, bearing in mind that it's virtually impossible to achieve peace and unity in diversity without absolute JUSTICE. We have discussed this in great detail in the chapter entitled, "The Universal Prayer". Therefore, the exact challenge of the Qur'an, in Islam, is to achieve the global perspective of SUBMISSION to the Will of One God in the DIVERSITY of our creation and to maintain PEACE and UNITY with utmost JUSTICE. It is wrong to use jihad to promote Islam but it's correct to use jihad to defend Islam against injustices, oppression and aggression. If otherwise, we defeat the whole object of Islam.

The most important aspect of the Shariah is the universal interpretation of the Qur'an, which provides guidance to the people of all cultures, customs, traditions and compartments of our lives without showing any bias to any of these. If we cannot get that right then everything else we say and do in the Shariah will be wrong. SUNNAH, for example, is practice of Qur'an in the form of the believer. It has to be completely in harmony with the interpretation of the Qur'an, otherwise the believer will be a believer only in name, like the ummah is today, completely divided in almost every issue of life.

Unfortunately, when the Sunnah does not collaborate with the true teachings and practices of the Qur'an, it does not only distort the true knowledge and universality of Islam in world events, but it also divides us into different sects, madhabs, silsilas and khanqahs, which causes the loss of our leadership and direction in our lives. In addition to this, there are also other repercussions of not practicing the Sunnah according to the true teachings and universal practices of the Holy Qur'an. It distorts the meaning and definition of the Sunnah and makes the Sunnah and bid'ah (innovations), what is not Sunnah and bid'ah, causing complete confusion in the knowledge, understanding and practice of true Islam.

Therefore, when people like myself, who are sometimes called modernists and secularists state that it's not Sunnah or compulsory for a Muslim man to keep a beard, wear a kurtha, etc, or for a Muslim woman to cover her face or head in public, we do not do this to collaborate with the Zionists or Americans or have any sinister motives to do so. All we wish as sincere Muslims is to preserve the pure and universal teachings and practices of the Qur'an and Sunnah, both in the interpretation and practice forms, entrenching a very solid ground in the post modern era, which is now ready to embrace Islam. Thus, with the advent of the new world order of Islam, all those Muslims and their ulama, who promote and propagate Islamic religious extremism and fundamentalism will perish. And, we do not wish to be party to those, whose religion and way of life will perish with them.

Nevertheless, it is important to know that even if we establish the true teachings and practices of the Qur'an and Sunnah according to all the dynamics of the Shariah, it will not be acceptable as the Shariah unless the majority of the Muslims are prepared to accept it through mutual consultation (shurah) and consensus (ijma) in the Assembly of the Ummah. Hence, about two to three years ago, when there was a massive "No" to the Shariah law in Turkey, they were right within the dynamics of the Shariah not to accept the fundamentalist and extremists versions of it because, they, like many so-called modernists and secularists Muslims throughout the world, were not consulted to be a party to such teachings and practices of Islam that exists in the Muslim world today. Similarly, I do not believe that what I have written in this book is Shariah. I will only accept it as Shariah when the majority of the Muslims accept it by the shurah and ijma of the ummah in the Assembly of the Ummah.

Therefore, according to the divine teachings of peace and Tawhid, it's important to charter the path that was followed by the Prophet (SAW) to develop the Sunnah and the Shariah according to the shurah and ijma of the ummah. In a diagrammatic form this is as follows:

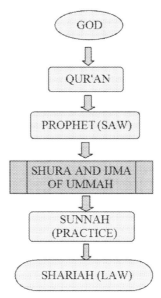

THE PATH TAKEN BY THE PROPHET (SAW) TO ESTABLISH SHURAH AND SHARIAH.

It is not easy to establish shurah and shariah with uneducated and ignorant masses, but this did not deter the Prophet (SAW). He had only pagan Arabs at his disposal, yet he managed to cultivate the shurah and ijma of these pagan Arabs who accepted Islam to create one of the most powerful, modern and democratic society in history. The people who are responsible for destroying the Assembly of the Ummah and usurping the power of the majority are our political leaders and religious leaders of the past, and present. We have no alternative but to fight for our rights and reinstate it. This can be easily done if trustees of all masajid are willing to corporate with us. It is their duty to do so because a trustee of the musjid is not only the trustee of a place of worship, but is also the caretaker of the Assembly of the Ummah, which is the nucleus of not only our religious development but also of our political, cultural and social development of the Muslim society in the vicinity of the musjid.

Therefore, before I explain what are the real duties of trustees in the musjid, it's important that I explain what are the merits of establishing the Assembly of the Ummah in the local musjid, and what is the real teachings of the shurah and ijma of ummah in Islam, because the ulama have their own explanations about these things to discourage us from forming the Assembly of the Ummah. Their fear is that if we put the teachings of the Holy Qur'an and Sunnah in the hands of the majority, we will distort the true teachings and practices of Islam, or, perhaps, they are afraid that they will loose their power and position in society that they enjoy at this present moment. Personally, I think the trustees should not listen to them. Things can't get worse than they are.

Hence, some of the merits of forming the Assembly of the Ummah at the grassroots level (of the local mosque) are as follows:

1. It does not contain any opinions of ulama of one sect and one school of thought or divide our masajid and brotherhood. It contains the opinions of all the people of all sections and compartments of our lives that live in the vicinity of our musjid (mosque).
2. It teaches us to respect the shurah (mutual consultation) and ijma (consensus) of the majority and brings about a unified and universal knowledge and understanding of the Holy Qur'an and

Sunnah, which does not divide us or our leadership and protocol in any way.

3. The generation gap in the knowledge, understanding and practice of Islam is closed. The younger generations grow up by participating in the proceedings of the assembly as observers at a very young age and at 15 are made fully-fledged members of the assembly with the right to deliberate and vote.

4. By participating in the assembly of the ummah, each individual is expected to research the Holy Qur'an, Sunnah and Islamic history. Even if he or she does not do so they will learn a great deal from the deliberations. Furthermore, true knowledge is expected to make Muslims less emotional, more rational and intellectual.

5. Muslims will learn to talk to one another in a more ethical and civilized manner. Today, majority of the Muslims think that they know it all. In the Assembly of the Ummah, they will realise that they are not as knowledgeable as they think. The ulama and muftis will realise their shortcomings, and humble themselves, hopefully, to accept what they do not know.

6. If any decision at one mosque is affected by the opinion of one sect, race, social or political group who are dominant in the vicinity of one mosque, it will be corrected by the majority at the regional and national level, by networking resolutions, mosque by mosque and region by region.

7. The division of the ummah and masajid, ulooms, etc., will be of no consequence. It will either wither away or disappear completely and there will be, in every dimension of our lives, unity of ummah.

8. The assembly of ummah will control all issues concerning the ummah such as halaal, hilaal, hajj, etc., so that no individuals or groups can monopolize them.

9. It will make the ummah active and organized in a more dignified, unified and constructive manner.

10. Those who attend prayers regularly (not necessarily five time a day) in the local mosque will only be eligible to deliberate and vote.

In a diagrammatic form, the four interpretation of the shurah given by the ulama are as follows:

INTERPRETATION 1:

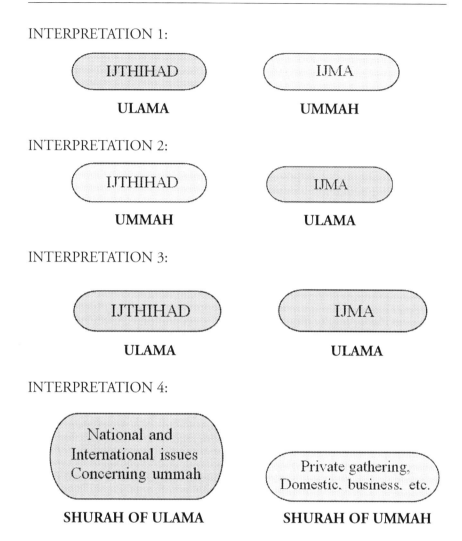

INTERPRETATION 2:

INTERPRETATION 3:

INTERPRETATION 4:

Logically, the Assembly of the Ummah should promote the shurah and ijma of the ummah, and not the shurah and ijma of the ulama. In addition to this, it is important to note that the shurah and ijma of the ummah in the Assembly of the Ummah should contain the most diverse opinion and experience of the ummah, and not the sectarian thoughts and experience of the ulama. Therefore, the correct interpretation of shurah in terms of the assembly of the ummah is as follows:

INTERPRETATION 5: (CORRECT INTERPRETATION).

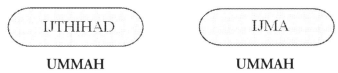

UMMAH   **UMMAH**

Since the true concept of shurah is very important for forming the Assembly of the Ummah and establishing Shariah, let's look at this whole episode of shurah in a more logical and scientific manner. The general mathematical formula of Shurah, for example, is as follows:

SHURAH = IJTHIHAD + IJMA.

Scientifically speaking, there should be only two interpretations of shurah. These should be as follows:

1. SHURAH OF ULAMA = (IJTHIHAD + IJMA) OF ULAMA.
2. SHURAH OF UMMAH = (IJTHIHAD + IJMA) OF UMMAH.

In the context of the above, the other two interpretations of shurah do not make sense. These are as follows:

1. SHURAH = IJTHIHAD OF ULAMA + IJMA OF UMMAH.
2. SHURAH = IJTHIHAD OF UMMAH + IJMA OF ULAMA.

Note: It is wrong to associate the Assembly of the Ummah with the ijthihad and ijma of the ulama. It is proper to associate the Assembly of the Ummah with the ijthihad and ijma of the ummah, because the Assembly of the Ummah represents the ummah and not the ulama, especially because the ulama have become priests, not scholars, and are sectarian.

Unfortunately, some ulama do not agree with any of the above concept of shurah. They state that in a small gathering or private gathering where the ummah as whole is not involved, the shurah and ijma of the ordinary Muslim is valid, whereas in all other matters involving the ummah as a whole, no ordinary person in the ummah has a voice and only the ijthihad and ijma of the ulama is valid.

Nevertheless, although this explanation of the shurah by some ulama might sound rational and feasible to many Muslims, according to shariah it is not valid. Some of the reasons for this are as follows:

1. In our attempt to promote the worldview teachings of peace and Tawhid and the unified field theory in all the compartments and levels of our lives, we oppose the quantum theory that states that there are different set of laws for small and large samples. We have only one Qur'an and one Sunnah. Therefore, whether we operate in a large assembly or a small gathering, the laws of shariah are the same because the guidance of the Holy Qur'an and the Sunnah are the same for all time and place. Do not the individual and small gatherings and families make up the community or society? In Islam, the individual and community cannot function differently. It is against the divine teachings of Tawhid to do so. In Islam, our democracy begins at the grassroots levels and not from the top. This is the big difference between Islam and all other systems of life. Therefore, there cannot be one shariah law for a small gathering of private individuals and another set for the nation, and the international Muslim community.

2. During the time of the Prophet (SAW), only the Assembly of the Ummah existed. Sometimes, ordinary Sahaba (RA) questioned the Prophet (SAW) whether what he was saying and doing was wahy or his own opinion. When the Prophet (SAW) said that it was his own opinion, the Sahaba Ikram (RA) would make suggestions, and on many occasions the Prophet (SAW) would accept their recommendations or proposals in place of his. During the time of the Prophet (SAW), only the shurah, ijthihad and ijma of the ummah existed. There were no such complications as having a different set of laws for a small gathering and another for a large gathering. The Muslim ummah was one, in all knowledge and experience of the Shariah.

3. The musjid represents the 2nd pillar of Islam and is the center or nucleus of all our development. The musjid cannot be the center or the nucleus of our development unless it is the Assembly of the Ummah. It was here that the Prophet (SAW) deliberated with those who were regular in salaah and established the shariah. In salaah if all men are equal then in the Assembly of the Ummah

there should be absolutely no discrimination and the voice of all the people there over the age of 15 should be respected. This is the ultimate democracy of Islam, where all laws of shariah are made, and approved by the majority without any party politics or sects. In our situation, where there are more than 500 mosques in our country, we should network our resolutions and leadership mosque by mosque, region by region, etc.

The Assembly of the Ummah is the ummah's brain. Working without the Assembly of the Ummah is like having no brains. It is like letting our friends and relatives to run our lives. At this moment in our history we do not have an Assembly of the Ummah. We have become the most backward people in the world, and it seems like we are suffering from brain damage or have retarded brains. It is obvious that this has happened to us because we have allowed the ulama of the different sects, schools of thought, tribes, etc., to control our lives with their own Islamic concepts and ideas of religion. Therefore, it is about time that we put our foot down and establish the Assembly of the Ummah.

It is important to state that we must not fall in the trap of any muftis of any sects and khanqahs. They will not only try and confuse us with their versions of shurah and ijma, but they will also trick us to accept the teachings of a particular sect by telling us that all sects are doing the same work but by different methods. They will say take a farmer for example, if he does not have the capital to buy machineries to plough his land, he will use hand labour, and he will achieve the same result.

This is exactly like saying that all religions are the same because they achieve the same purpose, but, we know this is not true because if a bad Muslim who has joined the Tabligh jamaat and a bad Christian who has joined the church have become good people, it's not the same because their beliefs contradict one another's beliefs. In Islam, we know that not all people of all sects will enter jannah. The Prophet (SAW) made this very clear. Only those who have true knowledge and understanding of Qur'an and Sunnah will enter jannah.

Therefore, the ultimate question is not only about becoming good or bad, but it's also about establishing haqq (the truth) from baatil (falsehood).

If a Muslim sect has made a person a good person in Islam, it's no better than a Christian or Hindu sect doing the same thing, because they are all sects who have deviated from the truth (haqq) in many different ways, and made their communities fundamentalists, extremist, and not true believers.

CHAPTER 9

The Vision And Mission Of Prophet Abraham (PBUH)

All organizations, religious or otherwise, usually have a founding father or fathers, who usually have a vision and make a statement of intent. If we do not know what are the visions and statements of their intent, it is hardly likely that we can make a success of their organization, religion or systems of life. The Islamic way of life that intersects the secular with the religious is no exception. Therefore, when the Holy Qur'an states that Islam is the deen (way of life) of Prophet Abraham (PBUH), it expects us to know, among many other things, the following:

1. That Prophet Abraham (PBUH) is the founding father of the Islamic way of life. He had a vision, and made certain founding statements about it.
2. That Prophet Muhammad (SAW) is "the final Prophet" and "the universal Prophet", who was given the task to complete and perfect the teachings and practices of Prophet Abraham (PBUH) in modern history, according to the divine teachings of peace and Tawhid, in the context of all diversities that exist in our creation.

In this book, one of our task, is to establish the founding statements and visions of the Prophet Abraham (PBUH) about our religion and Islamic way of life because without it, how are we expected to know what the final objectives of Islam is, and how to fulfill them?

Normally, in any organisation or system of life, the statements of the founding fathers do not give us all the clues about the organisations, and how to handle and make them work. Sometimes, we have to look at the objectives of the organisations and occasionally these are also vague. Hence, we have to look at the constitution and the plans of the organization for more details. And finally, it happens that we have to look at world events around us to know how to shape the organisation so that it is meaningful to our way of life, for all time and place.

According to the above, there is no doubt in our minds that Islam is a well organised way of life, which does not only have a founding father and a statement, but, it also has a very comprehensive constitution, and a very specific objective. Thus, the biggest difference between Islam, all other man made religions, and systems of life is that Islam is a partnership between man and God. Since the mission and vision of Abraham (PBUH) is that of man, and the objectives and the constitution of Islam, is the guidance of God.

In this partnership between man and God, man is made "the friend of Allah (SWT)" or aulia or wali-Allah, and it was for this reason that Abraham (PBUH) was given the title of Khalilullah (the friend of God). In order to understand the true teachings and practices of Islam, we have to know what was the mission and vision of Ibrahim (AS) because without this, we will not know what are the real objectives of Islam, and how we are supposed to apply the Qur'an in our lives.

Honestly, I don't think that as an individual, I have the capacity and the capability of establishing the true founding statements and visions of Abraham (PBUH) in their completed, perfected and pure form or of determining the real objectives of Islam and the true teachings and practices of the Holy Qur'an and Sunnah. Such a task requires a group of people who have a legal mind, political experience and a thorough knowledge and understanding of the Holy Qur'an and Sunnah.

My capability and potential as an individual only allows me to inject new ideas and thought to the ummah so that they may become free thinkers, and find a way forward for the ummah, and humanity as a whole. Furthermore, it does not matter what is the source of my knowledge. It's the rule of Shariah that it should be deliberated in the Assembly of Ummah before the Muslim majority accepts it as the Word of God, because it is the Assembly that decides what is Qur'an and Sunnah and what is not.

In my previous book, I stated many important teachings and practices of Abraham (PBUH) in his way of life. Some of these were his founding statements and vision in his religion and way of life. And, one of this is the faculty or institution of reason. I don't doubt that the majority of the Muslims and the ulama believe that the institution and faculty of reason is very important in the Islamic way of life, but the tragedy of the situation is that they say and do everything in religion, and the Islamic way of life, that is contrary to reason.

This is not just an oversight on their part, for they have a habit of doing such things. They talk a lot about the Sunnah, for example, but they say and do almost everything in the Islamic way of life that is contrary to the Sunnah, which is practice of Qur'an and not Hadith, in the context of time and place. Likewise, they will tell you that Islam is not a religion, but a way of life, yet they will say and do everything that is religion. We have explained these weaknesses of the ummah in great detail in a previous chapter of this book.

According to the true teachings and practices of Abraham (PBUH), the faculty or institution of reason should begin with the concept of God because this is the first article and principle of all religions and way of life. If the first article and principle of our way of life is contrary to reason, then whatever we say and do after that does not make any sense. We can see a very good example of this in the Christian religion of the Christian Church. Although, Christianity, for example, is a sister religion of Islam, the Christians believe Jesus is God and the Son of God against all reason. Some Christians like the Jehovah's Witness and some Anglican Church leaders are against the worship of Jesus, and state such a worship of Jesus is a myth.

When Abraham (PBUH) broke the idols of his ancestors, he was not only against the worship of the idols, but he was against all the concepts of God that was against the institution and faculty of reason. He did not only question the religious leaders of his time about their beliefs and practices but he also questioned kings, atheists, agnostics and himself about the true teachings and concept of God. I spoke a great deal about these teachings and concepts of God in my previous book. Allah (SWT) also speaks a great deal about this in the Holy Qur'an. I hope the ummah will probe into the matter and establish a concept of God, not only suitable for religion, but, also suitable for the secular aspects of our lives, according to the haqq of our creation.

Under the circumstances, here comes along Pope Benedict XV1 who worships Mary and believes that Jesus is the Son of God, against all the faculties and the institutions of reason, to advice Muslims how to reason in religion and all the matters of their way of life. How can we ever take advice from a man who is still living in a period of jahilyah (ignorance) by worshiping Mary and believing that Jesus is the Son of God, according to the dogmas and doctrines of the Christian Church? In fact, there is absolutely nothing in his religion that makes sense to us, because the very first article of the first principle of his faith does not stand the test of time or reason.

Perhaps, that is why the majority of his people are becoming atheist or reverting to Islam. Usually, when we ask the Christians who have reverted to Islam, why they have renounced Christianity, without hesitation they state that they are not happy with their triune (trinity) concept of God (Father, Son and Holy Ghost). It makes no sense because it is against all reason. It is just like believing that the light pole outside their house in the street is their God. All we can say about the people that believe Jesus is God, and the Son of God, is that they are ignorant of the truth.

The Pope Benedict XV1 is definitely ignoramus, not only because he does not know how to reason in his religion, but he also does not know how to reason in history. He quoted a 14th century emperor who was an enemy of Islam to state that it was a historical fact that Islam was "a war mongering nation", and the Prophet (SAW) "is an evil war mongering person". How can the quote of a 14th century emperor who is not a historian, but an enemy of Islam be a historical fact? What about the real scholars of history like Lamartine, Edward Gibbon, Simon Ocklay, Bosworth Smith, etc? Do they not count when they state that the Prophet Muhammad (PBUH) was the greatest person in history because he was the only one who was "most extremely successful in both the secular and religious levels"? No wonder the Mail and Guardian had a cartoon depicting the Pope as "The Holy Goat" in the triune (trinity) concept of the Christian Godhead!

Actually, the Pope is also a mischief maker. He states that he has studied Islam. This is a lie! If he studied Islam would he state that Islam was a religion of violence? Could he not see the fact that Islam was an Arabic word meaning SUBMISSION, which was derived from the root-word S'LM, pronounced "salm" meaning PEACE? Furthermore, did he not ask himself why Islam is not Mohammedanism, like Christianity, Judaism, Buddhism, Hinduism, etc., which are names of a religion that belonged to a specific person, tribe or a place? Or did he just study the works of a 14th century emperor who was an enemy of Islam to find out what were the true teachings and practices of Islam? Bush, Blair and Benedict make very good company. They are all idiots, liars and constitute the triangle of evil of the modern world. How will they answer to God for their wrong doings?

Let alone Pope Benedict XVI, we expected him not to know how to reason in matters of faith because he worships Mary (peace be upon her). But, what about the great Muslim ulama, muftis and saints of the past and the present? Do they not know what is the difference between taqleed (the blind following of religion) and the Quranic teachings of ilm-ul-yaqin (certainty of knowledge by inference or reasoning), ayn-ul-yaqin (certainty of knowledge by seeing and observing) and haqq-ul-yaqin (absolute knowledge, like this is a pen, this is a book, etc.)?

Can they not see that Islam is not a religion based on blind faith but a way of life, which intersect the secular with the religious according to the secular and Qur'anic teachings and practices of ilm-ul-yaqin, ayn-ul-yaqin and haqq-ul-yaqin? Likewise, can they not see that the Sahaba Ikram (RA) followed the Prophet (SAW) according to the teachings of the Qur'an? And, not according to taqleed because every now and then they asked him whether what he was saying was wahy or his own opinion? Unfortunately, it seems that the ulama do not have enough knowledge of the secular to understand the common ground between the secular and the religious in the Islamic way of life.

Another very important aspect of the life of Prophet Abraham (PBUH) is that he added the dimension of works to his faith in order to establish a very strong relationship between his beliefs and practices. Therefore, he SACRIFICED his wealth, health, pleasure, time, family, etc., to spread the true teachings and practices of his Islamic way of life, not only amongst those who did not believe in the existence of God, but also amongst those who believed, to show them "the straight path".

In addition to this, he also prayed to Allah (SWT), as the founding father of Islam, to make imaams of his descendent's so that his Islamic way of life could spread from generation to generation. This covenant of Abraham (PBUH) with Allah (SWT) is also recorded in the Genesis of the Bible. In religion it's a major proof of the existence of God because it existed in the Bible thousands of years before the Holy Qur'an was revealed to the Prophet (SAW). According to his prayer, different Prophets that descended from different generations highlighted different teachings of the same religion and way of life.

The five major Prophets and their teachings are as follows:

Noah (PBUH)	:	BELIEF in the unity of God.
Abraham (PBUH)	:	SACRIFICE.
Moses (PBUH)	:	COMMANDMENTS.
Jesus (PBUH)	:	LOVE.
Muhammad (PBUH)	:	UNITY.

Hence, the religion of Islam developed as follows:

Noah (PBUH)	:	B
Abraham (PBUH)	:	B+S
Moses (PBUH)	:	B+S+C
Jesus (PBUH)	:	B+S+C+L
Muhammad (PBUH)	:	B+S+C+L+U.

Where B = the BELIEF taught by Noah (PBUH), S = the SACRIFICE taught by Abraham (PBUH) and so on and so forth.

In my previous book I stated that there were many other Messengers in between the above five major Prophets in the religion of Prophet Abraham (PBUH) and the Islamic way of life. Furthermore, stating that when we combine the different teachings and practices of the different Books and Prophets in the religion of Prophet Abraham (PBUH), we establish the true teachings and practices of all the Books and Prophets of God. In the context of the BELIEF taught by the Prophet Noah (PBUH), we cannot translate the teaching of LOVE taught by Jesus (PBUH) to mean Jesus is God and Son of God.

Furthermore, we stated that the teaching of LOVE should not precede the teachings of the COMMANDMENTS in our religion. The people who celebrate the melaad and perform salaami, for example, state that they LOVE the Prophet (SAW) yet the majority of them neglect many important COMMANDMENTS of God such as performing their five daily salaah. According to the true teachings of Islam, we cannot show true LOVE to God and the Prophet (PBUH) without having true BELIEF and practicing the true teachings of the COMMANDMENTS. This does not mean that the Tabligh Jamaat who spread religious extremism and fundamentalism contrary to the true teachings and practices of Qur'an, are any better.

In addition to the above, some other important missions and visions of Prophet Abraham (PBUH) are as follows:

1. To establish Makkah Mukarramah as international capital of the ummah.
2. Make the Kabaa or the qibla a symbol of unity for all the people of this world because it was the first mosque or place of worship built by Adam (AS), who was the father of human kind, making Islam the brotherhood of the ummah within the brotherhood of humanity. This means that the mission and vision of Islam is the mission and vision of all peace loving people of this world who wish to establish peace according to the divine teachings and practices of Tawhid, which are the prime objectives of Islam.
3. To establish the rights of women and their liberation in the Islamic way of life. For example, Abraham (PBUH) married Bibi Sarah (RA) and Bibi Hajira (RA) and the part they played in forming the true teachings and practices of Islam. The Wahabis have a lot to learn from these founding statements on how to treat a woman in modern times within a post modern system of life like Islam, which was revealed in the full face of modern history.

In my previous book, I explained in great detail how all our mosques were organised internationally throughout the world by facing the Kabaa or qibla and that although we wore different clothes, spoke different languages, in the different mosques of different countries, it made no difference to our BELIEF, hence, our imaan. We worshiped the same one God of Prophet Abraham (PBUH). Therefore, to relate our beliefs and imaan to the clothes that we wore, language we spoke, or the customs and cultures (sights and sounds) we practiced in the different countries, did not make sense.

Likewise, it is important that we remember that our mission and vision in Islam is to establish a brotherhood of Islam within the brotherhood of mankind according to the divine teachings of peace and Tawhid and not to separate ourselves from humanity as a whole and make ourselves completely different from their way of life. If we did, we would not be serving the true purpose of Islam. When people like Jack Straw (foreign secretary of UK under Blair) state that we should find a way to assimilate with all the people of our global society, we should not take offense to such statements, but find a way to be part of the global society without losing sight of our beliefs, morals and the pure teachings and practices of the Holy Qur'an, because all our teachings and practices are universal.

Therefore, making the headscarf, niqab, burqa, beard and kurtha an issue of our faith does not make us different, but makes us irrational because none of these are commandments of Allah (SWT) in the Holy Qur'an to either the Prophet (SAW) or to us. It would cause no offense to Allah (SWT) and Prophet (SAW) if we said that it was the right of a person to do so, and not his or her religion to do so, because this is exactly how the Qur'an expects us to believe in what is said.

Nevertheless, I regret that in my previous book, I did not tackle the issue of Muslim women, their rights and liberation, in greater detail. There were many reasons for this. One being, that at that time when I published my previous book, women's right and liberation was not a global issue, but rather a tribal one, and not a major problem of Islam. Hence, I condemned the Taliban on this matter, but not the ummah as a whole.

Now, that I have become aware of the fact that it is not only a tribal but also a global issue, which concerns the Muslim ummah and humanity as a whole, I will, insha-Allah, tackle this matter in a global perspective in the remaining chapters. However, in this chapter my main ambition is to make the ummah aware of what the mission and vision of the founding father were on this very important issue of the Islamic way of life.

Many Muslims may ask where in the Holy Qur'an does it state that the Prophet Abraham (PBUH) made any statements about women's right and liberation? And, if such statements were made by him four-to-five-thousand-years-ago, how relevant are those statements today in the 21st century context? Alhumdolillah (by the grace of God), I am blessed by God to see greater meaning of the Holy Qur'an than many of the ulama that are not blessed to see in the pages of the Holy Qur'an. I am blessed with the worldview teachings and practices of peace and Tawhid, which make it very clear to me why the present day ulama are not the real scholars of Islam, and why taqleed, sainthood, priesthood, silsilas and khanqahs, etc., are completely against the true teachings and practices of the Holy Qur'an.

I have explained many of these teachings and practices of the Holy Qur'an in great detail in this book on how we do not agree with the ulama in almost every issue of Islam. Likewise, when we are instructed in the Holy Qur'an that God has made Safaa Murwah compulsory for us in hajj and umrah, we feel very strongly that we are instructed by God to respect the right of the women in the way that the Prophet Abraham (PBUH) respected their right at the highest international level when he agreed to include the Safaa Murwah as an important ritual of the hajj and umrah.

Initially, Allah (SWT) did not command Ibrahim (AS) to make Safaa Murwah a ritual of hajj and umrah. He only gave the instruction of tawaaf of Kabaa. When Abraham (PBUH) was given this instruction of tawaaf, he disclosed the commandment to Bibi Hajira (RA), and when she told him of her experience in Safaa Murwah, he incorporated her experience in the rituals of hajj and umrah. Hence, for us the message of the Holy Qur'an is very clear that women are equal partners in the shurah and ijma of the ummah at the highest international level. Allah (SWT) has incorporated this request of Bibi Hajira (RA) in the Holy Qur'an and according to this, it would be a major sin not to make women in our communities equal partners in all the levels of our shurah.

Furthermore, we are encouraged by the fact that we have seen our forefathers who came to this country about a hundred years ago respect their womenfolk in this way. We stated this in the first chapter that our forefathers made shurah and ijma with their womenfolk at the highest community level, concerning all developments of the ummah from secular to religious.

In addition to the above, not only does the Safaa-Murwah symbolizes the fact that Muslim women are equal partners in the shariah making process of the ummah at the highest international level, but when women make tawaaf and Safaa Murwah, they make it together with men. There is no screen or purdah between them where women walk on one side of the screen, and men on the other side.

Therefore, when we do such things or tell them to cover their faces and not to mix with men at their work place, at religious lectures or functions, in the bazaars and supermarkets, or even in mosques, etc., then we are telling them to do something that is not according to the true teachings and practices of the Holy Qur'an and Islam. Of course, they are instructed to cover their bosoms in public, and like men to lower their gaze, and not to fornicate and commit adultery, but, they are not forbidden to work with men in a professional manner for the betterment of their society or nation.

Unfortunately, the majority of the Muslims do not agree with me when I give a very liberal account of women's right in Islam. They think that I wish to have a good time with women and it is for this reason that I am collaborating with the permissive western society to liberate Muslim women. I really feel pity for them for their narrow mindedness. Can they not see that Islam is a moderate system of life that enjoins what is good and forbids that which is evil? In the West, for example, they have two very distinct opinion of God. One is a very extreme secular point of view that God does not exist and the other is a very religious point of view that Jesus is God and Son of God. The Holy Qur'an does not agree with both these extremes and human points of view. It states that the truth is that God exists and that it's possible to explain His existence through the knowledge of the seen like we have done on a number of occasions in this book.

Likewise, God want us to see the two extreme viewpoints of women's liberation and oppression in this world and admonishes us to take "the middle path" according to the divine teachings and practices of Tawhid. Hence, this moderate path of the Qur'an allows a Muslim woman to drive a car, go to school, work with men, etc., as long as she covers her bosom, and both men and women "lower their gaze" and do not fornicate, etc. Thus, it is a fallacy to state women should only go to work unless it is absolutely necessary for her to do so. How would she know that she will become a widow at the age of 30 or 40 or get divorce, and that she has to educate herself at an early age to get a decent job and experience?

In the same way, some people might argue that the times are not right for a woman to go to work. This does not mean that we should change the word of God to suit the times. The right thing to do is to make their environment more conducive for them to work, by implementing stricter laws of marriages, sexual harassments, adultery, abortions, etc. We want the Western world to take note that our women are liberated just like their women, but unlike them our women can retain their morals and conduct when they step outside their homes. Is that not what we wish to show the world? There was a time when many of their girls 'fell for our boys' because of their exemplary Islamic behavior.

Thus, while I agree with the secular Muslims and the West that it is not religion for a woman to cover her head or face in public, not to go to school, work with men, drive a car, etc, I disagree with them that it is not religion not to make them the head of a state or the church. This means that there are some restrictions on women in Islam, but not due to male chauvinism or culture, custom and tradition. It is due to the knowledge and wisdom of God. And, it is for both, men and women, to recognize what are these restrictions and what is the reason and wisdom behind it.

According to all the Books of God, Torah, Bible and Qur'an, it is very clear to us that God created man, not woman, as the vicegerent (caliph or deputy) of God on earth. Furthermore, it is made clear that before

Adam and Eve discovered their ha-yaah (shamelessness), Eve was made "companion" of Adam. This meant that before she became his wife, she shared his burden, not as a wife, but his deputy to God. Hence, the difference between them then was that he was answerable to God and she was answerable to him and not God. This did not change when she became a wife and mother or when he became a husband and a father.

Thus, in the Islamic way of life, if men and women do not wish to get involved in any kind of gender disputes or controversies, then the best thing for them to say and do is exactly what is written in the Qur'an. If the Qur'an does not compel a woman to cover her face or head in public or does not stop her from going to school, work, drive a car, etc, then it is wrong to state that it is religion to do so. Similarly, if the Qur'an allows a man to have more than one wife then it is wrong for a woman to question such an injunction of the Qur'an because it was not man who granted such a privilege to himself but it was God Who did so in His infinite wisdom and knowledge. In the same way if Allah (SWT) tells us in the Qur'an that the boys must be given two thirds share of the inheritance and the girls one third, and that two women must sign a legal document in the place of one male, then it is wrong to question the wisdom and knowledge of the Almighty in the matter.

Likewise, in the Islamic way of life, it does not mean that if a woman cannot become the head of the state or the church that she has no right to voice her opinion on any of the affairs of the state or church. As the deputy of the caliph, she has all the rights to do so. Therefore, when the majority of the ulama don't allow Muslim women to perform salaah in the main section of the mosque and address the congregation from the podium, it is against the rule of the Qur'an to do so. This does not mean that if the women did not address the congregation during the time of the Prophet (SAW) that they should not be allowed to do so today. This argument would be no different if it was argued that it was not Sunnah to keep a beard. Hence, such acts are not against the Sunnah or the true teachings of the Qur'an.

Similarly, secular Muslims or non-Muslims who ignore the true teachings and practices of the Qur'an in the other extreme are not any better. They are just as ignorant because they defy the fact that women are not the vicegerents of God on earth and are not answerable to God. And, therefore, they cannot be made head of state of the church. Let alone women, men are employing gay men as imams (leaders) of their mosques (church). They have absolutely no idea that Allah (SWT) has made man not woman, the vicegerent of God and it is here that He has drawn the line between the duties and functions of man and women on this earth.

According to the Qur'an, these lines between men and women are clearly visible and can be understood in every issue of our life. All Muslims have to do is understand the true teachings and practices of Islam only according to the Qur'an. There is no other book in this world other than the Qur'an, which can provide us with such an accurate and perfect guidance in every issue of our lives. The reason for this is that only Allah (SWT) and nobody else not even the Prophets have knowledge of the truth unless it was revealed to them by the All Wise, the Creator and the Lord of all the worlds.

Therefore, I consider it my duty to appeal to all the Muslims of this world, to start a shura at the local mosque level, to establish the fact that only the Qur'an and not the Hadith is the only source of knowledge in all the affairs of our lives. Unless we do that, we cannot make any progress in our lives!

CHAPTER 10

Sunnah Of The Prophet (Saw)

There are many things to consider when we try to understand the Sunnah of the Prophet (SAW). Some of these things are as follows:

1. He was the descendant of Prophet Abraham (PBUH).
2. According to the prayer of Ibrahim (AS), he was supposed to fulfill all the ambitions of Prophet Abraham (PBUH) like all other Prophets of God.
3. His Sunnah had to be centered on the Sunnah (mission and vision) of Prophet Abraham (PBUH).
4. As "the last Prophet" of God and "the universal Prophet", he had to "complete and perfect" all the teachings and practices of Islam, in the most modern and universal manner.

There is a very big difference between the Sunnah of the Prophet (SAW) and that of Prophet Abraham (PBUH). This difference is that the major part of the Sunnah of Abraham (PBUH) is the desire of man and the major part of the Sunnah of the Prophet (SAW) is the guidance of God. This means that the major function of the Prophet (SAW) was to purify all of man's knowledge and experience in this world according to the ambitions of Abraham (PBUH) and the guidance of God. Therefore, to understand the Sunnah of the Prophet (SAW), we have to understand what part of the Holy Qur'an deals with the desire of man and what part of it is God's guidance.

In Abraham's Sunnah, not all of it was the desire of man. Some of it, like the building of the Kabaa, the symbolic sacrifice of his son, circumcision, etc., was God's desire to fulfill the needs of man. Therefore, in order to establish the Sunnah of the Prophet (SAW), let us reiterate some of the desires of Abraham (PBUH) that represents the needs of man. Some of these are:

1. Exercising sound reason and logic in all matters of his life and not emulating other people's religion blindly;
2. Not separating the secular from the religious. He questioned both: the priest (religious leaders) and the king (secular, agnostic and atheist rulers), about the concept of God;
3. Championing the rights of women, and admitting their shurah at the highest international level of haj and umrah;
4. Entering into a partnership with God to establish the truth, and
5. Desiring to have a brotherhood of Islam (peace loving people) to do good within the brotherhood of mankind.

Note: Some Muslim might not think it's proper to state that Abraham (PBUH) entered into a partnership with God to establish the truth. They might believe that Allah (SWT) appointed him as His Prophet and commanded him to establish the truth according to revealed knowledge like He did with the Prophet (SAW). But this is not true. If Islam was a religion then we would have accepted such a concept of Prophethood. Since Islam is a way of life, it is appropriate to think that the initiative of SUBMISSION came from Abraham (PBUH), as a representative of man, out of his freewill, for SUBMISSION to be meaningful. Otherwise, the other option left to God was to make all the people of this world Muslim by force, the same way in which angels are made pure.

To explain this, let's take for example our attempt to unify the ummah. For the last thirty to forty years, many of us have made many different attempts to unify the ummah, but have failed to do so. In the process many of us have given up the attempt, but some of us are still continuing, hoping that one day we will succeed. I am one of them. I have not given up and will never give up. This is because I know for sure that Allah (SWT) wants us to succeed in every issue of our life, but by our own effort by knowing what works and does not work for us as human beings. Perhaps, I am lacking something in my knowledge of Islam or my approach to the Muslim majority is incorrect. Or it may be that the majority of Muslims are complacent, not knowing that their unity is more important for their survival in this world than some of their rituals.

Insha-Allah, one day all these issues will synchronize and all issues of unity will prevail within the ummah. Until then, all of us have to commit ourselves to unity because Allah (SWT) has made it very clear to us in the Qur'an that He will never change our condition unless we change it ourselves with our own souls. In other words, Allah (SWT) is Most Merciful, but sometimes He has to be cruel to be kind like we are to our children in order to bring them up properly. Hence, the desire to change has to come from us, but we cannot do so, especially in diversity, without the guidance of God.

Furthermore, it is important to acknowledge the fact that most of the truth in the creation of human life is abstract, due to the diversity of its creation. In other words, most of the truth in our way of life in the diversity of our creation is not haqq-ul-yaqin. If we separate, for example, the boundaries of the secular and religious, then reason will not apply to religion, it will only apply to the secular. It is only when we acknowledge the worldview teachings and practices of Tawhid (unity and universality), we take the option of reason in religion to secure the intersection of the secular with religion. If Allah (SWT) did not support us with this fact in the Qur'an, we would not know what the truth of our religion is.

In the context of the above and the fact that Prophet (SAW) was given strict instructions not to say or do anything in his life that was not revealed to him, the Sunnah of Prophet (SAW) was limited to the Sunnah of Abraham (PBUH) and the true guidance of the Holy Qur'an. The only difference between the Qur'an and the desire of man is that the Qur'an fulfills all the desires of man according to the instructions and guidance of God in a partnership with man, no more, no less. This is very different from the secular constitution of our government, which does not enjoy the benefit of God's guidance. In other words, Abraham (PBUH) wanted a constitution like the one we have in South Africa, but with God's guidance, recognizing the sovereignty of God, separating truth from falsehood.

Therefore, the Ahle Sunnah are all the people of this world that descended from Abraham (PBUH) according to his mission statements and guidance of God, and the Prophet (SAW) was one of them. This means that the Ahle Sunnah are not Ahle Hadith because they are the followers of all the Books and Prophets of God according to the mission statement of the Prophet Abraham (PBUH). In contrast, the Ahle Hadith are not, because they contradict many mission statements of the Prophet Abraham (PBUH), injunctions of the Holy Qur'an, and overall meaning and message of the Qur'an with time and space. In other words, Hadith is the practice of the time of the Prophet (SAW), which, within the diversity of our time place, we are not compelled to practice as Sunnah today. For example, he used the sword to fight wars, and we use gunpowder. Likewise, he used scribes to write the Qur'an, and we use the printing press.

It seems from the above that Abraham (PBUH) was a very rational and intellectual person. Although, he was born in a religious family who ran a temple, he was absolutely not interested in any kind of childish beliefs and practices in religion and priesthood like most rational and intellectual people do today. Hence, without any instructions from God, he destroyed all idols in the temple except one, and tied the axe around its neck. A religious person wouldn't do such a thing unless God told him or her that it was correct to do so. The Prophet (SAW) broke all idols in the Kabaa after the conquest of Makkah Mukarramah because he knew that he had to do so in the context of the knowledge and guidance of the Qur'an and Tawhid.

Abraham (PBUH) did it purely on the basis of reason. He was not instructed by Allah (SWT) to do so. Likewise, if we tell some of our people purely on the basis of reason that the forty days fatiha and one year ceremonies that they do for the dead people is insignificant and un-Islamic, they will not believe us. Religion is like that, once we are indoctrinated, it is very difficult to overcome it. Many Christians know in their hearts of heart that TRINITY is wrong but it is very difficult for them to give up their belief because they have been indoctrinated to believe that it is wrong to reason in matters of faith. And, their confusion in the matter is not due to the Bible, but, it is due to Satan.

The majority of Muslims are also trapped in many such issues by the indoctrination of their religion. If you do not believe in Hadith or pirs (spiritual leader of different sects) and saints you are considered to be a munafik (hypocrite) and a collaborator with the West. The sum total of this indoctrination is so great and so devastating that it has not only divided the ummah but it has also distorted "the all truth" to such an extent that it is now difficult to tell the truth from falsehood or to convince any Muslim on the matter. If it were not for the teachings and practices of Tawhid, I would be completely lost in the matter.

In Islam, we are totally forbidden to believe in religion that is based on blind faith, priesthood or the dogmas and doctrines of their sects, madhabs, silsilas and khanqahs. In Islam we are commanded to reason and rationalize in every issue of our life according to secular instructions of ilm-ul-yaqin, ayn-ul-yaqin and haqq-ul-yaqin. It is for this reason that the Christians think that we follow the Devil's religion. They say that only the Devil reasons, rationalizes and intellectualizes in matters of faith. They state that it is against religion to do so, which according to Islam is totally untrue in our way of life.

Unfortunately, majority of the Christians and Muslims who follow religion are unaware of the fact that Abraham (PBUH) practiced haqq (truth) according to the abstract knowledge of Tawhid, and not religion when he questioned both the priest and the king who was not a religious person and himself, about the truth of God. Hence, haqq is not limited to religion but, it also applies to secular people and rulers of our lives. Actually, when we apply haqq according to the worldview teachings and practices of Tawhid, we discard almost all of religion and accept most of the secular way of life.

In Islam, reason is associated with secular and haqq. And, blind faith is associated with religion and mythology. Some non-Muslims who have become Muslims purely because they reasoned that Islam was telling the truth recognize this fact. One of them is Ruqayyah Waris Maqsood. In her paper entitled, "The Islamization of the Social Sciences: Can We Take for Granted the Theory of Evolution", associates reason with the haqq of the Qur'an, as follows:

> "Many people coming into Islam as converts, like myself, without the background of Muslim acceptance and respect for the Holy Text ingrained into them from infancy, would tell you that if they found one single thing in the Qur'an that did not tie in with logic and reason, they would then disbelieve it as the "Word of God" and cease to be Muslim. They would do this for the very reason that this search for logic and reason that made

sense was the probable reason for their leaving the Christian church, or for coming into Islam from any other background. The happy fact is that the Qur'an **stands the test.**"

Hence, according to the above, the Sunnah of the Prophet (SAW) has certain conditions attached to it. Some of which are as follows:

1. It has to be rational, logical and intellectual;
2. It has to superimpose haqq;
3. It has to treat religion like it treats the secular;
4. It has to be a partnership between God and man;
5. It's teachings and practices must not be limited to time and space;
6. It must champion the rights of women among many other things;
7. It must encourage shurah and ijma of king, priest and that of the ordinary people, and
8. It must link all teachings and practices of Islam with the true teachings, and practices of the Qur'an, nothing more, nothing less.

Therefore, in the context of the above, another very important way to understand the Sunnah of the Prophet (SAW) is by explaining the meaning of the Arabic word Sunnah, which has two distinct meanings. One is "the path" and the other, "the practice". Mathematically, this can be represented as follows:

SUNNAH = THE PATH + THE PRACTICE.

Usually, "the path" refers to the source document, and "the practice" refers to the practice of the source document. Another name for the source document is the constitution. In Islam, undoubtedly, the Qur'an and not the Hadith is the source document unless the fundamentalists think that the Qur'an is the constitution and the Hadith is the Sunnah (practice of the Qur'an) by the Prophet (SAW), although almost all the teachings and practices of the Hadith contradict the true teachings and practices of the Holy Qur'an and Sunnah, with time and space.

What the fundamentalists and extremists do not understand is that you cannot write one thing in your constitution and say and do another thing in your practice. If the Qur'an is your constitution and Hadith is Sunnah (practice) of the Prophet (SAW), then you cannot say and do one thing in the Qur'an and say and do another thing in the Hadith. For example, the Qur'an recognizes the diversity of our tradition and does not compel us to keep a beard, wear a khurtah, etc., yet the Hadith ignores the diversity of tradition and compels us to do so. Likewise, the Qur'an prohibits us to believe in sects and madhabs but, the Hadith compels us to believe in sects and madhabs and so on. In Islam, this is wrong because we cannot say and do one thing in the Qur'an and say and do completely another thing in the Hadith, which fundamentalists believe is Sunnah of the Prophet (SAW). This distorts the true knowledge and understanding of the Qur'an and Sunnah, which is Shariah.

A very good example of a person that works very strictly according to the constitution is the judge of a court of law. When Judge Nicholson passed his judgment in the infamous trial of Jacob Zuma that led to the "recalling" of President Thabo Mbeki, Judge Nicholson had the following to say when he was questioned about his judgment:

> "As judges we only have one master, that's the constitution and we should not respect persons at the expense of the constitution".

Unfortunately, for Judge Nicholson, his judgment was overturned in the Appeal Court. The Judge in the Appeal Court found that he did not follow the proper procedure in hearing and judging the case. This greatly damaged our trust in his judgment, but not in his word about the constitution. Then again, to state that politicians do not influence judges of the Appeal Court, etc, is doubtful. The Heath commission exposes some of the corruption.

Nevertheless, the big problem in the Muslim world is not only that they show great respect for persons (ulama, saints and muftis), who divide them into the different sects, madhabs, silsilas and khanqahs, which is totally contrary to Qur'an, but they also have two source documents, one in the form of the Qur'an and the other in the form of the Hadith, and they both contradict one another, with time and space. We have already discussed these contradictions in many chapters of this book. In Islam, we have to sort out whether we are going to respect and follow the so-called ulama, saints, muftis, their book of Hadith, which was written by man, or are we going to respect and follow the Sunnah, according to the true teachings and practices of the Holy Qur'an and the shurah and ijma of the ummah?

Having two constitutions that contradict one another is such a bizarre experience that even judges can make mistakes. Take for example the judgment that was given against an Indian schoolgirl for wearing her nose ring as her cultural practice in school. The judge in the magistrate court stated that according to the constitution of the school the girl was wrong to practice her culture in school. Likewise, when the case went to the appeal court, the same thing happened. The judge of the appeal court said that the judge of the magistrate court was right. The girl had violated the constitution of the school.

But when the case went to the constitutional court, the verdict was reversed. The constitutional court discovered that the constitution of the school was written according to the White culture, when only White students were privileged to attend school during apartheid time, and that the school's constitution did not cater for the new political dispensation. Therefore, it had to be scrapped, and that girl had to be readmitted to school, according to the South Africa's new constitution.

Unfortunately, I do not agree entirely with the above Constitutional Court's judgment on the nose-ring saga. I think that an Islamic Sharia Court would have gone further to examine whether the school's constitution really reflected the European culture of the apartheid era or was purely secular in nature. If it was purely secular, based on the teachings of ilm-ul-yaqin, ayn-ul-yaqin and haqq-ul-yaqin, the Sharia Court will not allow the girl to wear the nose-ring in school because the school was a secular institution reflecting the right, title, interest, claim and demand of the secular way of life according to all the terms and conditions of the Qur'an. Furthermore, as caliphs (deputies) of God on earth, we are supposed to know that the nose-ring is tradition and not religion.

In Islam, we do not have any problem with the so-called "secular Muslim" and "modernist Muslim". They know that the Qur'an is their constitution and their master. They understand it in a very universal manner, with time and space, and the dominant secular base of the Islamic way of life. Therefore, they do not only reject the Hadith but, they also reject the mullahs, their saints and kitabs, which has caused a great deal of confusion in their lives. My only advice to the modernists is that they should not give an interpretation of the Qur'an only according to their knowledge and experience of this world, and the secular constitution of the West.

By all means, take into account what is going on in the world, but also take into account the fact that Islam is a mission for world peace, in the context of Tawhid and the diversity of our creation, and interpret all the teachings and practices of Islam to fulfill these objectives, according to the true Word of God found in the Qur'an in this context. In other words, they should avoid forming a brotherhood of like-minded Muslims around the Internet, because in Islam, we are advised to form our brotherhood around our local musjid, according to the shurah and ijma of all Muslims that live in the vicinity of the musjid, for this is where the real diversity of our lives lays.

Furthermore, we should not assume that our interpretation of the Qur'an is the final interpretation of the Qur'an unless it is approved by the shurah and ijma of the ummah. This will not happen until the majority of the Muslims establish the Assembly of the Ummah. Until then we will have to exercise patience, and promote our own individual thinking in the diversity of our creation, and in the context of the peace mission of Islam, not enforcing it as Shariah, but enlightening the ummah to be more open-minded and universal in all the matters of their faith.

Thus, in this book, although I have given a very strong viewpoint why Muslims should reinstate the Qur'an as the source document to establish the Sunnah, the fundamentalists and extremists Muslims do not consider it a good enough reason to abandon the book of Hadith. Unfortunately, to complicate matters with fundamentalists and extremists Muslims, the religious leaders of Turkey wish to solve the problem of the Hadith by rewriting the book, accepting only those Hadith that collaborate with the

Qur'an, and rejecting those that do not collaborate with the true teachings and practices of the Holy Qur'an.

It's like writing the many different versions of the Bible, and the Hadith has its limitations. If they rewrote it, it will still not explain the Sunnah with time and space, in a universal and rational manner according to the worldview teachings and practices of Tawhid, like I have done in this and my previous book.

Therefore, it is for this reason that I am not interested to preserve the book of Hadith in any form. I wish to take the stand that Hazrat Abu Bak'r (RA) took in the matter. Just before his demise, he took all 500 Hadith, written by him and burnt them. Hence, our objections to the book of Hadith are as follows:

1. Contrary to the true teachings of the Holy Qur'an, it does not allow many important teachings and practices of Islam to progress and develop with time and space.
2. It does not contain "the completed and perfected" knowledge and guidance of the Holy Qur'an.
3. It distorts the true definitions of Sunnah and bid'ah. It makes Sunnah and bid'ah, what is not Sunnah and bidat, and vice versa.
4. We have absolutely no confidence in the science of Hadith. It relies very heavily on the reputation and status of the narrators, and not in the value of the narrations.
5. It divides the ummah into sects, madhabs, silsilas and khanqahs.
6. It contains inaccuracies and interpolations.
7. It encourages religious extremism and fundamentalism.

Mathematically the Hadith is represented as follows:

HADITH = PART QURAN
+ PART ARAB CULTURE & CUSTOM OF THE
TIME OF THE PROPHET (SAW)
+ RELIGIOUS EXAGGERATIONS AND MYTHS
+ SOME PERSONAL LIKES AND DISLIKES OF
THE PROPHET (SAW)
+ INACCURACIES DUE TO NARRATIONS OR

SCIENCE OF HADITH
+ INTERPOLATIONS.

The biggest fault with the book of Hadith is that it introduces words like bidat, madhabs, taqleed, etc, to the Islamic way of life which are totally alien to Islam and the Qur'an. For example, if we did not have Hadith, the word bidat (innovation) would be totally foreign to us because according to the Qur'an, if we do not experience the dichotomy of the secular and religious and all injunctions of Qur'an are not affected by time and space, then, how does the word bidat apply to any issue of the Qur'an and Sunnah? Similarly, the words madhabs and taqleed are foreign to Islam. The Prophet (SAW) and Sahaba Ikram (RA) did not engage in madhabs and taqleed, where one madhab performed salaah and calculated zakaat differently from that of the other.

Another very big fault with the Hadith is that it is completely against the diversity of all cultures, customs, traditions and compartments of our lives. All Muslims who believe in Hadfith believe in an Islamic sign, symbol, identity, dressing, sight, sound, politics, culture, custom, tradition, economics, education, etc. This is totally wrong because as caliphs of God on earth, we have to be completely neutral to all diversities and are duty bound to preserve and purify them according to all the injunctions of the Qur'an and the Sunnah of the Prophet (SAW) that collaborate with the Qur'an and not the Hadith.

The diversity of our creation is very important for the understanding of the Qur'an and Sunnah or Shariah in our Islamic way of life. It helps us to understand Islam in a simple, humble and rational manner, in the diversity of our creation. Whether such a knowledge and understanding of Islam deals with the socio-economical, political and religious aspects of our life is of no consequence. In order to explain this, let's take for example our daily salaah. The Qur'an compares the shadows of our salaah with those of inanimate objects as follows:

> "Do they not look at Allah's creation, among things, how their shadows turn round, from the right and the left, prostrating themselves to Allah, and that in the humblest manner?"
>
> (Al-Qur'an 16: 48).

Thus, according to the global perspective of the Qur'an and the diversity of our creation, for our salaah to be accepted by Allah (SWT), it has to constitute only our submission to the Word of God according to our rukhu and sujood, nothing more, nothing less. Therefore, it does not matter how we replicate our salaah and what name we give it, example, fard, sunnat, nafil, etc, it makes no difference, like it makes no difference to the inanimate objects that perform their salaah from dawn to dusk. In addition to this, it is also obvious that inanimate objects do not perform their salaah according to any madhabs. Therefore, how come our salaah is fard, sunnat, nafil, etc, or Shafi, Hanafi, etc?

Therefore, it is our humble appeal to our brothers and sisters in Islam, not to make fard, sunnat, etc, or madhab an issue of our salaah that divides us. Let's behave like inanimate objects and become very simple and humble in our salaah, where these acts of salaah do not compromise our salaah in any way if we unify them to eliminate the madhabs. Let's come to the conclusion that the truth in our salahh and everything else besides what is absolute haqq (haqq-ul-yaqin) is abstract, and we cannot understand it unless we submit to the knowledge of Tawhid (the divine teachings and practices of unity and universality) in the diversity of our creation.

Unfortunately, the majority of the Muslims and their ulama do not understand that in order to have the most accurate knowledge and understanding of Shariah, we have to have the most accurate knowledge and understanding of the Holy Qur'an and Sunnah, where the Sunnah is the most accurate practice of the Qur'an, with changes in time and place. For example, to state that to keep beard, wear kurtha, kneel and drink water, etc., is Sunnah and Shariah is wrong because the Qur'an does compel us to do so. All the injunctions of the Qur'an apply to all the people of this world immaterial of the fact that they keep a beard, wear the kurtha, etc. Likewise, to state that secular education is western, Christian, worldly and un-Islamic is Sunnah and Shariah is wrong because it is totally against the Qur'an to do so.

According to the above, Sunnah, Shariah, Qur'an and haqq are one and the same thing in different forms. For example, the Qur'an is the **word of God** and the Sunnah is the **exact practice** of the Qur'an like the Prophet (SAW) was the walking, talking Qur'an. Likewise, the Shariah is the **law** according to the Qur'an and the Sunnah and the haqq that emanates from this is the **reality** of our creation and nature. According to the divine teachings and practices of Tawhid, which are the prime objectives of Islam, if we do not make sure that there is an accurate relationship between the Qur'an, Sunnah, Shariah and haqq, we are not good Muslims, and we are not following the true teachings and practices of Islam. Mathematically, this relationship is written down as follows:

Qur'an = Sunnah = Shariah = haqq (the absolute truth and reality of our creation).

CHAPTER 11

Quran And Science

In my previous book a similar chapter dealing with science was entitled, "Religion and Science". I thought that in view of the worldview teachings and practices of Tawhid, I had made a mistake to title the chapter in the way I did in the previous book, because the core teachings and practices of religion was opposed to the core teachings and practices of the secular. And, such a union between religion and science was impossible to achieve in any religion except the Islamic way of life, where only that part of religion was acceptable to the secular, which was thoroughly compatible with science, according to the knowledge of the Qur'an.

When I reviewed this chapter, I thought that the appropriate title should be "Islam and Science". Ultimately, I decided that even this title was not appropriate, mainly because there were two versions of Islam, one fundamentalist and extremist, which believed that everything in this universe was created from the noor of the Prophet (SAW) or nothingness, and the other, which was Qur'anic, stated that everything in the universe was created from "a mist" (gases) that existed in the universe before God created it. Hence, in order to distinguish haqq from Islamic religious extremism and fundamentalism, I had to title this chapter, "Qur'an and Science".

Thus, what I wish to demonstrate in this chapter, like in all other chapters, is that our worldly knowledge in science, religion, business, politics, etc, does not create haqq (truth). Only God's wisdom and knowledge can tell us is what haqq in them. For example, if Allah (SWT) tells us in the Qur'an that He created Adam (AS) and each species of creation from the soil of this earth, then that's it, that is haqq, whether scientists agree with it or not. Similarly, if a religious person wants us to believe Jesus is God and Son of God or that Prophet Muhammad (SAW) was not an ordinary person because he did not have a shadow, we cannot agree because we would in contradiction of haqq.

This means that the mistakes we human are making is that we are seeing haqq through the distorted knowledge of our science and religion, where science does not agree with religion and vice versa. What we should be doing is looking at our human knowledge of science and religion through the haqq of the Qur'an, finding the truth in them like it is demonstrated in this chapter in the many issues of science and religion. Muslim trump card from this point of view is that we are the only people in this world who possess the revealed knowledge of God in its most pristine form.

Explaining anything from the perspective of haqq is very difficult in the Islamic way of life. For example, the Prophet (SAW) predicted that his ummah will divide into 73 sects and only one will enter jannah. He made this prediction from the perspective of haqq. When we try to interpret his predictions from our distorted knowledge of religion, not knowing the haqq of the Qur'an in the matter, we will never be able to establish the sect that will enter jannah. From this point of view, all sects believe that they will enter jannah. If they only knew what haqq was by studying the Qur'an, they would know how to correct themselves. But, unfortunately, they are no better than Iblis (Satan), who without haqq stated that he was better than Adam (AS) because he was made of fire and Adam (AS) from dust.

Thus, it is very important that Muslims exhaust the knowledge of the Qur'an in every issue of their life, and understand exactly what haqq is in every situation of their lives. Because, if they don't, they will never know how they have deviated from haqq and how to correct themselves. For example, when I discuss the high divorce rate, the disunity of the ummah and the harm it is doing to the ummah, etc, the majority of the Muslims fail to see the causes of these problems in the ummah from the perspective of haqq. All they can say to contribute to the discussion is to say, "Make dua", as if dua will solve the problem. What they are required to know is that Allah (SWT) will not change these conditions of the ummah unless they are prepared to learn haqq from the Qur'an and rectify their situation accordingly. Hence, understanding haqq and not making dua is a means of solving our problems and getting rid of myths in the Islamic way of life.

Allah (SWT) used haqq to create this universe. Therefore, there are many reasons to believe why Islam and science do not differ in principle and methodology or fail to intertwine faith with reason. And, under the circumstances, to contradict one of them without the knowledge of haqq is totally un-Islamic. Some of the reasons for this are as follows:

1. It is a requirement of Tawhid to have absolute unity between the Word of God and the Work of God in the signs and science of nature and in the history of religion.

2. In both, Islam and science, certainty of knowledge is due to ilm-ul-yaqin, ayn-ul-yaqin and haqq-ul-yaqin and not according to taqleed, aqeeda, sainthood, priesthood, etc, which are the core teachings and practices of religion.

3. The union of the secular and religion is the most important feature of Islam in world history. The Prophet (SAW) was the only one who was "most extremely successful in both the secular and religious levels".

4. It is not against the Sunnah of the Prophet (SAW) to develop human life according to science, with time and space. For example, he used the string as an instrument of science to determine the time of fij'r and maghrib, and the sighting of the moon to determine the months of the lunar calendar. According to the Qur'an, we are persuaded to use astronomical calculations, to achieve the same results.

5. In the context of diversity, some of haqq (truth) is absolute and some of it is abstract. Both, Islam and science agree on this very important issue of life. We have explained this in great detail in the previous chapter.

As of the above knowledge and understanding of Qur'an and science, I entered the 2002 evolution and creation debate in 'The Star' newspaper (Johannesburg). My letter was entitled, "**Godless science is an impaired vision**". Some of the things that I mentioned in the letter are as follows:

1. According to the divine teachings of Tawhid (unity and universalism) in Islam, it is imperative that we have as much knowledge and understanding of religion as we have of science. If our knowledge and understanding of science is greater than

that of religion or vice versa, we are bound to differ and end in conflict.

2. It is a myth and misconception in religion that God created something out of nothing. Scientifically, it is also not possible to create anything out of nothing. Scientists themselves are not able to create a single living cell out of anything. From the Holy Qur'an, God did not create this entire creation from nothingness. There is not an instance or a verse in the Qur'an in which God says that He created anything out of nothing. Not only did He create the universe from a mist, but He also created Adam from the soil of the earth.

3. Science has proven that matter is eternal. According to the Holy Qur'an, before the Big Bang took place, the universe existed in a mist form and when the term of the present universe expires, God will fold it and evolve it to a higher form. This means that existence of matter is, and will be eternal. Hence, religion confirms what modern science holds as true and correct.

4. From the above, science has proven that matter is not only eternal, but it is living. The Qur'an states that matter is not only living but it is also conscious—conscious of the command of God. The Qur'an further states that before the Big Bang, the "mist" was actually gas moving at a very high speed in space. Since, there is no friction in space; it was hardly likely that the gases were going to form anything. God called forth to these gases to come willingly or unwillingly. The gases replied that they came willingly. Hence, the planets follow a fixed path in orbit because they are conscious of, and submit to the will of God.

5. From the above, we can deduce that since matter is living and conscious, it cannot be subjected to any shape or form, which is against its nature. Otherwise, it would be rebellious. Therefore, all primeval matter or basic matter has to be created in a more advanced form from its original nature. God created all living and plant matter from primeval matter and not from the origin of the previous creation. According to the law of entropy, all living matter dies, disintegrates and decays. Religion confirms this law, but goes further and states that such decayed matter will be resurrected again from primeval matter.

In the Holy Qur'an, the following four verses of surah Al-Anbiyaa (Surah 21) demonstrate some of the major sequences of events that were used by God to create our universe:

Verse 30: Do not the unbelievers (evolutionists) see
That the heavens and the earth
Were joined together (as one
Unit of creation), before
We clove them asunder?
We made from water
Every living thing. Will they
Not then believe?

Verse 31: And We have set on the earth
Mountains standing firm,
Lest it should shake with them,
And We have made therein
Broad highways (between mountains)
For them to pass through:
That they may receive guidance.

Verse 32: And We have made
The heavens as a canopy
Well guarded: yet do they
Turn away from (the signs
Which these things (point to)!

Verse 33: It is He Who created
The night and the day
And the sun and the moon:
All (the celestial bodies)
Swim along each in its
Rounded course.

Hence, according to the above, the different stages of our creation developed as follows:

1. The heaven and earth were one.
2. The heaven was space and earth was smoke (gas), and it was not easy to distinguish the one from the other;
3. God compacted the gas into a liquid and solid forms, thus, making the earth distinct from the heaven (sky);
4. Then He created life from water;
5. Made the ground firm beneath us by making mountains;
6. Likewise, He made the sky or the heaven as a canopy above us to secure the earth in space;
7. Created the sun, moon, planets, day and night, and
8. He organized the planets to swim in a rounded course.

Recently, in the year 2010, there was a debate on science and faith in the 'Muslim Views' of Cape Town. The debate was not centered around the argument whether primeval matter had an eternal existence or whether it was created from nothingness. It was centered around the argument whether it was wise to link the revelation with science or not. Some people thought it was not wise to do so because science and revelations were two separate entities, which did not agree with one another on methodology. Surely, I was not going to support such a concept of creation. Therefore, my reply to the debate was as follows:

"I disagree with Professor Mall's article, 'Science not to be linked with revelation' (Muslim Views, July 2010).

In contrast, my knowledge and experience of the Qur'an on science and faith is as follows:

- Initially, primeval matter existed in the form of a 'smoke' (gas).
- It could not create itself without the help of God.
- In all its form it functions according to the laws of physics and mathematics.
- God used the same laws of physics and mathematics to create it, except where it was not possible to do so.
- Every living thing was created from water and each species of creation was created from primeval matter and not from the origin of the previous species.

- Hence, it is He Who causes the rain to fall, the seed to sprout, the sun to rise in the east and set in the west and so on, and it is we who have learnt science from His creative powers.
- Likewise, He did not supply us with our cars, household appliances, furniture, etc. He gave us the resources and the intelligence to do so.

All aspects of our lives, whether it is socio-economical, political, religious or otherwise, cannot function in the long term without the teachings and practices of science because it is the nature and character of our universe to function in that way.

Even the garden mole uses science to air condition its burrow.

Similarly, the bee extracts honey for shifa.

Hence, the Qur'an encourages us to establish the teachings and practices of science where we do not have the knowledge of science and provides the appropriate guidance when we have the knowledge of science.

Therefore, it is unlike us not to donate body parts for transplant, do stem cell research, produce an atom bomb, make test tube babies, etc.

If there are weaknesses in this creation then they are due to the weakness in the origin of the primeval matter.

God will amend the quality and nature of the primeval matter in the hereafter for a permanent and perfect creation.

All knowledge and guidance of the Qur'an that applies to science applies to faith because in the Islamic way of life there is a very intricate balance between the knowledge of the seen and the unseen, the secular and the religious, the material and the spiritual, this world and the akhirah (hereafter) and so on.

I think we should not worry about the ulama, their ulooms, the Hadith or any unfounded knowledge of religion. We should just acquire knowledge from the cradle to the grave or be it in China and then apply the guidance of the Qur'an periodically, like Allah (SWT) did from time to time with people of this world, by the shurah and ijma of the ummah so that we can enjoin what is good and forbid what is bad in every aspect and level of our life."

In addition to the above, we are required to believe that man was appointed as the caliph (deputy) of God, and it is within his means and capabilities to emulate all the attributes of God to a certain extent as the caliph of God. If he fails to do so, he will fail in his duty to God.

Thus, to end this conversation on science and faith, the following verse of the Qur'an, should convince us that we cannot survive without science and the guidance of God:

> "So set thou thy face
> Steadily and truly to the Faith:
> (Establish) God's handiwork according
> To the pattern on which
> He has made mankind:
> No change (let there be)
> In the work (wrought)
> By God: that is
> The Standard Religion:
> But most among mankind
> Understand not."
>
> (Al-Qur'an 30: 30).

We agree with Allah (SWT) that majority of the people of this world do not understand the true teachings and practices of "the standard deen" in relation to human nature, its origin, existence and duty as caliph. They use their Books and Prophets wrongly to establish their religions wherein they differ with one another instead of establishing "the all truth" and reality of their creation by acknowledging the divine teachings and practices of Tawhid, as it is explained in this book.

Thus, in this book, it is our duty to persuade all the people of this world (both Muslims and non-Muslims) to establish the true teachings and practices of their way of life according to haqq and science, which is found in the Qur'an, and, not according to the distorted knowledge of science and religion, and to perform their duties as caliphs. Otherwise, how else can they succeed in a way of life, where there is no dichotomy of the secular and religious?

CHAPTER 12

Sports And Recreation

Usually, the ulama make all modern sports like tennis, soccer, cricket, etc., haraam (impermissible). They state that it is a waste of good time, and will not help us in the akhirah (hereafter). Therefore, they state that only those sports like archery, wrestling, horse riding, fencing, javelin throwing, etc., that were played by the Sahaba Ikram (RA) to help them prepare for war are permissible. Hence, some Muslims play modern sports like tennis, soccer, cricket, etc., but with great reservation, doubting whether it is permissible or not, undermining their passion for the game.

Likewise, Muslims are misled to believe that secular education is only good to get a job, and would be of no benefit to them in the akhirah. Hence, they go to universities to achieve minimum qualification to get a job, with the belief that by becoming an Aalim or a hafez they would be better off in the akhirah. Unfortunately, after they were devastated in the war in Afghanistan after 9/11, they realized that Muslim should learn science, not to advance the knowledge of secular development of the ummah, but to build a bomb. Nowadays, they advice Muslims students on campus about Islam without true knowledge and understanding of haqq (truth), and one day this will also have its repercussion on those students that follow them. Read chapter entitled "Why Religions Fail", in my previous book.

The ulama are living in the past. If I did not write in my previous book "An Islamic Revolution for Peace and Unity", that it was important to intersect the secular with the religious to prepare for all eventualities of the akhirah, many more Muslims children would not be attending school today, and the ulama would be still living in the past with their distorted teachings and practices of the Qur'an and Sunnah. It is important that the ulama realize that we do not fight our wars with swords, bows, arrows, spears, etc., or on horsebacks today, and that the sports that they recommend we play today, to prepare for war, are totally irrelevant.

In modern-day wars are fought with war tanks, warplanes, cluster bombs, guided missiles, war ships, drones, etc. Therefore, it is a great joke when the ulama state that when Jesus (PBUH) will come, he will call for his spear and his horse and use these to kill the anti-Christ. For more information on this subject refer to their book, titled, "Besti Zewar". The ulama have no authority to tell us that modern sports like soccer, tennis, etc., is haraam and will not help us in the akhirah. The Holy Qur'an and the Prophet (SAW) did not tell us such things were haraam. Therefore, by what authority are they telling us that modern sports like tennis, soccer, cricket, are haraam and will not help us in the akhirah?

What the ulama have failed to understand is that modern sport is big business. It does not only generate a huge amount of income but it also creates a huge amount of halaal (permissible) employment for a decent living for people who have talents to play and administer sports. In other words, it is a more legitimate way of earning a living than running a brothel, selling drugs, pornography, gambling or running a business by selling back-door goods, under-paying the staff, etc.

Can the ulama not see that sport is a means of creating work and earning a legitimate income? For example, if you were a sports person, you could own a construction company to build stadiums and sports facilities, manufacture or retail sports equipments and outfits, work for an association or club as an administrator, physician, coach, referee, umpire, player, etc. Besides, there are sponsors, and if you are good player you can get huge endorsements.

Unfortunately, the ulama posses a very negative attitude towards sports in general. They state that by playing sports or working for sports, we do not gain any spiritual benefits. They state that the biggest sponsor of the prize money in sports is the brewery. Therefore, spectators are not prohibited from consuming alcohol on the grounds and to make matters worse they intermingle with the opposite sex, and create certain social problems that end in immoral ways.

Furthermore, they state that modern sports is corrupt because it is tainted with betting, bribery, dishonesty, etc., where umpires, referees, players, coach, etc., sell or fix the match. In addition to this, spectators run riots and many lives are lost and properties are damaged. The so-called "alleged murder" of Bob Woolmer, (coach of the Pakistan cricket team), was the last straw. The ulama used the occasion to condemn the sport altogether.

Many Muslims are unhappy with the general verdict of the ulama on sports. What the majority of the ulama fail to realize is that all compartments of our lives have an evil, bad and a negative side and, a good, positive and progressive side to it. And, it is an essential part of a Muslims duty to enhance the positive and suppress the negative. Take for example, the business and political compartments of our life. Every other month it hits the headlines for corruption. In one month alone there was the bread price fixing saga, and a case against Jackie Selebi, the Minister of Law Enforcement in South Africa, who was charged and tried for bribery and corruption.

Thus, bribery, corruption, fraud, murder, etc., is also rife in business and politics. Therefore, why single out sports only? Can we not make everything in sports as legitimate as we can make them in all the other compartments of our lives? Our real challenge in Islam is not only to give legitimacy to all the compartments of our lives, but also to use the Qur'an and Sunnah to conquer all the negative challenges of all the compartments of our lives, and find winning ways in all of them.

Sport is a very important activity of our life. It is a way of keeping us fit and providing us with some entertainment and employment, especially for our children who are not good at schoolwork but are very talented in sports. It is an activity that we would like to keep at all cost. We know what happened to our ancestors in this country when they chose to send their children who did not do well in school to India to become Aalims and hufaaz. They destroyed the entire deen. Refer to chapter one for more information on this matter.

If our children are not talented in sports, we should encourage them to play sports or have some kind of extra curricula activity like arts, music, sculpturing, cycling, swimming, karate, etc. It is a kind of therapy that gives them a break from their normal schoolwork, and other obligations and calms them down. Actually, we should not only encourage our children to play sports and engage in other extra curricula activities, but we should also put in a lot of our effort, and money into these activities in our local areas instead of building, and maintaining large ulooms, and jamiats, that teach, and practice false teachings and practices of religion.

There is a greater benefit in promoting sports and extra curricula activities that establish true Islamic knowledge and benefit humanity, than building ulooms and jamiats that divide humanity and promote false teachings and practices of religion. Sports, besides creating therapy and employment, also keeps them away from drugs, mischief, unruly behavior, etc, improves their discipline, and helps us to understand many of the finer teachings and practices of Islam.

Therefore, we do not only support sports because it fulfills certain of our worldly ambitions, but also because it exposes certain teachings of religion that are un-Islamic, sometimes difficult to understand and explain in any other compartment of our life. For example, in the previous year's Curry Cup Rugby finals match, the captain of the winning team thanked God for winning the trophy during the presentation ceremony. Some people objected, saying that God was also the God of the losing team. Therefore, it was inappropriate for the winning captain to imply that God had favoured only the winning team, and not the losing team, because God had nothing to do with the match.

Likewise, in business, it did not mean that God favoured only those people who succeeded in business, and did not favour those who did not succeed. On many occasions we find that those that are un-Godly succeed, and those that are Godly fail. To make matters worse, the winning captain wore a T-shirt with the inscriptions "Jesus is Lord". Many people objected. They said that not all the fans of the winning team believed that Jesus was God, and that it was wrong for him as the captain of the team to wear the T-shirt, especially during the presentation ceremony in a country as diverse as ours.

In Islam, like in sports or in any other compartment of our life, we have to be very careful how we bring God and religion into our lives. In business, we will be just as ignorant as the winning captain of the rugby team if we claimed that our business was successful because God blessed us, and our other brother lost his business because God punished him. Therefore, our success in this world in our businesses, marriages, as a nation, etc., has very little to do with God and religion except for His guidance, but has a great deal to do with hard work and winning ways of a particular situation. Allah (SWT) makes it very clear in the Holy Qur'an that He will not change our condition unless we change it ourselves with our own souls.

During the first Pro 20 cricket tournament here in South Africa, Pakistan needed only six runs in four balls to win the match. Everybody knew that it was possible but Pakistan lost the match. The prayer of the man on the Pakistan bench was not answered not only because God was neutral in the matter but also because the best Pakistan player in the tournament who was on strike lost his nerves or played the wrong shot. Therefore, this did not mean that the God of the Hindu team that won the tournament was the real God, and the God of the Muslims was false.

It was foolish for the Pakistan man on the bench to make such a mockery of God and religion. But, then again to come to think of it religion is like that. It makes us look foolish on most occasions, and Muslims usually forget that Islam is not a religion, but a way of life based on pure logic, reason and haqq taught by the Qur'an. In addition to the fact that Allah (SWT) will not change our condition unless we change it ourselves, He also states that most of what goes wrong with our lives is due to our own doings.

In Islam, it is usually important for us to keep religion out of our life like it is important to keep it out of sports, and limit our religion to only the injunctions of the Holy Qur'an. Firstly, because Islam is not a religion, and secondly, because most of what Muslims say and do on the sports field like keeping a fist-length beard, kneeling and drinking water, etc., is Wahabism and not Islam. Therefore, whatever we would like to say or do on the sports field should be said, and done in a very special and universal manner, as a way of life rather than a religion.

If we do not wish to wear the "Lion Ale" badge on our shirt, (just like cricketer Hashim Amla playing for South Africa) we should make it clear that we do not wish to wear it because alcoholism is a major social evil, and as Muslims, we are totally against it. By doing so it would not make alcoholism an exclusive problem of the Muslim ummah, but would also make it a major problem of the entire human race. By saying that it's our religion to do so, very few non-Muslims will sympathize with us on this very important issue of life, not because they hate Islam, but because religious beliefs of a particular religion do not mean much to them, especially if their faith does not restrict them to do so and it is not haqq for them to do so.

In a way of life such as Islam, where we have very little to do with rituals and religion, we are encouraged to live a life based on science according to the guidance of the Holy Qur'an and true Sunnah of the Prophet (SAW). Muslims will have to come to terms with such a concept of Islam because it is this idea and concept of Islam that makes us different in world history or rather through which the Prophet (SAW) is recognized as the greatest person in world history. In Islam, to get involved in any kind of religious teaching and practice based on blind faith of the Hadith or any tribal leaders and saints that contradict the Holy Qur'an and Sunnah, is absolutely foolish, (like reciting a dua or reading darood sharief before playing a cricketing shot), unless it reminds of God, not to fight, cheat, show descent, be racist, etc.

If we had no idea that we were playing spin bowling, and played the shot against the spin instead of playing it with the spin, and we got out, how can we claim that we got out because our prayer was not sincere enough? This kind of a thing always happens in all the compartments of our lives whether it is politics, business or sports. Let's take a doctor for example. Whether he is a Muslim or non-Muslim, whether he recites bismillah or not, the injection or the prescription will work according to science, and not according to our religious beliefs. Otherwise, why would we place our lives in the hands of a world-renowned physician who does not believe in God or believes in another god other than God? In Islam, we are commanded to get involved in only that part of religion that is compatible with science, reason, history, experience, etc, based on the haqq of the Qur'an. By doing this, we are following the true teachings and practices of Islam, not something that is contrary to Islam.

Yes, it is true that the Qur'an commands us to recite bismillah and to say masha-Allah (glory to God), insha-Allah (if God willing), etc, but not to change the laws of cause and effect but to establish a tradition of God consciousness in whatever we say and do, so that we may recognize the truth that is revealed to us in the Qur'an and not distance ourselves from it. In the Qur'an, all those that deviate from the truth with or without the consciousness of God's Word are evil and wrong-doers. Furthermore, it is obvious that if the recitation of bismillah, masha-Allah, insha-Allah, etc, had the power to change the laws of cause and effect, or the natural laws that govern our lives, then science, logic, reason, etc, will cease to exist. And, in the Qur'an, the truth is associated, very strongly, with science, reason, and logic.

Unfortunately, the majority of the Muslims think that the success of our lives in this world is associated with the recital of certain religious verses of the Qur'an, and not with the laws of cause and effects. They associate their and our imaan (faith) with their religious beliefs, and not with the reality of our situation, and the laws of causes and effects that are associated with it. They fail to differentiate between the abstract and absolute teachings and practices of the Qur'an based on the secular teachings and practices of ilm-ul-yaqin, ayn-ul-yaqin and haqq-ul-yaqin. It is for this reason that I have great hatred for Muslims who state, "Make dua", when I talk to them about many of the issues like the high divorce rate, the disunity of the ummah, etc. Some of them even go to the extent of telling me that we should not waste our our time with modern inventions and technology because God created the non-Muslim world to do that for us. If this is the kind of world in which the Muslims are living in, then I have nothing to do with them. Please refer to chapter 7, which is titled, "The Articles of Our Faith", for more information on this subject.

In the post modern era of Islam, if Muslims are unable to distinguish their imaan from the falsehood of this world, in terms of the Qur'anic teachings and practices of ilm-ul-yaqin, ayn-ul-yaqin and haqq-ul-yaqin, they will actually lose their imaan, like the majority of the Jews and Christians are doing in Europe today. They have to understand, that, in Islam, they have to be rational, intellectual and universal in every issue of their lives. For example, dead meat and swine meat is made haraam for health reasons, and not for any religious reasons. Likewise, cow or goat meat is made haraam for a religious reason when other than the name of Allah (SWT) is invoked. It is logical that the laws of cause and effect cannot be changed

155

by the recital of Qur'an or Bismillah or vice versa, unless it is an injunction of the Qur'an.

Our success in this world depends very heavily on our knowledge of science based on haqq and not on any prayer other than those recommended in the Holy Qur'an. And, there are very few of these. For example, in cricket we have to stay fit for long periods of time and on overseas tours that last the period. We have to be careful what we eat, the kind of exercises performed and how to space them. Likewise, we have to be always focused on the game, and sometimes get psychological treatment because once form is lost, it's difficult to get back on 'track' for the fear of losing one's place in the national or provincial team. Just reciting verses of the Qur'an in a religious manner won't help.

Similarly, if the captain of our team is required to make a decision whether one is going to be batting or bowling first, he will have to do so based on certain scientific facts, such as cloud cover, moisture on the pitch, etc. And, there are also other factors, like whether the pitch will deteriorate, consider a spin attack, or is it always necessary to vary our bowling attack with a good spin and pace, etc. None of these things have anything to do with religion. If we engage in Islam in this way, we are not doing anything in contradiction of the Qur'an and Sunnah. Actually, functioning in this way is "the standard deen" prescribed for us in the Qur'an, but we are reluctant to do so because we enjoy religion that is shrouded in myths and mysticisms.

We are proud, that there was a time in Pakistan cricket, under Imran Khan, Javed Miandad, Wasim Akram, etc, that Pakistan cricket was world class. The irony of the situation was that they concentrated less on religion, and more on the game. They did not keep a beard, knelt and drank water, made sajda on the grounds, etc. They concentrated on the game, and it was they who introduced pure science to the game (example, reverse swing bowling, the doosra, etc). At one time they were the most glamorous side in world cricket and big money spinners. In addition to this, some Muslim cricketers like Nasser Hussien of England, Muhammad Azaruddhin and Nawab of Patudi of India, and of course Imran Khan, Wasim Akram, Javed Miandad, etc., of Pakistan, have shown great leadership qualities in world cricket, and displayed great potential to lead any country or nation in the game, Muslim or non-Muslim.

We believe that the Muslim ummah have such kinds of talents and potentials in all the compartments of our lives, that is required to rule the world once again, if Muslims are willing to get educated in secular schools and universities, rather than in the ulooms. This does not mean that we are against the basic study of the Qur'an and Sunnah. We are not. We only wish that it should be done in an Islamic manner and not in a religious way. We are sad that in the last 20 to 30 years, the majority of Muslims joined the Wahabi sect, and made not only sports haraam, but also made secular education haraam. It's because of this that our most talented players are not playing sports anymore, and the majority of the ummah is not educated enough in both the secular and religious to rule this world.

In addition to the above, sports like Islam, does not tolerate racism. Usually, we get away with what we think are petty acts of racism in our businesses, homes, religious institutions, etc., but when we are on the sports field and on TV, then a very petty act of racism which we think is petty can become a very big issue and we may be fired or suspended from our club. In the second cricket test match in Australia between Australia and India in 2008, Harbhajan Singh of India called Symond a "monkey". This turned out to be a very big racial issue because Symond was the only Black player in the Australian team. Otherwise, it would have been different.

On the sports field racism is such a big issue that FIFA made the theme 'SAY NO TO RACISM' of their soccer world cup tournament of France in 2006. It was also the theme of the last T20 cricket match in the Carribean (2010). This did not only mean that one player of one race could not hurl racial abuses to another player of another race, but it also meant that players of all race throughout the world should be given equal opportunity in the game, and must be selected on sheer merit and nothing else.

In Islam, we are also persuaded to be very sensitive to racism. In order to overcome our problem of racism, we have been persuaded to stand shoulder to shoulder together with our Black Muslim brothers five times a day in our daily salaah. But, unfortunately, it seems that that is not enough, because as soon as we leave the mosque we are back to our old ways (of being racists). We seem to think that the Black people do not have enough brains to make any significant contributions in our lives, because of what we think is their inferior race.

This is extreme foolishness on our part because they are not any inferior or superior to us in any level or aspect of our lives, and definitely not on the sporting fields. The likes of Nelson Mandela, Edson Arantes (Pele), Muhammad Ali, Sir Garfield Sobers and many others are super legends. Hence, if Black people are given equal opportunities in any aspect or level of our life, they have the ability like anybody else to become the best amongst us. Therefore, it is our duty to give all equal opportunity in every aspect and level of life, and trust them in the highest office, like we trust everybody else.

Thus, if there is any compartment of our life in which we can explain the true teachings and practices of Islam in great detail, then it's sports. In no other compartment of our life could we have explained the most intricate balance and equilibrium between science and religion, like we explained it in the sports compartment, showing very clearly that science, not religion dominates our life. And, that we accept only that part of religion that is compatible with science, reason, history, experience, etc., and, not any religious belief that makes no sense to us. In Islam, we could not have explained racism in a better way than explained in this compartment.

Similarly, sexism is a very big issue in sports and Islam. Firstly, because in the inheritance law, the Holy Qur'an gives the female child only one third of the inheritance while it gives the male child two thirds, and when we are asked to sign a legal document, the Holy Qur'an states that if we do not have two male witnesses to sign the document, then two women may sign it in place of one male. Secondly, to make matters worse, the Saudis do not allow their women to drive a car, and when there was a gang rape on a young Saudi woman recently, she was given a severe sentence for breaking the Saudi law for being alone in a car with a person who was not her relative. Furthermore, Muslims are accused of oppressing Muslim women in many other ways like it was discussed in this book.

Usually, the Quranic laws of inheritance and the requirements of two female witnesses for one male witness do not sound discriminatory in an Islamic society that does not show any other form of discrimination against Muslim women that extremists and fundamentalists Muslims show towards their women. During our forefathers time, when there was no restriction on a woman to drive a car, wear the scarf, go to school and pursue a career, the Quranic laws of inheritance and witnesses were not regarded as discriminatory because women were treated as equal in every compartments of their lives. Today, in the context of the Saudi and Wahabi culture, it has become very difficult to defend the Qur'an where it should be defended on merit, because the majority of Muslims and non-Muslims believe that the Saudi and Wahabi culture is Islam, which it is not.

In Islam, there is no discrimination against sexes any more than that which we experience on sports field in a Western society, where women play against women and men play against men. This cannot be regarded discriminatory in the Western society because women are free in every other aspect of their life. Similarly, the Holy Qur'an also differentiates between men and women in a very few instances, for very good, and logical reasons. An example of this is in the inheritance law, where the male child is given more than the female child because the male child is expected by the Qur'an to take the responsibility of maintaining certain parental needs, and requirements as caliph, which the female child does not have to, from the financial point of view.

Unfortunately, recently one mother felt that this law was unfair because all her sons took their shares and left with their wives leaving her daughter to support her. Will Allah (SWT) ever forgive her sons for taking two thirds of the share and not performing their duties to their mother? They have put a black mark of disgrace on the Qur'an by their action which is totally contrary to the Qur'an. If they performed their duty to their mother like the Qur'an commanded them, the mother would have praised the Qur'an for her good fortune. Similarly, non-Muslims say many bad things about the Qur'an, such as it teaches violence, because a lot of Muslims behave in that way.

In the Holy Qur'an, we do not experience any discrimination of woman because the Holy Qur'an does not stop a woman from driving a car, going out and studying or working with men or compels her to cover her head or face. In addition, the Holy Qur'an does not stop her from conducting her own business, owning property, etc. In almost every aspect of life, she is equal to a man except for the few things that the Qur'an says that they are not like we discover physically on the sports field.

The Prophet (SAW)'s first wife, Bibi Khadija (RA), owned her own property and business when she employed the Prophet (SAW) to work for her when he was an eligible bachelor at 25 years, and she was a widow of 40. Who cares whether she was a widow, and fifteen years his senior? A man is a man and a woman is a woman. They could have lived in sin, but they feared God, and got married. Therefore, in any secular society, a Muslim woman who is upright should not fear to work with men, because the secular law gives her plenty of protection, which unfortunately, today, many Muslim countries cannot give her with the kind of shariah they prescribe for her!

Therefore, it is important to know that Islam, like sports deals with almost every important issue or aspect of our life. It does not deal only with issues of racism, sexism, halaal employment, balance between science and religion, but, it also deals with the subject of our discipline, commitment to our team, flag, nation, etc., and our dressing, custom, tradition, culture, etc. We learn to come for practice in time, to play the match or for meetings. And, we learn how to respect our coach, captain, the management, etc, and, learn not to show descent to the umpire's decision. We are taught not to cheat, For instance we are out while batting in cricket we must learn to "walk" or if we took a very low catch and the ball touched the ground, we must be pious enough to admit that that the batsman is not out.

Similarly, we must not fight with our teammates, resolve our differences with them in a friendly way, and not hit the player with a bat like Akthar meted out to Asif. In addition to this we must dress properly for each sports, not insist on wearing the kurtha to play sports like soccer, tennis, cricket, cycling, etc. We must teach our children that in Islam there is no such thing as Islamic: dressing; science; business; politics; language; etc. Our teachings and practices in all the compartments of our lives are universal according to true teachings, and practices of the Holy Qur'an, which is based on haqq, our diversity and science, because we are created from a primeval matter which operates according to the laws of physics and mathematics.

Unfortunately, the majority of Muslims will not agree with what I have written in this book. They think that my imaan (faith) is weak because of my western education. Hence, they put greater faith in their ulama and saints of past and present, and state that not all of them can be wrong. Therefore, in my defense, I would like them to consider this:

1. I love them as much as I love to go to jannah (paradise), but my brotherhood with them is not based on love alone. It is largely based on the unified knowledge, understanding and practice of the Qur'an and Sunnah.

2. According to true teachings and practices of the Holy Qur'an and Sunnah I am compelled to establish shariah according to the shurah and ijma of the ummah, and not according to that of the ulama who are sectarian. I have explained this in great detail in this in both our books.

3. Allah (SWT) did not create our compartment of science, politics, business, sports or religion. We created it. All He does in the Holy Qur'an is give us guidance, which is the same for all compartments; cultures, traditions and customs of our lives, over all time and place. I am only obeying His injunctions.

4. When I establish all the injunctions of the Holy Qur'an in all compartments of my life, I establish a very intricate balance, and equilibrium within, and between all of them. Therefore, it does not matter whether I enter Islam through the compartment of politics, science, religion, business or sports, it is all the same.

5. The intricate balance between the secular and religious compartments of my life make the secular compartment of our life the dominant compartment of my life, because the secular accepts only that part of religion that is compatible with science, reason, experience, history, etc. How can I contradict it?

6. Thus, Islam does not deal with the religious perspective of our life. It only deals with the life perspective of life. It is an established fact that Islam is not a religion, and there is no priesthood in Islam. I am not in contradiction of this fact.

7. A comprehensive teaching and practice of unity and universalism support all missions of world peace. In the Islamic mission for world peace, the divine teachings and practices of Tawhid (an Arabic word for unity and universalism) are a comprehensive solution for world peace. I see it as the cardinal teaching and essence of Islam.

CHAPTER 13

Assembly Of Ummah

I feel very unhappy with the present situation of the Ummah. Some of the reasons for this are as follows:

1. It's sectarian;
2. Extremist and fundamentalist;
3. Does not intersect the secular with the religious;
4. Does not include the Assembly of the Ummah, where all Muslims are made to accept the one true knowledge, and understanding of the Qur'an and Sunnah, according to the shurah and ijma of the majority of Muslims, at the grassroots level;
5. Does not contain the true knowledge and understanding of the Qur'an and Sunnah;
6. Each sect and madhab runs its own hilaal, halaal, zakaat, education, welfare societies, etc, contrary to the concept of the ummah. We are required to be more constructive, efficient and brotherly.
7. Due to the division of the ummah, we are unable to recognize the true leadership of the ummah;
8. We are developing in every aspect of our lives without true guidance (knowledge and understanding of the Qur'an and Sunnah), leadership, professionalism and direction;
9. It is not the way in which the Prophet (SAW) and the Sahaba Ikram (RA) functioned;
10. It is definitely not the way of the Qur'an according to the worldview teachings and practices of Tawhid (unity and universality), which are the prime objectives of Islam;
11. It does not give power to the people at the grassroots level;
12. It maintains the status quo of the different ulama of different sects, madhabs, silsilas and khanqahs in their communities and followers.

There are many causes for the above problems of the ummah. The sensible thing to do is to sit down together and find out what the cause of each problem is and how to cure them. The world-view teachings and practices of Tawhid make clear the causes and provide divine solutions. We have no other option but to use it to secure our unity.

Let's take the first problem of the ummah, which is the root cause of many of the problems of the ummah, namely, that of sects, which is totally forbidden by the Qur'an. This happened not because the Prophet (SAW) predicted that it would happen. It happened because all of us do not have the same knowledge and understanding of the Qur'an and Sunnah.

To illustrate this point, let's take the Deobandi school of thought. The majority of them believe that it is religion for men to keep a beard and women to cover their head and faces in public. Not many sects besides the Wahabi Deobandi sects believe in such teachings and practices of religion, which are totally contrary to the true teachings and practices of the Qur'an according to the true Tawhidi definition of the Sunnah.

I have discussed many of these differences between all the sects and madhabs, in great detail in this book, and have come to the conclusion that not all of them can be right, but all of them can be wrong. And that their major problem in the Islamic way of life was that they have deviated from the universal teachings and practices of the Qur'an and grossly distorted the true definition of the Sunnah, by stating that it was the verbatim practice of the Hadith, and not the Qur'an.

Therefore, it is very clear from what I have stated in this book, that if we do not have unified knowledge and understanding of the Qur'an and Sunnah according to the world-view teachings and practices of Tawhid, by shura and ijma of ummah, mosque by mosque and region by region, we cannot solve any of the problems of the ummah in the above situation of the ummah.

Nevertheless, it does not matter, what I have to say or how I think we should solve the above problems of the ummah. What matters most is what the Qur'an has to say about the best method of establishing the unified knowledge and understanding of the Islamic way of life and its problems, for us to find a way forward.

Let's start with the injunctions of the Qur'an, which deals with the shura and ijma of the ummah. In surah Al-Imran verse 159, Allah (SWT) states:

> (O Prophet), it is only due to the great mercy of Allah that you are gentle with (the believers), (O Muhammad) if you had been harsh and hard-hearted towards them, they would have certainly dispersed and scattered away from you. So pardon them and overlook their shortcomings, and pray to Allah to forgive them, and **consult** them in (matters of the moment). And when you have come to a **mutual decision** (ie after due consultation), then put your trust in Allah, for Allah loves those who put their trust in Him."

According to the above verse of the Qur'an, there are three very important issues or commandments that we are required to follow when we consult with our Muslim brothers and sisters in the affairs of the ummah. These are as follows:

1. Before we enter into consultation with them on any issue of our life, we must be humble and positive in our approach and attitude towards them, of gentleness, kindness, love, brotherhood, etc. In other words, not to be hard on them if they are unable to express themselves but always try to understand their cause and intentions in the most positive and articulate manner.
2. After mutual consultation there has to be a mutual decision. This means that even if we do not like the decision of the majority, we have to respect it and not condemn or attack it in any way, but wait for consequences to bring it up again, at an appropriate date, when the climate is right.
3. We must not assume that the shura (mutual consultation) and ijma (consensus) of the ordinary members of the ummah are not good enough to make a difference at the highest levels in our lives. We have discussed this in great detail in this book in the diversity of our creation. Hence, Allah (SWT) assures the Prophet (SAW)

and us that we should not fear the shura and ijma of the majority and trust in Him, because He is most Knowledgeable and Wise to recommend it.

Sometimes, it is very difficult to understand some of the commandments of Allah (SWT), like the shura and ijma of ummah in the context of our diversity. Therefore, in such instances Allah (SWT) tells us that we should "trust Him". In other instances, He might state that there is greater meaning in it for men and women of understanding. But, none of these are difficult to comprehend in the long term, when we infer that what has been said has been said in the context of the Islamic mission of PEACE in the diversity of our experience and life.

Unfortunately, the fact of our life is that whatever our interpretation of Qur'an and Sunnah, we cannot claim it to be Shariah, unless it is approved by the majority of Muslims in the Assembly of the Ummah. This is not only the commandment of the Almighty but it is the universal demand of all the diversities of our creation. And, it is in this process of nature, that Allah (SWT) takes into account our interpretation of the Qur'an and Sunnah, which makes the Shariah compatible, not only with all the aspects of our lives with time and space, but, it also makes it irresistible to both Muslims and non-Muslims in the post modern era.

Therefore, whether we like it or not, we will have to establish Shariah by the shura and ijma of the Muslim community that lives in the vicinity of our local masjid, and not by the majlis of the ulama, whom I consider are priests and not scholars. Even if they were scholars, neither the Almighty nor the due process of nature in the diversity of our creation, would allow them to dictate the Shariah.

In addition to the above, I regret that I initiated and supported the formation of the Islamic Council of South Africa (ICSA), some forty years ago. I have since learnt by experience that none of these organization like ICSA, Unity Council, United Ulama Council or even Vision 20/20, etc, will work until they represent our local communities, at the grassroots level, in all the affairs of our lives, not only, the Shariah making process.

It was in the context of this knowledge and experience with the Muslim ummah of South Africa, that I wrote the following letter to the Muslim Views, which appeared in the May issue of 2011, as follows:

Our unity starts in the community

The letter by Abdul Kamal Fryddie, "Let's have Unity Day", (MV, April 2011), refers:

In the most basic teachings and practices of Islam, our unity is not dependent on the unity of the ulama. It is dependent on the unity of our local Muslim community that lives in the vicinity of our local masjid.

The starting point is the congregational salaah.

In order to understand the significance of the congregational salaah, it is important to understand the most basic meaning and message of all salaah, which is no more than submission (by ruku and sujood) to the Will of one God (by the recitation of the Qur'an, not Hadith or kitab of any saint, aalim or jamiat of ulama).

Hence, the congregational salaah is a prelude or stepping stone to the

Assembly of Ummah, where the individual and the community commit themselves to the Shariah (Qur'an and Sunnah) by the shura and ijma of the ummah, not ulama.

The Sunnah (practice of the Qur'an) is the variable term of the Shariah, which makes the practices of the Qur'an compatible with the diversity of all cultures, customs, traditions and compartments of our lives, over all time and place.

The Prophet (SAW), for example, fought his wars with sword, we use gunpowder: he used scribes to write the Qur'an, we use the printing press: and so on.

Likewise, according to Surah 69 verses 43-46 and Surah 10 verse 15, he did not say that it was his Sunnah to keep a beard, wear the kurtha, etc, because it was not an injunction of the Qur'an for him to do so.

The Shariah, therefore, is Islamic law and jurisprudence, which helps us to decide what is Sunnah and what is not, in the diversity of all cultures, customs, traditions and compartments of our lives, with time and space.

Like it is difficult to establish Shariah, without the true knowledge of the Qur'an and the proper definition of the Sunnah, it is difficult to establish unity of the ulama without the unity of our local community.

Similarly, our congregational salaah is rendered useless without our individual and collective commitment to the Assembly of the Ummah.

Furthermore, it is important to appreciate the fact that the shura and ijma of the ummah at the local mosque or grassroots level, in all the affairs of our lives, is the most ideal form of democracy. It starts from the bottom going up, rather than the top-bottom system of western democracy, where the people in the echelons of power cannot reach the people on the ground.

All that Muslims have to do to achieve national and international unity is to network their resolutions and leadership, mosque by mosque, area by area and region by region.

If Muslims follow the above path of Qur'an and Sunnah, they will be guaranteed not only unity but also become the best example of a plural society and democracy in world history.

Today, no nation has grassroots structures of democracy and Book of Guidance like we have.

There are many other rules of the congregational salaah that we are required to add to the rules of the Assembly of the Ummah, which I did not mention in the above letter to the Muslim Views, because of space restrictions in the letters column. Among these include the membership of the Assembly, with the right to deliberate and vote in all issues and affairs of the ummah. For example, only members who perform regular congregational salaah, with the jamaat, in the local masjid, are allowed to become bona fide members of the Assembly.

The Qur'an does not stipulate the age at which people who are regular at salaah, can become bona fide members of the Assembly. It is left to the majority of the Muslims to decide at what age they should become bona fide members of the Assembly. Normally, all Muslims above the age of fifteen should become bona fide members of the Assembly. And all Muslims over the age of ten, should be allowed to become observers so that when they turn fifteen, they will know how to conduct themselves in the Assembly. This helps us to close the generation gap in all the affairs of the ummah, over all time and place.

Another very important aspect of the congregational salaah, that is relevant to the Assembly, is that all men among men and all women among women are equal. In other words, we cannot assume, think or conclude in any way that what an elderly person, rich person, Aalim or doctor, etc, is saying is of greater significance than the voice of a younger person, poor person, uneducated person, etc. The voice of every person, male or female, must be equally respected in the context of the debate and the universal teachings and practices of the congregational salaah.

The benefits of the Assembly are virtually endless. I have discussed a lot of it in this book, but, in my opinion the most important of these is that no enemy of Islam can infiltrate the higher echelon of our power to harm us in any way or control us in any way, because our grassroots structures are too complex for them to infiltrate. We will not spell out the details of this. Let the enemies of Islam take centuries to find out. Furthermore, it is inevitable that they will not be able to penetrate our power base, not only because of the complex nature of the power base but also because the Almighty Who is the architect of our Assembly will make sure that no evil person with evil intention will be able to infiltrate it, because it was He Who recommended that we use the shura and ijma of the ummah in this manner.

Generally, it is very easy for anyone to tell the majority of the Muslims what are the true teachings and practices of the Qur'an and Sunnah, but who will listen. The majority of them have their own belief systems, which they think are right and all others are wrong. They will find faults in everything we say and do. For example, how can we tell the so-called Sunnis that the protocols of the Assembly demand that they attend the mosque nearest their place of residence for the congregational salaah. They will reject it saying that it is haraam to perform their salaah behind a Wahabi imaam.

What they don't understand is that it does not matter who is the imaam in our congregational salaah, as long as we performs the congregational salaah according to the Shariah (Qur'an and Sunnah) exactly like Allah (SWT) wants us to do, we should not fear whether it is accepted or not. In other words, we must have absolutely no doubt that Allah (SWT) will accept our congregational salaah, because we performed it exactly like He commanded us to do, and we obeyed Him and not those religious teachers who state that it is haraam to perform our salaah behind the imam of another sect. And as long as we do what Allah (SWT) wants us to do, we should not fear that what we have done is wrong.

This is exactly like going to the Assembly of the Ummah, where we are given all the privileges to deliberate by mutual consultation, but the majority vote does not go in our favour. We should not feel bad about it because Allah (SWT) showed us the procedure how to conduct ourselves in the Assembly. As long as we have conducted ourselves like He wished that we conduct ourselves, we are blessed. Even if the decision by the majority is wrong, Allah (SWT) tells us in the Qur'an that He will overlook it and forgive the majority because it was His idea that they should conduct themselves in that manner, and He is pleased that they obeyed Him.

Similarly, it does not matter who is the imaam of our local musjid. Whether he is sufi, "Sunni" or Deobandi. What matters most is that we have to adhere to the protocols of the congregational salaah and the Assembly of the Ummah, which have been laid down by Allah (SWT) and was practiced by the Prophet (SAW) and the Sahaba Ikram (RA). If we don't, we will be in problem in the akhirah for making our own rules and not doing what Allah (SWT) and the Prophet (SAW) told us to do. Therefore, those who think that their aqidah and imaan are greater than the protocols of the congregational salaah and the Assembly of the Ummah, are the ones who really lack imaan and carry no blessings, both in this world and the akhirah, in whatever they say and do.

Likewise, it does not matter what is the topic of our discussion in the Assembly of the Ummah, we are commanded to discuss it in the context of the Qur'an, not Hadith or the kitab of any saint, aalim or scholar. This is because, in our congregational salaah, we committed ourselves to the congregation, by submitting to the Will of God by reciting the Qur'an, and not the Hadith, etc. If the congregation does not adhere to this condition of the congregation salaah, then we have the right to walk away from the deliberations and not recognize their Shariah binding on us or anyone else, because our condition of our congregational salaah with them was to submit to the true teachings and practices of the Qur'an and not the fabricated teachings and practices of the Hadith or any other book.

In the same way, the interpretation of the Qur'an is also controlled by certain objectives that are revealed in the Qur'an by Allah (SWT). For example, He gave the name ISLAM to the Islamic way of life. We didn't, nor did the Prophet (SAW). Therefore, since the Qur'an is the Book of God, which explains the Islamic way of life, surely, the word ISLAM should tell us what we wish to know about the objectives of Islam, and what we should be looking for in the Qur'an, to teach us more about the Islamic way of life, that Allah (SWT) wants us to know to provide the appropriate guidance that make us Muslims.

From this point of view, the first issue of concern to us is PEACE, because the Arabic word ISLAM is derived from the root-word S'LM, pronounced "salm", meaning peace. Therefore, before we discuss the Arabic word Islam, which means SUBMISSION, we are required to investigate all the natural issues of our lives that are involved with the mission of PEACE, not only within ourselves, but also within and between our families, communities, nation and the international community. This then is the foundation by which we determine what Islam is and what are the true teachings and practices of the Qur'an.

In this book, I have already stated that the two most important components of PEACE are DIVERITY and UNITY, which cannot be achieved without absolute JUSTICE. Therefore, unless we identify these two dimensions of PEACE in this world in its world-view context according to the guidance of the Qur'an, we will find it very difficult to answer all the questions on SUBMISSION, such as "Submission to Whom? Why? When? Where? etc?". In a diagrammatic form all teachings and practices of PEACE that are found in the Qur'an can be represented as follows:

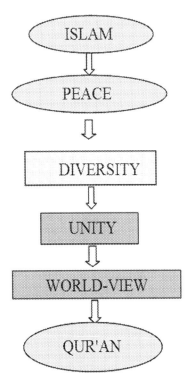

**THE QUR'ANIC CONCEPT OF PEACE
IN THE DIVERSITY OF OUR CREATION.**

In addition to the above, it is important to understand that our mission of SUBMISSION in the Islamic way of life, is not associated with the blind faith of religion. This is because Islam is not a religion but a way of life, which does not only not tolerate blind faith but is dead against the division of the secular and religious, which is totally against the Qur'anic knowledge of reality.

Therefore, in Islam, the factor that binds the secular and religious, is the consensus of all naturally existing diversities, which agree by mutual consultation and accord, by sound reason and logic, that the solution for the problems of their diversity can only be found by submitting their will to the Will of one God. According to them their choice of God is the God of Abraham (PBUH). This is because the God of Abraham is not only the God of the Christians, Jews and Muslims but is also the God of all the other nations of this world. In our previous book, "The Islamic Revolution for Peace and Unity", we stated that the God of Abraham (PBUH) sent Prophets to all the nations of the world. For example, in Hinduism, the story of Brahma, paryapathi (father of nation), is almost identical to that of the Prophet Abraham (PBUH), in the Bible and the Qur'an.

In a diagrammatic form, all the teachings and practices of SUBMISSION that are found in the Qur'an can be illustrated as follows:

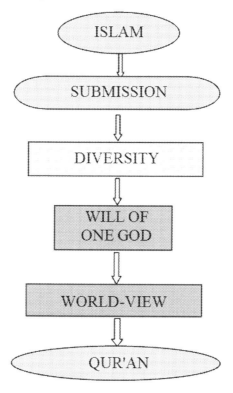

QUR'ANIC CONCEPT OF SUMISSION IN
ITS MISSION FOR PEACE.

Finally, to establish the undisputed fact that Islam is not a religion but a life of PEACE and SUBMISSION, it is important to demonstrate how the Qur'an provides guidance to both the secular and religious, and what are the dominant features and common grounds in them. In a diagrammatic form, this can be illustrated as follows:

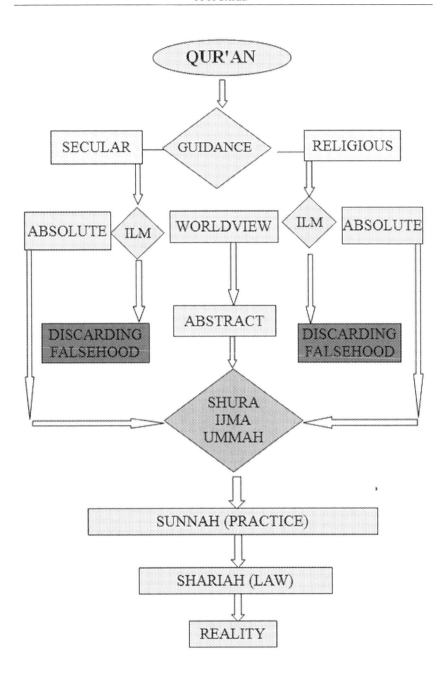

**ISLAMIC CONCEPT OF LIFE ACCORDING TO
THE DIVINE KNOWLEDGE OF PEACE
AND SUBMISSION.**

Unfortunately, throughout history, the majority of Muslims, especially the ulama (religious leaders and priests, not scholars), did not understand the secular and religious balances taught by the Qur'an. They always thought that it was a contradiction of the 7th century Islam of the Hadith, which was more traditional and religious. Hence, they fought against every secular institution and government in Islamic history that tried to teach a very rational and intellectual interpretation of the Qur'an that outdated many of the teachings and practices of the Hadith, because of its false definition of the Sunnah, and distortion of both, the Shariah and reality, with time and space.

Therefore, the most important task of the Assembly of the Ummah is to reinstate or re-establish this secular and religious, or material and spiritual, balance amongst the ummah, in an everlasting life of progress and development, according to the Qur'an and Sunnah (Shariah). Allah (SWT) and the Prophet (SAW) did whatever they had to do to establish this very intricate balance of the secular and religious, like giving us a Qur'an and Sunnah (example) of the Prophet (SAW), restricting or limiting religious teachings and practices to that of the Qur'an, allowing us to establish the most practical explanation of Shariah (Qur'an and Sunnah) that met the demands of our progress and developments in all aspects of our lives in the most diverse manner by shurah and ijma of the ummah at the grassroots level.

Hence our major task in the Assembly of the Ummah, at the grassroots level, is to make people aware that Islam is not a religion, but a way of life, both secular and religious, where religion is limited to the injunctions of the Qur'an, in order to develop the exact perception and reality of the Islamic way of life. To demonstrate how the perception of reality changes with religious beliefs and practices that contradict the Qur'an, let us take the religious perspective of the greatness of the Prophet (SAW). In religion, if we do not claim that he was imaam of all the Prophets of God, or that he did not have a shadow, etc, we have very little to claim his greatness in a universal way.

Now, let us look at the same perspective of the Prophet (SAW) in world history. He was greatest because he was the only one who was "most extremely successful in both secular and religious levels". There was no other person. Thus, world history appreciates the fact that the Prophet (SAW) was the greatest person because he paved the way to the post modern era of human development, which found common ground between the seen and unseen, secular and religious, individual and community, national and international, this world and akhirah, etc. And not for any religious reasons based on the religious teachings and practices of taqleed, aqidah, etc, which were contrary to the teachings of the Qur'an and world history, based on the worldview teachings and practices of ilm-ul-yaqin, ayn-ul-yaqin and haqq-ul-yaqin.

Similarly, in Christianity, the religious perspective of Jesus is that he is God and Son of God. World history does not take this religious perspective of the Christian faith to assess whether Jesus was the greatest person in world history, above that of Prophet Muhammad (SAW), who was not the incarnate of God or the Son of God. It took into account that he was not greater than the Prophet (SAW) because he did nothing to enhance a post modern perspective of life, as was in the case of the Prophet (SAW).

Thus, Islam has the very perspective of reality that world history seems to aapreciate. It is a way of life, in which, we can integrate and assimilate our Islamic way of life with the international community. For example, in Islam, like in world history, mysticisms and myths of religion, which are not reflected in the Qur'an about the Prophet (SAW), like he did not have a shadow, or that he was not an ordinary person or was the imaam of all the Prophets of God, etc, should not matter to us. What should really matter to us is what the true perspective of reality is that the Qur'an wishes us to convey in order to establish the Sunnah and Shariah of our way of life.

This can be taught in almost every issue of our life that is taught by the Qur'an, like ibadah, salaah, masjid, aalim, imaam, zakaat, etc, and how these institutions are nation building institutions, which have very little to do with religion. Insha-Allah, in the next chapter, I shall elaborate a little more on these perspectives of reality that I wish to convey in this book, to make Islam acceptable to the post modern era.

CHAPTER 14

The "Middle Path" Of Halaal And Haraam

In all issues of halaal (permissible) and haraam (impermissible) acts, there is a "middle path", like in all other issues of our lives, where there is a secular and religious balance, except for those that are completely forbidden by the Qur'an. The consumption of blood, whether it is that of human or animal, even if the animal is halaal, is forbidden to us, but with all that we still buy red meat from the butcher, wash, cook and eat it. We do not complain that since the meat is contaminated with blood, which is haraam, we will not eat it. All we are interested is in the consumption of the meat, which is made halaal according to the Islamic way of life, and, not in the little amount of blood that is still left in the meat. We wash the meat to the best of our ability, cook and eat it, and fully satisfied that it's halaal. If Allah (SWT) did not tell us in the Qur'an that only the blood that pours out from tne animal when it is slaughtered is haraam, we would not know whether the blood that is left on the meat which we eat is halaal or not.

But, in complete contradiction of the above, we complain about the contamination of any haraam food in all the other issues of our lives, and we will not buy certain halaal foods from a non-Muslim manufacturer, for fear that it is contaminated with some of the haraam food that's in their place of manufacture. In food manufacture, we take the issue of halaal and haraam to such an extent that we force the manufacturer to have two separate sets of machineries, one for halaal and another for haraam products, otherwise we will refuse to purchase the halaal food, even if the machines are washed before they are used to manufacture the halaal food, like we wash the meat before we cook or braai it. We do the same with our maids at home. We tell them that they cannot use our plates and cups to eat their food. They are given their own plates and cups to eat their food, as if if they ate in our plates and cups, they would contaminate it.

Likewise, let's take the issue of the pig. According to the Qur'an, only the consumption of the pig meat is haraam, not the pig itself. If the pig itself was haraam, it would mean that Allah (SWT) created something haraam and we know for a fact that the quality and nature of Allah (SWT) is such that He can never create anything that is haraam. Unfortunately, like dead meat gets contaminated with bacteria, which even if you cook it and eat it will harm you or make you sick, similarly the meat of the pig is not good for our health. This does not mean that the pig itself is haraam. If a piglet came to you and wished to play with you, it would be rude for you to frighten it and chase it away, because you think it is haraam. It's not, for it is only a baby, and if you touched, petted and played with it it would not kill you or take your imaan (faith) away from you.

The story of the pig is a very big issue in Islam. It is a means of teaching us how to treat the whole issue of halaal and haraam in Islam in the most tolerant and civilized manner. For example, when someone leaves a pig's head in our mosque in the night, we should not go on a rampage the next day, destroying properties and killing those whom we suspect are responsible for committing such an impious and unpleasant act. Actually, when our enemies put a pig's head in our mosque, they expect us to get upset, destroy property and kill people, so that they can prove to the world that Muslims are violent, and that the Qur'an teaches them to be violent because it prescribes jihad (holy war). Unfortunately, this type of a behavior by majority of Muslims in certain areas of the world makes it difficult for genuine Muslim scholars of Islam to claim the fact that Islam is a world mission for peace.

Therefore, under the circumstances, the majority of the Muslims and non-Muslims have to be taught that the pig in itself is not haraam except for the consumption of its meat, and that we should not consider the pig's head in the mosque to be any different from the head of any other animal, which is slaughtered by a non-Muslim. Hence, if we do not make such issues that arouse our emotions an issue of religion, then it will not give our enemies an opportunity to tease us. Furthermore, we are told that the best dart board is made of pig skin. So what if we played or used a dart board made of pig skin? Will it be against our imaan to do so? Or is it the case that just eating the pig, and not the playing with a dart board made of pig skin is haraam for us?

Thus, the halaal and haraam issue is a very good way to demonstrate that Islam is not a religion but a way of life, which is universal and applicable to the post modern era. For example, dead meat, blood and pig meat is haraam for us not because of any religious reasons but because it contains impurities, which are harmful to us and which our bodies dislike and wish to get rid of anyway. Therefore, to state that our religion forbids us to eat pig meat is not altogether correct because there is no religious reason but a secular and health reason to do so, which in the Islamic way of life establishes a very intricate balance between the secular and religious. In contrast, certain foods, even if they do not contain any impurities that can harm our bodies, they can become haraam for us purely for religious reasons. For example, like Hindu prayer food, like parsaad, red meat, etc, where other than the name of Allah (SWT) is invoked.

The reverse of this is also true. The pig meat cannot be made halaal, even if we invoke the name of the one true God and slaughter it. This means that although God gave us permission to eat pig meat if there was no other means for survival, we cannot take it for granted that eating the pig meat under these circumstances will not be harmful to our health. As long it is temporary until we can find halaal food, because pig meat is less harmful than premature death under these circumstnces.

Likewise, in Islam, wine and alcohol, which are intoxicants, and gambling are haraam (prohibited), not for any real religious reasons, but only because these have a negative effect on our social lives. Therefore, to state that we do not consume wine and alcohol because our religion forbids us to do so is incorrect. Initially, Muslims performed salah when they were drunk, but as soon as Muslims recognized the real social implication of these vices, liquor was prohibited. Therefore, when Allah (SWT) prohibited wine and alcohol or gambling, He did so because it was harmful to us at a social level, and not because it harmed our imaan (faith) in any major way, except for the reason that it was prohibited by God.

Similarly, zina, murder, plundering, looting, fraud, etc, are prohibited because they have a negative impact on our lives and Allah (SWT) did not wish that we should live in this world in such an unruly manner. Hence, God's guidance is not only for religious compartment of our lives but for all other compartments like in science, where certain aspects of our evolutionary creation are correct. What the majority of Muslims have to understand when they apply any injunctions of the Qur'an in their lives is that Islam is not a religion but a way of life, where there is no dichotomy of the secular and religious. No injunction of the Qur'an should be promoted in the name of religion unless it is a specific religious injunction of the Qur'an, but should always be promoted as a way of life. In this way we will not only promote world peace, but also the Islamic way of life by submission to the will of ONE GOD.

When we integrate, assimilate and intersect with the non-Muslim in this way, it does not mean that we are getting weak in our imaan (faith in God), but, it means we are absorbing them to our way of life and acknowledging the truth about the Islamic way of life. Eventually, they will see the weaknesses in their religion and accept Islam. This means that they are no way near Islam because we are no way near Islam. In other words, if we become moderate, they will deal with us in a moderate way, and if we become extremists and fundamentalists, they will deal with us in an extremists and fundamentalists manner.

Nevertheless, not all issues that are haraam for us are mentioned in the Qur'an in the form of an injunction. Some of them are mentioned in an indirect manner. For example, it is not a direct injunction of the Qur'an that we should prohibit priesthood and all ultra teachings and practices of religion like taqleed, aqeeda, sainthood, silsilas, khanqahs, etc. But, the sum total of all injunctions of the Qur'an conclude without doubt that there exists a very intricate balance between the seen, unseen, secular and religious, and that according to these balances, there is no place for priesthood, and all ultra teachings and practices of religion, like taqleed, aqidah, silsilas and khaqahs, that contradict the true teachings and practices of the Qur'an, namely, that of ilm-ul-yaqin, ayn-ul-yaqin and haqq-ul-yaqin.

Similarly, it is apparent that if we do not teach and practice only what is written in the Qur'an about religion, we cannot achieve the truth about religion, and the true balance between the seen and unseen and the secular and religious. According to the Qur'an, the salaah constitutes facing the qibla, reciting Qur'an, bowing and prostrating. It does not include the burning of fire and god-lamps or blowing of the horn and ringing of the bell, etc. If we do such things, which are not written in the Qur'an, then it will be completely against the true teachings and practices of Islam, which is not a religion but a guidance to all the cultures, customs, traditions and compartments of our lives, (both secular and religious). This means that it accepts the diversities of the secular and religious, but in their pure forms, according to the injunctions of the Qur'an.

Therefore, in this relationship between the secular and religious, the Qur'an tell us in no uncertain terms, that all of religion is corrupt or haraam except for that which is mentioned in the Qur'an. In other words, all of secular is good except that which is un-Godly or untrue. This means that Islam is a guidance for all the people of this world in all aspects and compartments of their lives, (both secular and religious), without favouring either. All that Islam wishes to do is to establish the truth (haqq) in all aspects of our lives, (both secular and religious), so that we may progress and develop in all the aspects of our lives, in a very positive, and constructive manner, without any conflict with others and ourselves, who follow the Qur'an.

This also means that if Islam was a religion, and not a way life, then our situation in Islam would become hopeless. We would have to believe in everything that the majority of Muslims believe that contradicts the Qur'an. For example, we would have to believe in saints, and state that the Prophet (SAW) was not an "ordinary" human being like us, but a cosmic human being who did not have a shadow. Likewise, we would have to believe in 40 days and one-year ceremonies for the dead, urs, taqleed, silsilas, etc. If we did not, then just about any ignorant person will tell us that we do not have imaan (faith).

Thus, it was never my intention to discuss the halaal and haraam issue or any other issue like science, sports, recreation, the new constitution of the new South Africa, or even any articles of our faith, in any great detail. All I wished to do was to use these diverse topics to demonstrate facts that all injunctions of the Qur'an applied to all compartments of our lives, cultures, customs and traditions of this world. And, that as Muslims, we should not be saying and doing one thing in the mosque and completely another thing outside it. For example, we must not agree inside the mosque that God created each species of creation from primeval matter, and not from the origin of the previous species, and then go outside the mosque, and teach evolution. In Islam, such a dichotomy of the secular and religious is unacceptable, because the truth does not change from the religious to the secular or vice versa. It remains the same.

Therefore, when we are outside the mosque, we should not be shy to promote the idea or hypothesis that each species of creation was not created from the origin of the previous species, but it was created from primeval matter, like we did in "The Evolution and Creation" debate in 'The Star' newspaper. Refer to the chapter on "Qur'an and Science" for more information on this subject. Our (Muslim ummah's) reluctance to promote the truth in a universal manner has done great disservice to humanity and Islam.

Take for example, the halaal and haraam issue in general. Its teachings and message are for all the people of this world. Therefore, when we label halaal food, we should not label it with a moon and star symbol. This is not Islamic, because in the Islamic way of life, considering the fact that Islam deals with all the diversities of this world in its mission for peace, it does not favour one sign, symbol, dressing, culture, over that of another. Hence, the correct Islamic way of labeling halaal food in a multicultural and multireligious society would be to write "HALAAL" or "KHOSER" with the name of the organization that certifies it halaal. Likewise, we are required to take a universal approach to all the teachings and issues of Islam and life in general.

In conclusion, it has to be said that finding the true teachings and practices of Islam are not as easy as they seems, because the true teachings and practices of Islam are not found only by forming the Assembly of the Ummah or the shurah and ijma of the ummah. But, they are also to be found in the pure knowledge, and understanding of the Qur'an, without the influence of Hadith or kitabs of any of the ulama, past and present.

If the majority of the Muslims in the Assembly of the Ummah do not use the Qur'an as their only source document and constitution, but give preference to the book of Hadith or kitabs of certain scholars of Islam, that contradict the true teachings and practices of the Qur'an, like we have explained in this book, then such a shurah and ijma of the ummah even in the Assembly of the Ummah does not constitute the Shariah. Therefore, the proper procedure for establishing the true teachings and practices of Islam are as follows:

1. It must be pure knowledge and understanding of the Qur'an.
2. It must be established by the shurah and ijma of the ummah at grassroots level in the local mosque.
3. It must be finalized by net-working the resolutions of the local mosques, region by region, and nation by nation.

In a diagrammatic form, the procedure for interpreting the pure knowledge and understanding of the Qur'an is as follows:

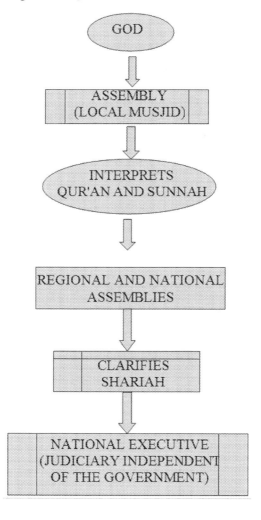

In the above path to Shariah, the teachings and practices of the Qur'an are not only made universal according to the diverse viewpoints of the Muslim ummah in the Assembly, but they are also made revolutionary with time and space. Although the injunctions of the Qur'an are universal, for all time and place, the Sunnah, which is the practice of the Qur'an, changes with time and space. For example, during the time of the Prophet (SAW), Muslims fought their war with swords, spears, etc. Today, we engage in modern warfare with sophisticated weapons, which were not used in those days.

Likewise, it's not wrong to use microphone in mosques to amplify the voice of the imaam or muezzin. Those ulama and muftis who state that it is against Sunnah to use the microphone in mosques and modern weapons in warfare, because the Prophet (SAW) did not use them, have very little knowledge of Islam, Qur'an and Sunnah. Similarly, those ulama who maintain that it's against Sunnah to print copies of the Qur'an in the printing press are not scholars, but priests, acting totally contrary to the true teachings and practices of Islam, with time and space.

The interpretation of the Qur'an, and the practice of Sunnah, is not only dependent on the diverse knowledge and experience of the ummah at a particular time and place, but it is also dependent on the diverse knowledge and experience of the ummah with time and space. During war, the Prophet (SAW) was told that it made no difference whether the Muslim army was small in number, and the enemy's army was large in number, because what mattered was their faith. We accept that the same injunctions of the Qur'an apply even today, but, only if the playing fields are level or we have the same kind of armaments that our enemies have. We cannot hurl a stone at an enemy's tank even with the greatest of faith, and expect the enemy's tank to explode.

When the mujahideen told us such stories when they fought and defeated the Russians, it was a lie. If they are talking the truth then why are they not doing the same thing to the Americans, and their allied forces? Muslims have to get more rational and realistic about the interpretation of the Qur'an and Sunnah with time and space. For example, it's not wrong to mechanize the slaughter of the chicken to cope with the massive demand and increase in population. Therefore, it is not against Shariah to invoke the name of Allah (SWT) only once for all chickens we wish to slaughter for the day. Like we perform one janaza salah or nikah for many people or couples with one prayer, we can do the same for the slaughter of chickens in abattoirs.

This also applies to stunning chickens on the conveyor belt. We should not argue that if the Jews are allowed not to stun chickens, we should have the same privilege. Our situation is different, because our system of life is much more comprehensive, universal, "completed and perfected" and our population is much larger. If the whole world will becomes Muslim, then what? Hence, it's about time that Muslims sat down like intelligent people, and used pure knowledge, understanding of the Qur'an to establish what is good and bad in our lives, and not be divided on issues that are irrelevant to the Qur'an. If dead meat, which is infested with bugs is haraam for us to eat because of health reasons, and not for a religious reason, then is it true to state that the dead chicken by stunning on the conveyor belt, which is not infested or a risk to our health, is haraam? Likewise, the final decision on this matter must come from the Assembly of the Ummah and not from the fatwa (religious decree) of any mufti.

The issue of halaal and haraam is a very contentious issue in South Africa. All three organizations that certify halaal food in our country have been in deep trouble one time or another for issuing halaal certificates for food that the majority of Muslims contended was not halaal. Therefore, under the circumstances, I do not claim that everything I have said about halaal and haraam in this book is Shariah and entirely correct. All I wish to state is that there is a "middle path" in this issue like all issues concerning the Islamic way of life. For example, Allah (SWT) does not mind if we cook and consume the blood left in the meat after we have slaughtered an animal. Similarly, Allah (SWT) tells us in the Qur'an that if the majority took a wrong decision in the Assembly of the Ummah by the process of shurah and ijma, He will forgive because it was He Who recommende that we function in that way. This means that since Islam is immersed in the teachings of unity in diversity, it cannot coexist without compromising the "middle path" in the post modern era.

CHAPTER 15

Summary And Conclusion

Islam is not a religion. It is comprehensive way of life, which requires a very comprehensive knowledge and understanding of all the affairs and activities of this world, with reference to the truth and reality of our creation. From this point of view, some perspectives of haqq that influence the Islamic way of life are follows:

1. Our universe is created from "smoke" (gas). Refer to the chapter on "Qur'an and Science" for more information on this subject. Hence, the primeval matter from which we are created is not only volatile in nature, but functions according to the laws of physics and mathematics in all the forms of our creation. Allah (SWT) used the same laws of nature to create it wherever it was possible to do so. Therefore, all aspects of our lives, whether it be socio-economical, political, religious or otherwise cannot function in the long term without the teachings and practices of science because such is the origin and nature of our creation. If it were not so, we would be forced to undermine science at the expense of religion and develop our lives in a very unscientific and un-constructive manner, according to some custom and culture of the past and present or according to some mindless dogmas of religion.

2. Man was created as the deputy of God (caliph). It was only after that that he was made a husband, father and son. Therefore, as caliph, he has duties and responsibilities to protect the right, title, interest, claim and demands of all the diversities in our creation, both seen and unseen. Furthermore, there is no knowledge in the Qur'an to state that only Muslim men are caliph of God in this world. All men that are the descendants of Adam (PBUH) are caliphs. Therefore, all men who violate their duties as caliphs are accountable for their crimes, both in this world and akhirah. In this respect, the mission of a Muslim cannot be separated

from that of mankind. It has to be neutral and universal at all times, without any favour for a Muslim or prejudice against a non-Muslim. Within each nation, direction, leadership and allegiance are found by shurah (mutual consultation) and ijma (consensus) of the majority.

3. The duties and responsibilities of the caliph cannot be accomplished without a good knowledge and understanding of the creation in all aspects of its life. Therefore, the first thing that Allah (SWT) told the Prophet (SAW) when He revealed the Qur'an was to "Read" and "Write" and educate himself. Usually, the ulama limit deeni talim (Islamic education) to knowledge that is acquired in the ulooms (religious schools) according to the religious system of preaching and following or the system of priesthood, which include the teachings and practices of taqleed, aqeeda, sainthood, silsilas, khanqahs, sects and madhabs. This is totally contrary to the Qur'anic system of education, which is heavily dependent on the teachings and practices of ilm-ul-yaqin (certainty of knowledge by inference or reasoning), ayn-ul-yaqin (certainty of knowledge by seeing and observing) and haqq-ul-yaqin (absolute knowledge, like this is a book, etc) in every aspect of our lives, be it in China. Hence, as caliphs, Muslims are commanded to be well educated and informed in every level and aspect of their lives, in the most rational and intellectual manner.

4. The main purpose of Islam is to achieve world peace. Islam is an Arabic word meaning SUBMISSION, which is derived from the root-word "salm", meaning PEACE. Therefore, in the context of the diversity of our creation, Islam is PEACE by SUBMISSION to the will of the Most High, the Supreme, the All Knower, the Creator, namely the God (in Arabic Allah). Furthermore, like all mission of peace, the Islamic mission for peace cannot be achieved without the teachings and practices of unity and universalism. In Islam, the divine teachings and practices of unity and universalism are found in the divine teachings and practices of Tawhid. Therefore, Islam is a brotherhood or movement for world peace within the brotherhood of mankind, according to the divine teachings and practices of Tawhid. Any Muslim who does not promote peace with absolute justice according to the teachings of Tawhid does not serve the real purpose of Islam.

5. None of the injunctions of the Qur'an are affected by time and space. This is because the dichotomy of the secular and religious does not exist in Islam, and there is no universal culture, tradition, etc, in the unified field of the Islamic way of life. For example, it does not matter in which period of history or compartment of life we exist or culture, custom and tradition we adopt, we are commanded to function in all aspects of our lives according to the divine teachings and practices of ilm-ul-yaqin, ayn-ul-yaqin and haqq-ul-yaqin and not according to the ultra religious teachings and practices of taqleed, aqeeda, silsila, khanqah, sainthood, sects and madhabs. This is the same as stating that the truth does not change with the different teachings and practices of the different cultures, customs, traditions and compartments of our lives with time or space. It remains the same. All Muslims who reduce the true teachings and practices of Islam to the time of the Prophet (SAW), according to the Hadith, are fundamentalists and extremists.

6. Woman was created as the companion of the caliph before she was made wife and mother. Her primary function in life was to fulfill her duties as the companion of the caliph, according to the Word of God found in the Qur'an. Therefore, it is compulsory for her to know what is written in the Qur'an, and what is not, and what is happening in the world. If there are any restrictions on her according to the knowledge of the Qur'an, then these restrictions on her are not due to male chauvinism or any culture, custom or tradition. It is due to the wisdom and the knowledge of God. Although, she cannot take the place of the caliph as the head of the state or the congregation in the mosque or the Assembly of the Ummah, she can become an official of the state or mosque and address the nation or congregation using the podium of the state or mosque. Thus, she has the right to use the main section of the mosque to pray with the congregation or pray at home, drive a car, go to school, work with men, etc. It is the duty of all men as caliphs to see that she is protected at all times from abuse, sexual harassment, etc. Men who fail to do so will be answerable to God.

The above revelations of the Qur'an is the haqq around which a Muslim is expected to establish the true perspective of Islamic reality according to which he or she is expected to conduct all the affairs of their lives and understand the world around them. And the revelations become more meaningful when we interpret the Qur'an in the context of the diversity we experience in our lives. For example, when I advised a young man who was about to get married to study part time and improve his qualification to improve his earnings, his father butted in and said that there was no need for that because Allah (SWT) provided rozi (his sustenance).

What the father failed to realize was that although Allah (SWT) provided the sustenance, many people in this world existed by rummaging the dirt bin for food. Some others earned it by begging and some by prostitution, stealing, etc. Therefore, in this context, all I was saying to the young man was that his salary was not enough to maintain a wife and a home because after paying his rent, etc, he would be hardly left with anything to make a decent living. Therefore, as a dispatch clerk, working for a small retail business, without a matric certificate, he did not have much of chance to improve his future if he did not improve his qualification. Hence, not establishing an Islamic reality in our way of life is our greatest downfall.

Understanding national, international and eternal reality is important to understand true reality of our creation, life and the correct interpretation of the Qur'an. For example, in the making of rain, the Aalim who quoted the Hadith stating that the Prophet (SAW) said that "those who stated that rain was made according to the teachings of science did not have imaan (faith)" had absolutely no knowledge of the truth. In chapter 4, which is titled "Islam is neither a religion nor a 7th century way of life", I presented a diagram in which the Qur'an refers to the different ayahs of science that Allah (SWT) used to create rain. Hence, interpretating Qur'an, without having knowledge of the universal and eternal reality pronounced by the facts of our life and creation, which are found in the Qur'an, is the single most important factor separating those who have knowledge of Islam from those who don't.

Similarly, separating truth from falsehood in every issue of our imaan (faith) is a very important teaching of Tawhid (unity and universality). It separates the false teachings and practices of religion distinguishing it from the true perspective of reality found in the Islamic way of life, which has very little to do with religion and blindfaith. For example, recently I advised a teenage lad who just passed his grade 9 exam to give more time to the study of maths because worldwide research has revealed that those children who did well in grade 10 maths had a high success rate in life. To this his father interrupted by saying, "His success depended in his faith in Allah and not in the study of maths". This was exactly like saying that Allah (SWT) did not use science to create rain. He just used His volition totally ignoring the nature and quality of primeval matter. This is not true because He created this world not for Himself but for human to live in it according to their intellect.

According to the Qur'an, the correct path in the intersection of the secular and religious is the secular teachings and practices of ilm-ul-yaqin, ayn-ul-yaqin and haqq-ul-yaqin and not, the religious teachings and practices of priesthood, sainthood, taqleed, aqeeda, silsilas, khanqahs, sects and madhabs. When such knowledge of the Islamic way of life is made clear by the Qur'an, we accept it as the truth because nobody knows better than God what the truth is. It's not only our faith to accept what is written in the Qur'an, but it's also logical in the context of our diversity and existence to do so, otherwise we will not progress in both the secular and religious.

The majority of the ulama are very afraid of all secular institutions that teach and practice ilm-ul-yaqin, ayn-ul-yaqin and haqq-ul-yaqin. They believe that these institutions are completely western, worldly, Christian and un-Islamic. This is their mistake, because any teachings and practices of the Qur'an that are recommended by the wisdom and knowledge of Allah (SWT) are never wrong, and can never lead us astray. For example, in the dispute on the Muslim Marriage Bill, I mentioned that I trusted the secular state institutions, which taught ilm-ul-yaqin, ayn-ul-yaqin and haqq-ul-yaqin in matters of our way of life rather than Muslim religious institutions, which taught the Qur'an in an un-Islamic and religious manner. This was mainly because the reality of haqq based on the true teachings and practices of the Qur'an, was completely different from that of religion based on human knowledge and blind faith.

To illustrate this fact, let's take the worst scenario of Godlessness in the western world, where the teachings and practices of ilm-ul-yaqin, ayn-ul-yaqin and haqq-ul-yaqin in all secular aspects of their lives? They believe in evolution but they cannot prove or disprove the existence of God. Hence, they teach evolution, but in the context of biodiversity and the natural process of natural selection, where it is made clear that evolution does not necessarily mean that man evolved from ape. It means that it occurs in the process of natural selection to establish the strongest varieties within species, over a long period of time. Among them, are those who refuse to admit the existence of God, and are too stubborn to admit the fact that evolution does not occur between different species, but occurs within varieties within species and God exists. But, at least, there are many in the worst scenario of Godlesness who also admit their mistakes.

Recently, CB Rogers, a former chemist and associate professor of organic chemistry at the University of KwaZulu Natal Westville Campus, wrote an article entitled, "Evolution needs a leap of faith", (Page 13, The Star, December 13, 2010). In it he stated that as a devout Darwinist and ardent atheist for 40 years (up until five years ago), he would have considered the teaching of any form of creationism at our schools a pure nonsense. All this changed five years ago when a young doctor challenged him to prove evolution was fact. At the end of his article he concludes, "As each tenet of evolution comes under fire, it seemed ironic that it has been advances in science that are responsible. As intelligent design gains credibility, one now needs faith to be an atheist". At least in the worst scenario of Godlessness people can be made to rectify their mistakes but not in religion.

Therefore, in view of the above, it is the duty of every Muslim, male and female, to preserve the purity of every secular institution eastern or western, with great sincerity and passion for the truth. When the French governments states that it is wrong according to their secular constitution to allow a female Muslim teacher and learner to wear a Muslim headscarf or niqab in school, or in secular institutions like hospitals, police force, etc, we should not object or retaliate to such a request by them in a negative manner. But, should help them to preserve the purity of their secular institutions, which conforms to the right, title, interest, claim and demand of the secular, which limits religion to the teachings and practices of the Qur'an

The reason for this being that their secular institutions, which are developed according to the Qur'anic teachings and practices of ilm-ul-yaqin, ayn-ul-yaqin and haqq-ul-yaqin, serve as a secular base for us to learn the pure teachings and practices of religion, in Islam, according to the pure guidance of the Qur'an. For example, it teaches us that in the balance between the secular and religious, it is not an injunction of the Qur'an or religion to wear the headscarf or the niqab but tradition, which can be practiced outside of the secular institutions. By stating that it is religion to do so does not only put the secular under strain, but also distorts the true teachings and practices of Islam, that establishes the true balance between the secular and religious.

It is about time that all Muslims are made aware of the fact that it is not the secular institutions that are un-Islamic, but it is all their religious institution, which function according to the ultra religious teachings and practices of taqleed, aqeeda, sainthood, priesthood, etc, that are un-Islamic. During the time of the Prophet (SAW), the mosque was not only a place of worship, but it was also the Assembly of the Ummah and the salaah was not performed for the sawaab of the akhirah but it was the prelude or stepping stone to the Assembly, where the voice of every Muslim was respected in the spirit of their brotherhood, and submission that was found in the salaah, in a rational and logical manner, making the mosque and salaah more secular than religion.

Thus, the legitimate purpose of the musjid was to establish consensus on Shariah and build our nation accordingly. Unfortunately, the musjid has lost that purpose and has now become purely a religious place of worship, which does not serve a single Islamic purpose. The same has happened to the Aalim. He has lost his place as a scholar, and has become a priest where there is no place for him in the real Islamic world. And it is this deep rooted religious sentiment of the ulama that make it very difficult for true Muslims to propagate the true Islamic reality based on the haqq of the Qur'an. This has happened simply because they have given preference to the religious teachings and practices of taqleed, aqeeda, sainthood, silsilas, khanqahs, sects and madhabs, which are totally contrary to the true teachings and practices of the Qur'an.

Unfortunately, not all the present Islamic religious institutions can be reinstated or reformed according to the Qur'anic teachings and practices of ilm-ul-yaqin, ayn-ul-yaqin and haqq-ul-yaqin. We can reinstate the mosque in its pure original form by reinstating the Assembly of the Ummah. But, we cannot say the same for the jamiats of the ulama, because these are bidat or un-Islamic bodies (innovations), which did not exist during the time of the Prophet (SAW) and the Sahaba Ikram (RA). Furthermore, the jamiats are divisive and sectarian, which is totally against the true teachings and practices of the Qur'an and Sunnah. These institutions are no better than the council of churches that exist in Christianity. In addition to this, these institutions serve no purpose in the presence of the Assembly of the Ummah, once the Assembly is reinstated.

Likewise, reforming the present day ulama is virtually impossible. They do not have a proper Islamic knowledge of both religion and secular, which requires a life time of experience and effort. Actually, their knowledge of Islam is not, only not secular, but it's circular. In other words, it is dogmatic and anyone who does not believe in what they believe is declared non-believer by them. Unfortunately, most of them are too old to reform and provide leadership. The greatest thing that they can do for Islam is to admit they are wrong, and allow ordinary people who have knowledge the space to rectify the situation. Allah (SWT) always forgives those who repent, Ameen.

The majority of the ulama and their followers might not agree with what I am saying about them. They might think that I have some ulterior motive or agenda, or am being paid by the enemies of Islam to destroy Islam from within. But this is not the case. They may think what they like. My ambition is only one. I wish to gain the former glory of the ummah and make myself worthy of my worship to my Creator, and the praise and salutation to the Prophet (SAW). In addition to this, I also desire to enter jannah. Besides this, I am also fully aware of the fact that it is bad commerce to sell my imaan for the temporal pleasure of this life.

Unfortunately, the road to jannah is very "steep". It requires a very comprehensive knowledge and understanding of Islam. These include the following:

1. The Qur'anic concept of Islam as it is stipulated at the beginning of this chapter in terms of of the knowledge of the creation, the role of the caliph, the objectives of Islam, etc.
2. Practical knowledge and understanding of Tawhid (unity and universalism). For example, how to intersect the seen with the unseen, secular with the religious, and so on and so forth, in term of the abstract and absolute knowledge of human life, and truth.
3. The fact that the Qur'an, Sunnah, Shariah and haqq are one and the same thing in different forms. The Prophet (SAW) was walking talking Qur'an and there has to be absolute unity between the Word of God (Qur'an) and the sayings and doings of the Prophet (SAW), etc.

In addition to the above, it is important to know that not all of the truth on the eternal plane is haqq-ul-yaqin (absolute). A lot of it is abstract, due to the teachings and practices of ilm-ul-yaqin and ayn-ul-yaqin. Thus, using the Qur'an in this world to learn the eternal truth is a way of preparing us to live in peace in an eternal abode in the hereafter. But, unfortunately, in Islam, we cannot find peace and success in the hereafter, if we have not found peace and success in this world, with the greatest of justice for all diversities.

Furthermore, the tricky part in diversity is that we cannot go it alone to attain success in the hereafter. We require the shurah (mutual consultation) and ijma (consensus) of the majority of the Muslims to agree on the truth, even if we agree with God as individuals. And, if we tried and failed, like we have done in this book, Allah (SWT) might consider us to be worthy of the eternal community of Islam, Insha-Allah, ameen. Actually, in diversity, all people who partake in the shura and ijma of the ummah with an open mind are blessed, even if they took the wrong decision on rare occasions, because they obeyed the way of their Lord.

The ummah has a lot to offer this world in science, religion, and all the other aspects and levels of our lives, such as politics, business, education, etc, which includes a very comprehensive nation building program. But, unfortunately, the majority of the Muslims and their ulama do not like the type of Islam based on the haqq of the Qur'an. They state that it does not give them that powerful feeling of spirituality that they get from the teachings and practices of the 7th century Islam of religious extremism and fundamentalism. They feel that that the Islam that I advocate in this book on haqq is a blatant compromise with the West, worldly and Christian way of life, which is totally oblivion of the 7th century Islam that was followed and practiced by the Prophet (SAW) and the Sahaba Ikram (RA).

What I do not understand about their argument on this issue is what has their feelings of spirituality got to do with any of the teachings and practices of the truth, or Islam. It has been mentioned in this book, a number of times, that it is great mistake to associate our knowledge of Islam with our appearance, dressing, race, status, qualification, position, feelings, profession, tradition, custom, etc, or even with natural disasters like earthquakes, tsunami, etc. The Qur'an did not take any of these things into account to reveal the truth. Therefore, none of these things can tell us, not even the ulama of the past and present, what are the true teachings and practices of the Qur'an and Sunnah except the true Word of God that is found in the Qur'an. Collectively, we should come to consensus on this matter using our intellect and not our feelings.

Using fear, emotion, status, etc, to convince people of their beliefs, is not the right thing to do. We have to use their freedom of thought and intellect to make them accept what is right and wrong, and we should convince them that in the context of the diversity that we experience in this world, the only source of true guidance is the Word of God, that is found in the Holy Qur'an, and to some extend in the Old and New Testaments of the Bible.

We are caliphs of God in this world. If we do not use the Word of God in the diversity of our creation in a rational and intellectual manner, how can we explain to all the people of this world, what is the truth and reality of our creation, and why we should not differ with one another and divide ourselves on any issue of haqq? The beard, hijab, feeling of spirituality in them, etc, has nothing to do with the true teachings and practices of the Qur'an and Sunnah, or even taqwa (piety), which is haqq.

Therefore, the most important issue of concern to us in our life is how to interpret the Qur'an to explain the truth about Islam. The Qur'an does not separate the secular from the religious in the Islamic way of life.

Therefore, when we translate the Qur'an into English, we will have to be very careful to take into account this fact, from both the secular and religious perspective.

For example, sometimes the ulama quote the following verse of the Qur'an to protect their integrity when they are exposed to the truth:

"Say, are those who are (truly) learned (ulama) equal to those who are not learned?"

In the above verse of the Qur'an, the ulama make sure that they stress on the Arabic word ulama giving it the best meaning like learned and scholar. But, in the Islamic way of life, where there is no dichotomy of the secular and religious, how can we accept their statement that they are learned and scholars when, they behave like priests in almost every issue of our life as it is explained in this book.

How can they claim that they are scholars when they believe that the Sunnah today is the 7th century Islam of the Hadith, and deeni talim is religious studies (not secular), which is taught in ulooms (religious schools) according to the religious teachings and practices of taqleed, aqeeda, silsilas, khanqahs, sects and madhabs, which are associated with the teachings and practices, of priesthood, and sainthood, and are totally against the true knowledge and understanding of haqq?

Similarly, in the chapter dealing with the subject of halaal and haraam, I explained that not all the issues of halaal and haraam were halaal and haraam because of religious reasons only. Many of them were haraam purely for health reasons and had nothing to do with religion. And, the ones that were haraam for health reasons, like the pig, could not be made halaal by slaughtering it in the name of God unless a person did not eat for more than three days. The diverse viewpoints of the ummah play a very important part to protect us from any false interpretation of the Qur'an and Sunnah.

Therefore, if there is anything that Muslims wish to know about Islam, they must use the Qur'an and not other sources like the Hadith, the books of their ulama, etc. Everything they wish to know about their life is in the

Qur'an. This is because the haqq of the Qur'an establishes a very different perspective of reality that cannot be found anywhere in the world except among those that place their entire faith on the Qur'an (the infallible Word of God). Take for example, the word for bid'ah (innovation). It does not exist in the world of haqq because the words secular and religion don't exist in the world of haqq. Besides, haqq is not governed by space and time, or the different cultures, customs, traditions and compartments of our lives. Hence, the question of bid'ah never arises in the Islamic way of life.

Since, the perspective of reality that is found by the process of the Qur'an, Sunnah and Shariah is different from the perspective of reality found outside of Islam and in the 72 sects that will not enter jannah, it is imperative that every Muslim who wishes to enter jannah, understands it in every detail of their earthly life. For example, he or she will have to understand in every detail of their life, who an Aalim is and who is not and all the reasons why and how an Aalim is not a priest. Similarly, he or she will have to know the meaning of deen (way of life) as opposed to religion practiced by the majority of the Muslims and non-Muslims of this world. I have explained all the relevant differences in this book. I hope the ummah will ponder over this important issue and come to some positive conclusion on the matter.

Human beings, as caliphs, have no excuse not to have an in-depth and critical knowledge and understanding of the Qur'an and Sunnah, in the context of all the diversities in our creation. It is their duty and responsibility to make life as comfortable and progressive for all of God's creation. They have to be very accurate in their knowledge of Islam with reference to Qur'an and Sunnah, haqq (truth) and batil (falsehood), halaal (permissible) and haraam (prohibitions), etc. They are required to know without doubt that our spirituality concerns that which is written in the Qur'an and not that which is advocated by our tradition, feeling, calamity, status, etc.

Definitely, the majority of the ulama of the past and present have failed us. They have created the despotic power of the ulama of the different sects and madhabs instead of the democratic power of ONE ummah, where the majority of the Muslims, including the ulama as ordinary members of the community, are given power to dictate Shariah and provide leadership and direction according to the consensus of the majority.

Therefore, let us now shy away from the norms of the last few centuries, that of the Hadith, priesthood and sainthood, and enter the domain that the Prophet (SAW) and the Sahaba Ikram (RA) had entered, which was based entirely on the revealed knowledge of the Qur'an according to the shurah and ijma of the ummah, and nothing else. Remember, Qur'an, Sunnah, Shariah and haqq are one and the same thing in different forms.

Furthermore, another very important issue concerning the ummah about the interpretation of the Qur'an is that they must not form groups of like-minded Muslims such as the present jamiats of the different sects, madhabs, silsilas and khanqahs, etc, or some form of elitist movement of professional people in the guise of a club, or around the Internet, etc. The only legitimate interpretation of the Qur'an is that of the diverse opinion, shurah and ijma of all Muslims living in the vicinity of the local mosque, networking their resolutions, area by area, and nation by nation. I hope the ummah will consider and act upon them, doing things correctly from now onwards, Insha-Allah, ameen.

GLOSSARY

Aalim: Scholar according to the secular and Islamic teachings and practices of ilm-ul-yaqin, ayn-ul-yaqin and haqq-ul-yaqin. Priest—according to the religious and un-Islamic teachings and practices of taqlid, aqidah, sainthood, sects, madhabs, etc.

akhirah: the Hereafter

Allah: Arabic for **The God**, which is constructed from the Arabic word al meaning **the,** and ilah meaning **god**. This is in keeping with the universal teachings of Islam, like Islam is word for submission to the will of One God in the context of diversity and not Mohamedanism.

amal: practice.

aqidah: sectarian beliefs and practices, which includes all the major tenets of Islam.

ayn-ul-yaqin: certainty of knowledge by seeing and observing.

batil: falsehood according to the Word of God.

bid'ah: innovations due to the teachings of the Hadith, which has nothing to do with true teachings and practices of the Qur'an, where the dichotomy of secular and religious.

burqa or **burkha:** traditional dress code of Afghani woman, which combines the headscarf and niqab in one.

caliph: vicegerent or deputy of God on earth.

dua: prayer by lifting one's hands to God.

dunya: worldly.

faj'r: time for salaah before sunrise at dawn.

Furqaan: another name for the Qur'an, mainly because it is the only neutral and universal solution to all the problems of our diversity and division.

Hadith: recorded sayings and doings of the Prophet Muhammad (PBUH), not in the global perspective of the Qur'an, but in the context of the Arab culture and custom of his time, where the Sunnah is not a variable term of the Shariah, over all time and place.

hafiz:	one who knows the Qur'an by heart in the Arabic language.
Hajj:	pilgrimage to Mecca, which is performed only during the month of hajj.
halaal:	permissible according to the Word of God.
haqq:	divine truths, absolute and abstract, like it is explained in the worldview teachings and practices of Tawhid in this book according to the true teachings and practices of the Qur'an.
haqq-ul-yaqin:	absolute knowledge, like this is a book.
Hazrat Abu Bk'r:	first Caliph of Islam and bosom pal and companion of the Prophet Muhammad (PBUH).
hijab:	woman's dress code, which compels her to cover the whole body except face and hands to the wrist, according to tradition, not Qur'an.
hufaaz:	plural for hafiz.
ijthihad:	one's personal knowledge and opinion in shurah.
Imaan:	faith.
Islam:	an Arabic word meaning **submission**, which is derived from the root-word S'LM, pronounced "salm" meaning **peace**, a universal way of life for all of humanity. Those that think of it as Mohamedanism in the same way they refer to Judaism, Christianity, Buddhism, Hinduism, etc, have never understood the universal meaning and message of God's Word in any religion or way of life.
ijma:	consensus of the majority.
Ilm:	knowledge.
Ilm-ul-yaqin:	certainty of knowledge by inference or reasoning.
Imam:	in a religious sense, a religious leader who leads the congregational salaah or prayer. In the true Islamic sense he is a pious and intellectual leader and authority at the local and national level.
jamaat:	congregation.
Jamiat:	institutionalized body of religious leaders, which did not exist during the time of the Prophet (PBUH), especially divided by sects and madhabs.
jannat or **jannatul firdose:**	paradise.

Khabaa:	first mosque (see masjid) built by Prophet Adam (PBUH), then rebuilt by Prophet Abraham (PBUH), in Mecca.
madhab:	the four schools of thoughts, namely Shafi, Hanafi, Hambali and Maliki, which stems from the teachings of the Hadith, not Qur'an.
magrib:	time for salaah just after sunset.
masjid or **musjid:**	mosque, not only a place of worship but also the house of parliament at the local and parish level.
munafik:	hypocrite.
niqab:	woman's dress code, which compels her to cover her face in addition to the hijab, according to tradition, in contradiction of the hijab, where the woman's face is left open.
pir:	spiritual mentor of one's sect, madhab or even silsila and khanqah.
qibla:	in the direction of the Khabaa in Mecca.
salaah:	usually refers to the five daily prayer, but in the Islamic way of life, where there is no dichotomy of secular and religious, the salaah is not only a prayer, but a means of signifying one's submission to the Will of One God, by bowing, prostrating and reciting the Qur'an.
Sahaba:	companion of the Prophet Muhammad (PBUH).
Sahabi:	plural for Sahaba.
SAW:	peace be upon him (PBUH).
sawaab:	blessings.
Shariah:	Islamic law and jurisprudence based on the true teachings of the Qur'an and Sunnah, in its universal sense, which embraces all cultures, customs, traditions and compartments of life, over all time and place.
shura or **shurah:**	mutual consultation.
silsila:	religious dynasty of religious leaders of a order of a saint, dividing according to the teachings and practice of one's sect, madhab, etc.
Sunnah:	exact practice of the Qur'an in its global perspective explaining the Shariah with change in time and place according to the injunctions of the Qur'an.

sujood:	prostration signifying one's submission to the Will of God in the daily salaah.
SWT:	God Almighty, Most High.
taqleed:	blind following or imitation of religious beliefs and practice.
taqlid:	see taqleed.
Tawhid:	an Arabic word for unity and universality.
ulama:	plural for Aalim.
ummah:	Islamic society.
umrah:	lesser pilgrimage to Mecca, which can be performed in all months of the year.
zakaat:	compulsory financial assistance to next of kin, needy, poor, wayfarer, those in debt, etc.
zina:	adultery.